Two-Part Inventions

Two-Part Inventions

a novel

Lynne Sharon Schwartz

COUNTERPOINT · BERKELEY

Parts of this novel appeared, in a slightly different form,
in *Boulevard* and *The Northwest Review*.

Library of Congress Cataloging-in-Publication Data is available.

978-1-61902-015-3

Interior design by Gopa & Ted2, Inc.
Cover design by Faceout Studios

Counterpoint
1919 Fifth Street
Berkeley, CA 94710
www.counterpointpress.com

Distributed by Publishers Group West

Printed in the United States of America

10 9 8 7 6 5 4 3 2 1

Overture

THE HIGH PIERCING WAIL reached him even before he got to the front door, so jarring that he dropped his keys on the flagstones. The wail sounded like a small creature being tortured, a bird, maybe. A demented form of birdsong. But there was no pause for breath or change in tone, no hint of sputtering life. The shriek kept up at that bizarrely high pitch, the far end of the keyboard, while he fumbled at the door and finally rushed inside, dropping his briefcase and laptop on the shelf in the front hall.

Where was she? It couldn't be Suzanne. It wasn't a human sound. He followed it through the living room, past the grand piano with open sheets of music—Bartók, Poulenc, Stravinsky, he registered automatically—and into the kitchen, where billows of steam seethed and rose in clumps from the red teapot, already forming cloudy patches on the tiles behind it. He tripped over her body, stretched out flat on the floor, on her back. She looked like a ballerina who falls back in a firm, elegant line, confident that her cavalier will be there to break her fall and propel her on to her next step. But no one had been there to catch her. Before he knelt to see if Suzanne was still breathing, he stepped over her to turn off the flame under the screeching pot.

No breath, no pulse. This couldn't be. It was simply impossible. They had plans. . . . He had plans. Should he call for help? It was too late. And yet her face and hands were still warm. She couldn't have been lying there long; there was still water in the pot. The empty mug was on the counter, the one she liked, with the picture of Mozart, given to her, half-jokingly, by the director of the Vienna Conservatory when they visited a few years ago. A potholder lay near her on the floor. He stroked her face, as if he could bring her back to life, as if there were a grace period after death—ten minutes, fifteen minutes, and the loved one might return. But that didn't happen.

He had to do something, call someone. But he couldn't, not just yet. How could he even speak? And they would come and take her, and he couldn't let her go yet. His throat tightened with tears but he held them back; he hated to cry. Years ago, as a boy, he had once cried every night for weeks, then stopped abruptly and vowed never again to be so defeated. He held her large limp right hand in his, studying the long pianist's fingers, the carefully trimmed nails, short so as not to click on the keys, then placed it on the floor. If only he had gotten home ten minutes earlier, if only he hadn't made that last phone call from his studio to a new client—useless anyway, he'd left a message—if not for the interminable construction on the Thruway, he might have saved her, at least gotten help. What a cruel offense, he thought, that the last sound she heard was that dreadful screech. She with her musician's ears, her hatred of harsh invasive noises. In their apartment in the city in the early days, before they could afford this house, before together they began producing the CDs that made her reputation, she'd complained of the car alarms that punctured the dead of night, their maddening repetitive tuneless tunes and whines, as well as the police sirens and fire engines—they'd lived around the corner from a firehouse. They go right up my spine, she used to say, they're zapping my brain cells. She was awakened every Wednesday and Saturday at six thirty by the garbage truck under their window—audible even over the hum of the air conditioner in summer—the sound of the heavy bags being tossed into the truck's maw and crunched by its fierce teeth.

Sensitive ears. Small ears. He used to joke about her ears, so small and delicate. How could they hear so much, he'd ask, running his fingers along the rim. He ran his finger along her ear, still warm, then sat down on the floor beside her. What would he do now? He had made her ambition his life's work. What was left to do?

A *New York Times* was on a kitchen chair. She must have been about to read it while she had her tea. She never read the paper in the morning; it distracted her from practicing, she said. Late in the day, when she was done, she would sit down with the paper or a book before she started dinner. Now, as always, she liked to cook. Years ago, in the dark years of her despair, she had learned to cook elaborate dishes—she found companionship with Julia Child—simply to do something with her restless hands, and at last when the despair passed (because he found a way to lure her out of it, Philip liked to think), the habit of cooking remained.

The headline in the paper was about the election fiasco. The Supreme Court had declared George Bush the winner, even though he most likely was not. They'd heard the news together on the radio that morning, Suzanne wrapped in a towel, just out of the shower, still so beautiful. The perfect skin and willowy shape, with a faint middle-aged droop to her body that he found irresistible. They were both angry and indignant, though only Suzanne was surprised. Philip had predicted the outcome. "How can they do it?" Suzanne asked. "How can they allow such an injustice? It's . . . it's a fraud. Pure fraud. We'll be calling him President but Gore had the votes. Everyone knows that."

"That's the way the world goes, sweetheart," he said, lacing up his shoes. "You of all people should know that." Those were almost the last words he'd spoken to her. He'd meant to call during the day, but things were so busy in the studio, a group working on a recording of the Archduke Trio, at it for hours, no break, sandwiches brought in at four, that he hadn't had a chance. Now the words scraped the inside of his skull. That's the way the world goes. You of all people should know that. He hoped those weren't the words she took with her to her death. He hoped she'd forgotten them. He hoped she'd forgotten their last argument, too, over a week ago; the memory was still raw. There had been a few days of coolness, but she couldn't keep it up. Though quiet and wary with new people, at home she was talkative, more and more as she got older. She spent much time alone, and in the evening she liked to tell him every small thing that had happened during the day. She talked most when things were going well; her reserve was saved for times of wretchedness—she had always been that way, even back in high school, where they had met. After the first few cool days, things were gradually returning to normal. Or so he hoped. She must be getting used to the idea, he thought, the matter they had argued over, and seen that it was the reasonable next step. Now he'd never know for sure.

The following weeks were a vast, gray-skied prairie of grief Philip Markon imagined he might be traversing forever. But in the emptiness of the landscape, broken only by work deadlines—there was no letting things go in the recording business—and by the buzzing of reporters' calls and emails, buzzards picking at the remains, he found a tiny place of shelter, like a prairie dog burrowing into an underground hole. Maybe this premature death—she was just fifty, a stroke, the doctors said, which might have left her partially paralyzed had she survived it—was lucky for Suzanne. She would not have to face the speculations—more than speculations, if he was candid—that had begun on the music websites. The same sites that had raved about her talents, Half-Note, Andante, Platinum, now were releasing a flurry of nastiness about her recordings that could grow into a blizzard as the zealots gathered their electronic evidence. Every day the computer programs became more sophisticated, able to compare speeds and pressures and dynamics, identifying performances and passages, printing the data as if they were running a corporation rather than dealing with an ineffable art and volatile artists. The technicians were glued to their consoles, and the critics, armed with the retrieved data, would have plenty to fill their columns and blogs. How they would gloat at destroying a reputation. How stunned their readers would be. No matter that he and Suzanne had worked so hard—*he*, especially, had worked so hard—to win her the recognition she'd spent years struggling for, that she deserved. She wouldn't have had the strength to withstand the ugly publicity, the notoriety that was sure to grow. Her strength was in her hands, in her wrists and arms, in her ear. There she possessed might and endurance. Otherwise she was naive, easily bruised, an innocent. He, on the other hand, was prepared for any kind of assault, any crude online chatter. Whatever his business might suffer, he could handle it. He was hard. Nothing could touch him. He was impervious, his defenses constructed in early childhood.

In those weeks after her death the phone rang so often that he was tempted to hurl it against a wall. He let the machine take the calls, and he returned hardly any, except those from close friends or family, certainly not the ones from music bloggers blandly offering condolences and hoping he'd answer just a few questions. He persuaded himself that he was impenetrable, and that was almost true when it came to the rumor-mongers, the pedantic technicians chiming in with their numbers and statistics. None of it mattered now: Suzanne was gone, the CDs were over, there would be no new ones. (Not that he wouldn't release the last, almost finished one, just a little more editing on the final mix.) He saved the messages, though; there might come a time when he'd want to answer them or need them to defend himself. For the time being he had nothing to say; he'd stonewall, and it would all pass. Fortunately, the obituary in the *Times* ("World-Class Pianist Known by Few") was nothing but admiring and respectful.

Of course, those obituaries were written well in advance. Weird, wasn't it, he mused, to think that all the famous people walking around were already memorialized in the files of the

Times, where the obits sat waiting for them to kick off. Then the people would be dead and the obits would come to life. Some intern must be assigned to keeping them up-to-date, like a hospital's life-support system. Well, that intern hadn't caught up with the online chatter about Suzanne, which started a week or so after her death. Most likely it was her death that got the serious listeners worked up again, though there'd been an earlier query or two, a few puzzled comments, on a couple of the websites. Nothing to worry about, he'd thought at the time. Naturally, he never mentioned anything to Suzanne. Now the rumors had slithered through the web—never had that designation, web, seemed so maddeningly apt—though the slower--moving newspaper of record had not yet caught up.

Despite his relief that Suzanne didn't have to face these insinuations—accusations, really—now and then came a creeping suspicion that she might have enjoyed the notoriety. He thought he had known her thoroughly, but you never know anyone thoroughly, do you? Even a wife or lover. Especially a wife or lover. Who knew him, for instance? No one. Suzanne had impeccable manners, the graciousness of a born aristocrat (where this came from was anyone's guess, certainly not her family). But he had seen her angry, and he knew how her will could harden. He had also seen her in moods of abject passivity—the obverse of her despotic ambition. He was the only one who had seen that in its raw state and it was awesome. Perhaps in some people the desire for renown—which luckily did not burden him—didn't distinguish between praise and opprobrium. Perhaps it was simply the name in the papers, or now on the Internet, that mattered.

But no, he couldn't seriously think that. Her passion for

music was so genuine and intense; she wouldn't have wanted to be seen as in any way subverting what she loved. He still wasn't sure how much she had known or suspected all along—except for that dreadful night last week, they hardly discussed the recordings once they were done—or how surprised she would have been at the lengths he'd gone to on her behalf. She had taken her knowledge or ignorance to the grave, or rather to the flames she told him years ago she would prefer, like her father.

Before long, he trusted, the right moment would come: He would find the means to clear her name, and his own as well. As soon as he recovered from the shock of her death. He could construct a story, a spin that would shift the interpretation of the whole affair.

He'd gotten in the habit, in those first few weeks, of checking the music sites, just in case. It was difficult to remain impervious when one afternoon, clicking from link to link, he came upon the interview with Elena in Andante. Elena, of all people. Anything for free publicity, he thought, yet it wasn't as if she needed it. She was doing a series of concerts at the Ninety-second Street Y this winter, and next fall at the Metropolitan Museum; her photo was splashed all over their brochures, still glamorous, the long blond hair swept back from her face, the stark, dark clothes, the aloof, intimidating look she affected for the camera. She had all the fame she could hope for, not to mention the financier husband and the Park Avenue apartment, but it was still not enough. And there was that semi-scandal linking her and her stepfather, which she sailed through until the rumors passed. But with all that, she had to exploit Suzanne's death, too.

He really shouldn't be surprised, he thought, going to the kitchen for some bourbon before he faced the screen. He must bear in mind that it wasn't really about Suzanne. Elena had had a grudge against him ever since he dropped her way back in high school. Christ, imagine a woman still clutching a rejection from over thirty years ago. Hell hath no fury, as the saying went. . . . They were practically children, playing at a teenage romance that lasted no more than a couple of months, if that; he could barely remember. He never slept with her—he would have remembered that—and a good thing, too, though at the time it was galling. She must have had plenty of experience back in the Soviet Union, so why shouldn't he get some, too, was his attitude. But there was never an opportunity. Her mother was always in the apartment, a skinny woman with wild fuzzy black hair and witchy makeup—chalky face, mauve lips. Elena told him the mother was a translator but she didn't speak much English to Phil, only grunts and frowns that made it clear he wasn't welcome. He should never have taken up with Elena, she wasn't his type at all, overconfident, full of herself, but he'd felt sorry for her at first. The new girl in the special high school, with her peculiar English, just arrived from the Soviet Union, where her life couldn't have been a picnic. She must be lonely, bewildered, or so he thought. He wanted to help. It wasn't long before he saw she was ready to use him in any way she could. That was the turnoff.

It was inevitable, in their work, that they would meet on and off over the years, always cordially, if not quite as friends. She'd been Suzanne's friend later on, at Juilliard, but not for long afterward. And now here she was online; when he clicked, bourbon in hand, the darkened screen lit up to show a large

photo in living color, to accompany her Q & A with the unctuous interviewer from Andante. It would appear in the print
version as well, the introduction said. Oh, terrific. Well, he'd
ride it out as he had the others. The classical-music world was
minuscule, really. It wasn't as if he couldn't go out of the house
without being accosted like a rock star. He must remember
how small and ingrown this world was, how few people cared
about classical music or musicians. And even fewer gave a damn
about the technical side—a few bars, or a movement borrowed
here or there, would hardly make a banner headline, like the
election of a phony president.

No doubt Elena, with her grudge against him, would make
Suzanne out to be his victim, the deluded innocent. Well,
innocence and delusions aside, any sensible person could see
how loyal and devoted he'd been, how he'd done everything
feasible to get her what she needed and deserved. They should
be applauding him, not making practically libelous insinuations. Even Suzanne, until her dying day, had been delighted
with the recordings, at least until quite recently. She'd been
willing, more than willing, ready and eager, to do the phone
and online interviews he arranged and to say what he suggested she say. When it comes to their background, he used to
tell her, all artists tinker with the facts a little bit; it makes for
a more intriguing story. So you say you studied in Paris with
Nadia Boulanger or at Juilliard with Olga Samaroff, drop a few
famous names. They're dead anyway, what does it matter? It's
the music that matters, and the music we don't tinker with. We
do everything to make it come out true and pure and perfect.

"That's correct, I was a close friend," the text of Elena's replies
began, "and yes, we did meet when we were very young, at the

High School of Music and Art in New York City, back when it was located uptown near City College. I was a newcomer, I'd just arrived from the Soviet Union with my mother, and Suzanne was kind to me."

Kind to her! Phil took a long swig from the bourbon and water. Suzanne? After a few weeks Suzanne became furious with Elena and didn't speak to her for the remainder of high school. She was nothing if not tenacious, and she, too, could hold a grudge. *He* was the one who was kind. Elena had managed to revise all that ancient history. Maybe she'd even convinced herself that her version was true.

"She intrigued me, her silences, then sometimes her exuberance. I could tell even then she was an extraordinary talent, even though she was modest about it in public. But she knew her worth."

"It's hard getting accurate information about her past." This from the interviewer. "There are so many different stories circulating, from the various interviews she gave. She's something of a mystery, isn't she? I mean, after those concerts in her twenties she stopped performing in public and was pretty much forgotten, and then years later those amazing CDs appeared. So what was she like back then?"

"Well, once you got to know her she could be very lively, enthusiastic. Fun to be with. But even so, there was something reserved about her. Kind of wary. It wasn't so much mysterious, I think, as that she was a trifle shy, hesitant. She didn't have the temperament of a performer, you know, thick-skinned, outgoing, you could even say aggressive, though she definitely wanted the rewards those traits bring. She was quite striking to look at, I don't think she knew how striking: great dark eyes, olive skin, that unruly mass of hair flying around when she played. She was tall and thin and affected an arty look that was in style then, you know—or maybe you don't—the black turtlenecks and dangling earrings, ragged jeans. Anyway, she was certainly one of the most talented, and fantastically ambitious, I realized when I got to know her. Yet kind of an innocent in some ways. I mean naive about the world. But as far as music, she knew exactly how good she was. Later we were students together at Juilliard and there, too, she stood out. We had a fantastic group of pianists, Emanuel Ax, Garrick Ohlsson, other names you'd recognize, but everyone knew she was outstanding. She was a born musician; she only needed to hone the technique."

"You must have expected great things of her. Do you have any idea why she stopped performing in public?"

"I was never clear about that. We lost touch shortly after Juilliard, so I really can't say what happened. She did those few recitals in New York where she wasn't at her best, but still, she could have recovered from that and kept going. She had plenty of contacts who would have helped her. I don't really know. I think she was ill for a while, something that prevented her from performing. But that's all rather vague. They were secretive about it, she and her husband, I mean. He was also her manager, you know. Philip Markon. As I said, she wasn't good at self-promotion. Maybe she got discouraged. In this business you have to be very tough. She just dropped out of sight."

Secretive? Was that what they called it now? Whatever happened to privacy? Wasn't Suzanne entitled to that? Hadn't the disappointment of the debut concert been public enough? Why advertise her weariness, her depression, the baffling weakness that overcame her unpredictably, for no apparent reason? And then the pregnancy and the miscarriage compounding things.

A run of bad luck until even he, Phil, with his boundless sympathy, had suspected what the doctors hinted at: a fleeing from the world, a kind of morose self-indulgence. It wasn't until years later that a doctor finally diagnosed her with fibromyalgia. By then Suzanne was almost ashamed of her intermittent symptoms; it was a relief to give a name to what had puzzled and plagued her for so long, frightening though the name was. The burden of shame and guilt slipped away and she was able to play again as best she could. On her best days she was as good as she'd ever been.

Elena had telephoned now and then over the years, but Suzanne saw her rarely, though Elena kept inviting her to lunch and sending tickets to her concerts. It wasn't only the betrayal Suzanne had felt over the affair with Richard—Philip was sure she got over that. It was Elena's persistent luck, the reverse of her own: the career, the flamboyant good health, the temperament made for the competitive life, the child. Nothing could jar or tarnish Elena; she was built of stone and steel. And of course it didn't hurt that her stepfather was a renowned cellist, so that all through her high school and college years musicians were dropping in at their apartment for dinners and postconcert get-togethers. No, Elena was the last person Suzanne wanted to see, the person who had appeared out of the blue and taken the life intended for her.

The last time Phil had run into Elena was maybe five years ago, during intermission at a concert at Avery Fisher, a chamber group he had an exclusive contract to record. It was a few years after Suzanne's CDs started getting those fantastic reviews, first online and then in print. Elena had asked after her and praised the recordings. She'd love to visit, she said. It had been so long and they'd been such good friends, once. Couldn't she drop in? Phil put her off, saying Suzanne wasn't well, wasn't seeing anyone. Maybe in a few weeks he'd give her a call. He waved to someone he knew across the lobby and dashed off.

"You say you lost touch not long after you both finished at Juilliard," the interviewer persisted. "Wasn't there some kind of rift between you?"

"That was a personal matter. I wouldn't call it a rift. A misunderstanding. It's a very busy life, lots of traveling, you can't keep up with all the people you'd like to. I didn't see her for a number of years but I got news through mutual friends, and when the CDs started to come out from Tempo, of course I listened to them. It was unusual, everyone knew that, even risky, an individual artist on a CD who didn't have a big reputation as a performer. But they were promoted and marketed well and turned out to be very successful."

Phil was surprised she would accord him this credit. Damn right they were promoted and marketed well. He knew his business better than anyone; he had run it single-handedly ever since he began. Even during hectic spells when he hired temporary assistants, he kept a close eye on everything. That was the only way. Marketed well, sure, but how about the music itself? No amount of marketing could sell a lousy CD.

"But the important thing," Elena continued, as if in response to his urging, "is that the playing was marvelous. Rigorous, unsentimental, fluid. It was much better than those early concerts, when the reviews complained that the rhythm was erratic and the interpretations bland. That was never the way I remembered Suzanne's playing. Those CDs were beautiful, and beautifully made, in anyone's judgment. I was happy for her."

"Still, wouldn't you say there was some sense of competition between you and Suzanne Stellman? After all, you'd studied at professional school together, one might say you were neck and neck in a very competitive world, you'd been involved with the same men, at least according to gossip, and it might be said that you attained the career she wanted."

"No, I wouldn't say that at all. We weren't competitive in the least. We were good friends, even after that gap. She always let me know she was pleased at my successes, and I did the same with her. I can speak for myself and, I think, for Suzanne, too, when I say that the main thing on our minds was always the music, not any kind of competition. It's not like the Olympics, you know. Getting the music right was what we cared about most."

She was obviously taking the high road, Phil thought, as he finished what was left of his drink. Well, good for her. She did always have dignity, he had to grant her that. And so far the interview hadn't been too bad. It could have been worse.

"Now, I'd like to ask, what was your reaction to the recent article in the *New York Times* regarding certain sections of Ms. Stellman's CDs?"

"Well, I was surprised, naturally."

No, you weren't, Philip thought. She'd fail a lie-detector test on this one. Now was where the interview would get sticky. He was at the bottom of the screen, his finger on the down arrow. He got up and went back to the kitchen. He needed some more bourbon before he scrolled down to see what she would do next.

The interview made him remember the day the idea had come to him, more than ten years ago. He was working in the studio he rented in the city, frustrated with the performance of a Polish pianist, Kosinski, who was in the United States on his first tour—no concerts in New York, but in several smaller cities. It hadn't been difficult for Philip to persuade him to do a recording for Tempo. Kosinski was barely known, and though he was promising, the bigger record companies were hesitant: They'd rather sign an artist after a public success than before. But Philip, although no longer a beginner—he had a solid reputation by then—was ever eager for business and was a good persuader. A good businessman, too, as he'd known he would be. All those hours spent listening to Uncle Mel hadn't been in vain, as well as the patient years learning the ropes and technology at RCA. When he first went out on his own—a phone and a bridge table in the bedroom of their Greenwich Village apartment—he rented studio space by the hour. In time he had no trouble affording his own place. Besides the recording work, the independent classical label he'd begun years ago was picking up. He never doubted that he could make a go of that; everyone he dealt with was impressed by his enthusiasm and competence. And no wonder. Besides doing an excellent job technically, he was never late, never impatient, and always returned calls. He knew exactly how to handle everyone, including himself.

He'd spent the previous two days with Kosinski, recording a selection of Chopin nocturnes, over and over. Though Philip kept his cool, the Pole grew more anxious by the minute, pausing to smoke French cigarettes whose bitter smell hung in the air, and drinking endless cups of coffee Philip brewed in the next room. Kosinski badly needed a shave, and by the second day his collar was curling at the tips. He had an irritating habit of tugging his ear before beginning each new take, as if he could correct his fumblings by clearing his ear. Philip had to use all his charm to keep him at it until they had a usable take. Like so many musicians, Kosinski didn't like to begin in the middle of a piece to repeat a few measures; he wanted to go back to the beginning each time, like a child who can't recite a memorized poem starting anywhere but the first line.

Philip recorded hours of repetitions. Sitting at the console with the score open before him after Kosinski left, his equipment lit up, he was attempting to piece together the best takes, adjusting the volume here and there. After several hours, he was nearly done, except for a few bars in the Nocturne in C Sharp Minor that were still not quite right on any of the takes. The dynamics were slightly off, the forte and fortissimo not clearly enough distinguished, though he might be able to fix that.

It was a warm late-October afternoon. Through his open windows wafted the delectable leafy aroma of autumn, but not yet its chill. The studio was in a brownstone on a narrow, tree-lined street in Chelsea. The leaves outside his third-floor window were just starting to turn, had reached a dun nameless color between green and gold. Tomorrow, if there was no rain or wind, the gold would emerge and dominate. It would be like gazing into a sun at eye level, just outside the window.

He was eager to get home to Suzanne, who hadn't been feeling well when he left in the morning. She lay in bed staring at the ceiling, pale, her dark hair stark against the white pillow.

"Are you okay?" he asked. "Can I get you anything before I go?"

"No, I'm fine. I'll be getting up in a minute. Go on." But five minutes later when he came to kiss her good-bye she hadn't stirred. He'd tried calling in the afternoon, but she hadn't picked up, was probably with a student—that was the most optimistic explanation. He hoped it wasn't one of those days when she barely dragged herself from bed; on those days, when he got home, he could tell by her slowness and vagueness that she'd just gotten up, for his sake. It had been going on like this for a long time now, the weeks drifting into months and then years, all of them the same. He didn't know how to break the pattern. Suzanne didn't even seem unhappy anymore about her dashed hopes, and that bothered him even more than the intermittent spells of apathy and weakness. She was agreeable and compliant, always interested in knowing how his business was doing, but the pianist part of herself, at least the ambitious part, seemed to have been stowed away in some attic of the soul.

The damn Pole was giving him grief. It looked like he'd have to return, and of course he, Phil, would be blamed. Unless there was some other way—shit, it would be so easy to drop in those few troublesome bars. . . . No one would ever know. He rummaged around the shelves and found an older recording of the nocturnes—another pianist, but luckily done here in the same studio, same room sound. He listened: It was a flawless performance. Tempting, and so easy, but no, he didn't dare. Things were going too well. His CDs were getting excellent reviews; there was no need to take such chances. He'd keep trying. Another half hour . . .

He played around with Kosinski's takes for ten more minutes, adjusting the volume and the reverb, and then he couldn't resist. Just on a whim, just to see how it sounded, with a cavalier flourish he got out the other Chopin CD, a Korean pianist, very fine but not very well-known, and plugged in the measures to cover Kosinski's awkward bit. It took almost no time. Amazing! A seamless job, and the touch was so similar that no one could ever detect the substitution. He wouldn't detect it himself if he hadn't done it. It was like a game, and he was master of it, a backstage wizard.

But enough of this wasting time. He wanted to get home. Just an experiment, he told himself as he shut down the equipment and got his jacket. Just fooling around, to test his skill. It was astounding what could be done nowadays. Same as with photography. Before the Berlin wall came down a year ago, he'd heard that in the former communist countries, in Kosinski's very own Poland, it was possible to lop off the image of a functionary who'd gone out of favor. Press a few buttons and the fellow was eliminated from memory as he'd probably been eliminated from life. Phil had seen the same kinds of wonders—though not of such grave import—in a photo shop on Madison Avenue where customers could play around with snapshots they brought in, killing off pesky relatives or wiping out their exes from the honeymoon. Sure, that sense of power was thrilling, but it was dangerous, too.

He left everything as it was—the Korean's CD out on the desk—so he'd remember to fix it in the morning. He'd have fresh energy for Kosinski; he'd get back to his editing and do the best he could.

Outside, on the way to his car, he felt again the warm, benign glory of the waning day. When he got home he'd take Suzanne out to dinner, maybe first a walk in the park near their house to look at the leaves. It was a number of years now since they'd moved from the Village apartment to the house in Nyack.

They'd stripped wallpaper and stained floors and gone around to garage sales, shopping malls, thrift shops, a few avid months of devotion to the house that brought them closer together again. It wasn't the kind of house he'd envisioned for so long—something like the house in Great Neck where he grew up—but Suzanne wouldn't want a house like that; in fact she probably would have preferred to stay in the city, though she didn't say so. This house was more distinctive than the one he grew up in, but he couldn't picture his parents and his brother, Billy, in it, as he might have done with a more ordinary house. But it did have grass around it, and Suzanne had taken to growing flowers on the front lawn and in the backyard.

But lately she looked pale and weary. She needed to get out, get fresh air, the world, people, activity. If she was reluctant, as she so often was during these bad spells—they lasted days, sometimes weeks—he'd think up something to be celebrated. He could tell her he'd gotten the contract to record the Atlantis String Quartet—that would do it. The deal was virtually settled; they only needed to iron out the final details. She took such pleasure in his successes. And why not, he thought with a tinge of satisfaction as he approached his car. It helped give her the time to practice, though he didn't really know how much time she spent practicing while he was gone all day. Or whether she even wanted to anymore.

She couldn't refuse a festive dinner, even if she didn't feel altogether well. Her illness—what they had gradually and tacitly agreed to call her illness—was mysterious, a combination of physical and mental symptoms, weariness, listlessness, weakness, pains that migrated from one part of her body to another, thankfully never to her forearms and hands. They'd been to several doctors but never gotten a precise diagnosis. The doctors, not surprisingly, still called it depression and she dutifully took the pills, but they didn't seem to alleviate her pains or weakness, just made her feel swaddled in gauze, she reported. Philip tried to be unfailingly sympathetic. He *was* sympathetic. Over the years his love for her, at first a mixture of passion, the desire to possess, and admiration for her gift, had become layered over with a protective sympathy, the kind of sympathy one feels for a child, unjustly handicapped, wistful, unable to run around with the others.

He had to park on the street because there was an unfamiliar car, a black Toyota station wagon, in the driveway. Most likely one of her students, though he'd never seen the car before. He heard the piano as he went up the front steps. In the foyer, pausing to hang his jacket on the rack, he knew at once it couldn't be Suzanne playing. The sound was without luster; it was the second movement of Beethoven's *Waldstein* Sonata— he remembered that had been on the program the day they first met, as teenagers at a Serkin concert. This was a far cry from Rudolf Serkin: The triplets were uneven, too loud and uncontrolled, with pauses and stumbling. Suzanne's students were usually more proficient. She got referrals from Cynthia, her old teacher, and from the faculty at Juilliard, who still remembered her as one of the star students. Great things had been expected of her.

Not wishing to disturb the lesson, Philip tiptoed down the hall and stopped at the archway of the living room, where Suzanne, dressed in snug dark slacks and a gray cashmere sweater he'd bought for her birthday last month, was standing slightly behind and to the left of the woman seated at the piano.

The woman's back was to him. Under her polyester pink shirt she had hefty, fleshy shoulders that sloped heavily into thick arms. Her hair was strawberry blond and curly, floating down to her shoulders. The triplets continued to give her trouble; she paused, her shoulders rising with a deep breath, and began the passage again.

Suzanne must have heard him, or sensed his presence. She turned and gave an abstracted nod and a faint wave of the hand, the long fingers fluttering in greeting. Although her face revealed nothing, he could imagine the frustration she must be feeling. Also the resignation. He raised his eyebrows and made a puzzled face, as if to comment on the woman's playing, but Suzanne simply turned back toward the piano. She stood erect, patient, alert, but that resigned impassive face gave him a twist in his gut.

Outrageous, he thought as he went into the bedroom to change. Criminal, that so gifted a pianist should spend her time on students like this one. There was no possible gratification to be found teaching someone on that level. That woman didn't need Suzanne; anyone would do. His Suzanne was meant for better things.

He went quietly into the kitchen to get a cold beer. Good. No elaborate dinner preparations; the kitchen was tidy, untouched. He stared into the refrigerator, braced by the chill. Then the idea came to him. Followed immediately by the wonder that he hadn't thought of it before. It must have been the Chopin nocturnes that sparked the notion. She could play those nocturnes every bit as well as Kosinski, even now. Better. She was a natural for Chopin—fluid, forceful, complex emotion delivered with subtlety and rigor. He'd heard her play the ballades and nocturnes dozens of times at home. It was only in front of an audience that she froze.

He had the means to do it. All he needed was her cooperation. Recording in the studio was nothing like playing in public; she knew that, of course, but he would reassure her. No one would be there but him, nothing at all to fear. She'd be at her best. And he'd take care of all the editing. She didn't even need to listen to the finished product if she didn't want to.

She wasn't the only musician who went stiff with panic on approaching the stage. For some, it lasted only the first few minutes, then they became absorbed by the music, they felt freed, and the panic slunk away like a thief deterred by bright lights in the house. For others, it dogged them the whole time, invaded, occupied, kept them at gunpoint. Each performance was an agony. Some, driven by ambition and desire, persisted, learned ways of routing fear, or at least accommodating it, bargaining, maybe with the help of drugs. Others cared less for the spotlight; they contented themselves with teaching or coaching, accompanying, glad to live their lives in music, wanting the music more than they needed the fame. And some gave up. Suzanne, his Suzanne, was a conundrum. Her need for glory—that was what she called it, to him, privately—was immense, torturing. It had been since early childhood. But she couldn't rout the fear. And then there was her illness, the weakness and lassitude. Cause, or effect, or neither, just a stroke of bad luck? That interfered with her playing, too. She tired easily; she wasn't always at her best.

Still, he couldn't bear the thought that Suzanne should be

one of those who give up. If he'd been blessed with her talent, he would never have given up. He hadn't minded so much, back in high school, when he understood that his talent was of the middling variety. He didn't lust for fame but for action, movement, power. He could find other ways. He would find a way to do it for Suzanne, get her what she craved. He would bring up his idea later, at dinner.

He stayed in the kitchen, leafing through magazines. The music stopped; the irksome sound of inadequate fingers wrestling with Beethoven's outlandish demands was replaced by Suzanne's low voice. He couldn't hear her words; no doubt she was gently making suggestions—she was always a gentle, patient teacher—explaining the trajectory of the notes, what they asked of the pianist they were entrusted to. For Suzanne saw her playing that way, as a composer's dream entrusted to her, willing her to honor that trust. Then the piano sounded again, Suzanne this time—a different universe of sound. Liquid sound coalescing into phrases, skimming off her fingers, telling a story no words could convey, the language of the inner ear, the contours of emotion. Could that woman even appreciate what she was hearing? When the music stopped he heard murmured voices, and very soon the front door opened and closed. A moment later he heard the car engine start up. Suzanne came into the kitchen.

"You're home early. I didn't expect you, or I would have scheduled the lesson for earlier."

"It was such a beautiful afternoon, I just felt like getting out. And I wanted to see how you were doing. Better?"

She nodded. "Fine."

"Who was that just now?"

"This was the first time she came. She's Lorna Fox's mother, you know, the girl who just graduated from Curtis and came to New York? She hasn't played in years and wants to take lessons again. So I told her to let me hear her."

"You're not going to take her on, are you? I mean . . ."

"I don't know. I said I'd let her know. It's money, isn't it?"

"We're not that desperate. You don't need to teach people like that. It's a waste."

She smiled wryly and leaned over to take a swig of his beer. The V-neck sweater pulled away from her skin and he noticed the curve of her breasts. Later, if she was not tired, he would put his hand there. She often said she was tired, but she was not hard to persuade. She was so porous, all the feelings close to the surface. "Let me twist your arm," he'd say sometimes, touching her thigh or shoulder. And a moment later she'd turn to him and murmur, "I guess you twisted my arm."

"Listen," he said, "I have an idea. I should have thought of it before. Let's go out to dinner, someplace nice, that new Greek place in town you liked when we took your brothers there. I'll tell you all about it."

"I don't know, Phil. I'm kind of tired. I could throw something together here." As she yawned and stretched her arms above her head, the sweater rose to show a strip of olive skin.

"You see? Students like that wear you out. Come on, rest for a few minutes, then fix yourself up and we'll take a little walk in town and end up at Aesop's Tables. A good new contract today. It's worth celebrating."

Over the first glass of wine, he made his suggestion. He was determined on his plan, no matter how she reacted. She would come into the studio and make the recording, and he would edit it, package it, and get it distributed. She wouldn't have to do another thing, no public appearances, no crowds. There was nothing to lose, he finished. The moment those words were out he was sorry he'd ended his pitch on that note. Nothing to lose meant she had no reputation to speak of, so why not give it a try? But she didn't take it badly, only tightened her lips for an instant and drank more wine.

He waited. Her face was unreadable, calm, full lips shut, her eyes slightly drowsy. She probably shouldn't drink while on the antidepressants, but he didn't want to appear to be monitoring her. If he couldn't persuade her on his own, he'd get Richard Penzer to help. She regarded Richard as some kind of god; his words were scripture, even back when he was an unknown composer. Now that he was one of the composers *du jour*, his operas and symphonies performed everywhere, the City Opera, the Philharmonic, his godliness was validated.

She was silent for so long that Philip expected her to resist, but in the end she didn't. She only sipped her wine, drummed the fingers of her left hand on the table in what looked like a series of up and down arpeggios, and said she'd think it over. "So tell me what happened in the studio. The contract."

The food came. He ate hungrily, and told her he'd just gotten the coveted deal to do a double CD with Atlantis, an up-and-coming young quartet making their first recording. If it was successful, they'd keep coming back—it would be steady, reliable income. Actually the deal was not quite closed; the agent had promised to get in touch by the end of the week. But he was almost sure it would work out. If it didn't, and if she remembered to ask, he would invent some last-minute hitch.

Suzanne was pleased for him, as she always was. She lifted

her wine and they clinked glasses. "That's great, Phil. I know they'll be happy with whatever you do. You do a great job."

And I can do it for you, too, he thought. But he didn't want to push things. Just take it slow. She didn't like to be rushed. Over the espresso and baklava, though, he couldn't resist. "So, have you had a chance to think it over?"

She smiled and blinked meaningfully, as if to say, How much time? A half-hour? But to his surprise, she agreed. "Okay, why not? You don't usually see CDs from people who aren't performing. But I guess it's worth a try. You're right. What's there to lose?"

Philip had been prepared to coax. He was almost disappointed that there was no call for his powers of persuasion, of figurative arm-twisting.

"All right, then. Great! Start with the ballades, and then maybe later we can do the preludes or some of the nocturnes. We'll figure it out, and you'll let me know when you're ready. You can start tomorrow. It shouldn't take long. You have them down pat already. I've heard you."

She gave that wry smile again. She was humoring him, he could tell, and for a moment the ambiguous dynamics of their marriage puzzled him. Who was humoring whom? Who was the protector, who the protected? "You sound like you're talking about an exam," she said.

"Well, you know what I mean, sweetheart." He took her hand across the table. "You always know what I mean, don't you?"

"Mostly," she said.

Before they went home they walked down to the river. There was still a trace of light in the sky. It wasn't too late, he thought.

He would do it for her. He should have done it long before. Look how easily she agreed. Once she heard the recordings she'd get as excited as he was, only he didn't dare show that excitement yet. She had that peculiar calm she'd developed over the last few years; he didn't know if it was medication or resignation or sickness, but he didn't like it. It wasn't natural to her, wasn't the lively Suzanne with the vivid, shining eyes he'd fallen in love with. What he'd seen in her from the very beginning was a simmering energy beneath the smooth lines of her face, a kind of volcano nearing eruption, or fireworks ready to spark up. He wanted to see that Suzanne again. Or re-create her, if he had to.

At home in bed, he began his usual seduction. He had to seduce her each time, but he didn't mind that. He thrived on effort. He was all effort, all action, whispering in her ear, suggestions, urgings, outrageous fantasies neither of them had any intention of acting out, used only to arouse. Pleasing her was his self-appointed task, the spur to his own desire. Suzanne, for her part, would start out languid, drowsy, abstracted as if in a caul, until she was engaged, until something seemed to click into place and then she could give herself over to want. She would spring into animation, like a doll infused with breath. The caul melted away and she would grow eager, ravenous. That Suzanne, the one who finally moaned on and on with pleasure through his efforts, he regarded as his creature. The vessel for his restless energies. It was a selfless task; he had no need to demonstrate skill and power, he craved only exertion and release. And to bring her out of her reverie and make her happy. He could create her as a sexual being, since she hadn't the will to do it herself.

He leaned over and began touching her breasts, her thighs, and when she turned to him sleepily, he murmured in her ear words he knew would stir her. "I'm going to make you famous. You'll see. The whole world will know who you are and want to hear you." And at those words she began to move under his hands, to reach for him. "'Suzanne, Suzanne,' they'll all say. They'll be dazzled by you, they'll . . ." Then there was no need to speak anymore. She was twisting and writhing, his fingers going deep into her; she was gasping. She grabbed his face and kissed him deeply and pulled him inside her. Then he could do with her anything he liked. She was his creature.

The phone woke them before the alarm: Suzanne's brother Gary, to tell them that their mother, Gerda, had slipped on a sticky patch on the kitchen floor and broken her hip. He was calling from the hospital, where they were taking X-rays. Suzanne was grabbing her clothes from the drawers before she even hung up. Phil couldn't let her deal with this alone, not with the way she was feeling lately. He sprang out of bed. "I'll go with you."

"You don't have to. I'll drive in with you and you can drop me off on your way to the studio."

"No, I'm coming."

They spent several hours waiting for Gerda to come out of the surgery, and once they were sure she was all right, they went around the corner to a diner for sandwiches with Gary and Fred. As often happened after an emergency, relief brought on a mood of adolescent hilarity—her twin brothers, when together, acted like adolescents anyhow, Phil always thought.

By the time he got to his studio it was midafternoon. There were half a dozen messages on the machine, all needing to be answered right away: offers of new work, the violinist from the chamber group bugging him for details about the concert schedule . . . Usually he loved the busyness, the sense of being overextended, not knowing what to do first. A manic energy propelled him, and he always got everything done. But today he was truly exhausted, what with the lack of sleep and the tense hours in the hospital.

When Kosinski telephoned, hoarse and impatient, Phil realized that in the flurry of returning his other calls, he'd forgotten to undo his switch, to remove the Korean's few bars from Kosinski's performance. When could he expect the final version? Kosinski wanted to know. Remember, he'd promised to messenger it over to the hotel around noon? Sure, sure, Phil reassured him. It's all done. I was just about to call for the messenger. It'll be right there. A half-hour at the most.

It was a pity to cut corners like that, but it couldn't be helped. He'd done such a good job, there wasn't a chance in the world anyone would notice. He mustn't do it again, he told himself. It was tempting, but far too risky.

Three weeks after Phil made his suggestion at dinner, Suzanne said she was ready. They drove into the city together. She was unusually quiet as he got her set up, and he wondered if she'd taken anything besides her antidepressants. Probably not. In the early days, when she was performing in public, she never wanted anything, not even the Valium he urged on her. She said she didn't know how it might affect her; who knows, it might make things worse, not better.

She wanted to play the first ballade before he began recording, just to warm up, but Phil said why not just record everything? If the first take turned out to be the best and they hadn't preserved it, they'd be sorry. That was what he told everyone, and on occasion it was indeed the first take they ended up using. She could warm up with a simple Mozart sonata, or something from the English Suites, to get the feel of the instrument. All right, she said. Again, he'd been prepared to persuade, but it wasn't necessary. She was agreeable, cooperative, businesslike. He'd never seen her so composed before playing, except at home. This idea of his might just turn out to be a stroke of genius.

The first ballade went beautifully: She was in fine form, in full possession of her gifts. He wished there were an audience to hear her. What would those reviewers think now? Afterward, as they put on earphones and listened together, they agreed on a couple of places where repeats were needed, a chord held a tad too long, a wrong note, a phrase just slightly rushed. Nothing out of the ordinary, nothing that would have marred a performance, but CDs had to be perfect. Superhumanly perfect—that was the tradition that had evolved. Misleadingly, as listeners ought to know but didn't.

She didn't object to the repeats, nor did she mind starting in the middle. She was wonderfully accommodating. He was impressed by how easy she was to work with, easier than most of the performers who came to the studio. Very soon he was sure he had enough to put together a perfect whole for each of the first two ballades.

But by the third she was starting to flag. Her energy level had sunk. She was playing too fast, as if she were trying to get it over with. She knew it, too. She stopped abruptly and looked at him behind the glass, where he sat at the controls. He switched everything off and came out to join her.

"Time for a break, right?"

"Yes, I think so," she said.

He made coffee, and when she asked about the technical apparatus, he was happy to show her how it worked, the elaborate board with its lights and switches and buttons, the undulating colored waves on the screen. She'd never shown any curiosity about it before, the few times she'd visited. Now she looked and nodded as if she were taking it all in, though he doubted she was following his explanations. She was trying to please him, doing it all for him. Well, she'd see. He'd put together something spectacular and make sure it got to the right places, and next time she'd be doing it for herself.

But when they began again he could tell she was too tired. She was straining against the music, concentrating too hard, and it showed. He suggested they try again tomorrow. No, wait, not tomorrow, he was booked all day. In a couple of days. Again she agreed, but frowning, clearly disappointed in herself.

"This is taking so much of your time," she said.

"What are you talking about? There's nothing I'd rather do. Anyway, you wouldn't believe how many times people have to come back."

"Really?"

"Really." That was not entirely true. People did have to come back, yes. But they usually lasted longer than this. All day, sometimes.

He and Suzanne had a late lunch at the café around the corner, and then she headed home. When she returned three days later, it was the same. She played well—wonderfully—on and off for nearly two hours. They did a few brief repeats, and that was all she could manage. "Don't worry," Phil assured her. "What we've got here is fine. Maybe one more session, and that'll wrap it up."

If he asked her to keep returning, she'd be worn-out and, worse, she'd lose confidence. That was the last thing he wanted. Especially as she had nurtured her ambitions for so long, long before he met her in high school. As far back as when she was a small child, she'd told him. No, he'd work with whatever he had, Philip decided. Anything that didn't pass muster, well, he'd have to find a way to fix it. He'd fixed Kosinski's well enough, hadn't he?

Part 1

I N HER EARLY years—alarmingly early, it would strike her later on, six, maybe five?—she was troubled by the notion that she might not be real. Everyone around her appeared to be real, her parents, her twin brothers, the children and teachers at school. Everything she touched was real. But she herself, just possibly, was not. She couldn't see herself moving through the world as she saw others. The mirror didn't count. The mirror was a tricky piece of furniture or a toy like a jack-in-the-box: There you are, move aside and there you aren't.

How could you be sure you weren't just a mind dreaming moment to moment, a mind dreaming up a mind? If she put her head on the pillow, it made a dent. When she dug her fingernails into the soft skin just above her wrist, white marks appeared, then vanished. If she ate a slice of bread, it was no longer on the plate but inside her. So there must be a "her" that could accommodate a slice of bread. She had an effect on the material objects of the world. But was that enough to make you real? What was "real"? What was "you," for that matter?

Real did not mean the ability to alter, or even ingest, objects in the physical world, which might itself be a dream. Her own dream. Real, she imagined later on, was something else; it had nothing to do with things you could touch. Real was being seen, noticed, acknowledged, and later remembered. Real was people thinking about you when you weren't in the room. If others thought about you, then you must be more than a made-up dream. You needed other people in order to be real, she decided. Otherwise you might be just a speck, an atom, inventing an elaborate story. It seemed like a paradox, yet it must be so. She knew other people were real because she thought about them. Her thinking of her parents and her brothers, her school friends, was proof that they were real. They were both outside and in her head. But how could she be sure she was in anyone's head?

When she played the piano, her doubts subsided. The music was undeniably real—it never occurred to her to question that. And if she was producing it, well, then, the music conferred its reality on her. Even more, her touching the notes in a certain way made something in the world happen—sound, music—and that in turn made something happen in people's minds. They listened and heard, they nodded, they smiled with pleasure and appreciation. If they were more than simple clods, they even felt something. The sounds she produced changed them. The making of the music and the hearing of it, and what happened inside the listeners—that was all real beyond a doubt. That was the kind of reality she could trust and rest in. It was *she* who made it happen, and it was their knowledge of that fact that confirmed her existence.

So when her father would summon her from downstairs, make her leave off reading on her bed or dressing her paper dolls, meticulously folding the little tabs at the shoulders and wrists and feet—the shoes were especially hard to do—and call her to entertain the visiting friends and relatives, even though she hated being displayed like a rare piece of merchandise that had miraculously fallen into his possession, she was lured as well. She slumped down the stairs slowly, like someone anticipating an ordeal, yet she knew that at the end of the ordeal would come the irresistible reward. It was not so much the attention, the astonished faces, the praise. It was the hugely satisfying certainty of her own existence—the music being heard, received, responded to. And so she colluded with her father at the same time as she resented his pressure, his vulgarity, his overweening pride in what he had nothing to do with. He was a musical dullard; the music genes came from her mother's side of the family, all of them good singers, a distant uncle even a cantor in a Queens synagogue.

There was no use protesting, in any case, at least not when she was so young. She could be stubborn but was no match for her father, older, bigger, with that deep hoarse voice. He never actually threatened her with any punishment if she refused—his worst punishments were the glares, the muttered words of his displeasure—but in the face of his badgering, sometimes accompanied by the badgering of the guests, her child's will deflated and collapsed.

When she was older, ten or eleven, she bitterly resented the command performances. The allure was gone; she no longer needed them. She could do it for herself, confirm her own reality, anytime she chose. But still she obeyed; it was habit, the easier path. And she was old enough and cunning enough to grasp that possessing her and putting her on display was her father's way of reassuring himself of his own reality. Still, when the brief performances were over—one piece was usually enough to prove his point—she was flushed with excitement.

Her eyes shone, her skin was lustrous. She was Suzanne, the prodigy, the child who had the special gift. Her gratification was utterly unlike her father's, more inward, more simple, less selfish.

Her mother had used that word, "gift," when she first discovered it. "She has a gift. A natural gift," she announced to the family. At the time, Suzanne was barely four. She thought a gift was something you were given on your birthday, wrapped in paper and tied with ribbons. A toy, a book, something to wear. You tore it open, shredding the noisy colorful paper, while people watched, and then you were supposed to say thank you whether you liked it or not. But this, she realized, was a different kind of gift. Something you already possessed without knowing it, something inside that you'd taken for granted as part of who you were. And there was no giver. It was just there, mixed in with the rest of you, the parts that were like everyone else's, but not everyone else had this. It made you special.

And so, after she played for people who recognized her gift, she could accept that she was real. It must be true. This was who she was: the girl with a gift. Then her native diffidence would peel away, she could smile and accept their praise and happily, even giddily, high on her own success, join them around the table to eat the platters of food her mother set out. And as she grew older she suspected that the food, which disappeared so quickly, to praise that almost equaled the praise for her music, was her mother's way of confirming her own existence. The notion that grown-ups, even her parents, perhaps everyone, needed some display to assure themselves that they were real and not mere pretenses, was consoling. She was not alone in her doubts. She played, she ate, she chattered. She would do her part in the great game, everyone tacitly agreeing to grant one another their reality.

They had begun, these command performances, a few years after the notable day her mother often referred to, talking to friends about Suzanne. Gerda was in the kitchen, singing as she often did as she went about her work, sliding a roasting pan holding a chicken into the oven. Gerda Stellman had a rich, husky voice, dense with emotion; the women she played bridge with urged her to try to get on one of the TV amateur shows, but she had no interest in performing in public. She was singing "Santa Lucia." Near the end of the verse she reached the high note, then the melody took a series of steps down, then back to the high note again. That was how it sounded to Suzanne, playing with dolls on the floor in the adjacent living room. She could see in her mind the melody tripping down and then up a staircase. Lately she had experimented at the piano, trying to pick out tunes, nursery rhymes, "Three Blind Mice," figuring out how the staircase of notes worked, how the white keys and the black corresponded to the notes of a sung melody, but she did it mostly when Gerda was out on errands, leaving her with her older twin brothers. They were willing enough to look after her but had an intense private fantasy life, replete with monsters, pirates, mercenaries, and the accompanying plastic paraphernalia, and so were glad when she could amuse herself.

As she listened to Gerda sing, Suzanne went to the piano and found the note that was the top step and then moved the index finger of her right hand down the keyboard, making the notes imitate the song's journey along the flight of stairs.

Her mother stopped singing and came into the living room,

wiping her hands on a dish towel. Gerda was a plump, fair-haired woman—colorful, Suzanne thought, with her pink cheeks and green eyes and not quite orange-gold hair. There was something doll-like about her—the creamy porcelain skin, the rounded cheeks, the wide-open eyes always looking surprised, or anticipating surprise, something like the dolls Suzanne dressed with care. Suzanne was nothing like her. She could see in the mirror—it might not be trusted for reality, but about appearances it did not lie—that she resembled her father, tall and olive-skinned, with black hair, the bangs reaching down to her eyes like a curtain. Sometimes her father's rough hand brushed the bangs away. "How can you see with all that hair in your face?" Joseph Stellman's body was heavy and coarse, though, and Suzanne was slender and would remain so.

"What are you doing, sweetheart?" Gerda asked.

"Playing the song."

"Let me hear it again."

"I don't remember it exactly. Sing it."

The melody lasted long, with much climbing and descending, but Suzanne listened intently and made it stay in her head the whole way through. Reproducing it was easy. The hard part was keeping it all in her head, like a story with many turns of the plot.

She couldn't understand why her mother got so excited. Gerda dropped her towel, hugged and kissed her and fussed over her. Then she asked her to play other tunes, simple ones: "Row, Row, Row Your Boat," "Frère Jacques." All perfect! The ear of a musical genius! Gerda couldn't stop exclaiming. How could she not have known until now? True, Suzanne could carry a tune remarkably for a four-year-old. But everyone in Gerda's family could sing. Even the boys could sing, though they had never shown any interest in music; their piano lessons had been given up after two pointless years of fumbling scales and arpeggios. But this, Suzanne at the piano. This was special.

She couldn't wait to tell Joseph when he came home from work. He grunted, skeptical as he always was of Gerda's enthusiasms, of most enthusiasms except those regarding business ventures. She was undaunted. Just wait and see, she said. Wait till after supper. In her state of exaltation, Gerda had left the chicken in the oven too long. Joseph and the boys, Fred and Gary, who were nearly fourteen, pronounced it dry.

"What does it matter? It's only a chicken. Dry!" Gerda said scornfully, though she was usually sensitive to comments about her cooking. "Do you realize what this means? She has a natural gift."

After supper, Gerda made Suzanne play for her father and brothers, who seated themselves patiently in the living room, indulgently, then listened in growing wonder. Tune after tune, with one finger: "Mary Had a Little Lamb," "The Itsy Bitsy Spider," "Twinkle, Twinkle, Little Star." In the midst of "Twinkle, Twinkle, Little Star" there came a whistle from the kitchen, ascending to a screech. Suzanne stopped; it was an adversarial music, ugly and unremitting.

"Gerda, the teapot," Joseph said.

"Oh, I forgot all about it." She'd been sitting entranced. She rushed into the kitchen and the noise stopped.

"Well, how about that," Joseph Stellman said at last. "How

about that. Come here and let me look at you," he commanded
Suzanne, and she obeyed. He placed his hands on her shoulders and scrutinized her, as if he could locate on her face some
physical source of the music. Then he hugged her roughly.
"That was very good. That was really something special."

He was a hulk of a man, hairy, solid, and muscular, with
thick impassive features in a face that looked always in need
of a shave, and hazel eyes that studied the world with wary
discontent, as though from long experience he expected it to
fall short of his requirements. The youngest child of a large
immigrant family, he chided his sons constantly for their lack
of ambition. Drive, he called it, reminding them that America
was the land of opportunity. "Look at FDR. You're probably
too young to remember, but he was a cripple. Did he let that
stop him? No. And you have your legs and arms and brains, so
use them."

He had taken pride in the birth of twin sons, as if the double-
ness implied his superior potency, and from the start nursed
the desire that they be special. Special. It was a word he used
often, for people in the news, feats of diplomacy or athlet-
ics, popular entertainers. Most people were run-of-the-mill.
Ordinary. Ordinary himself—and he knew this—he had contempt for the ordinary in public life. His sons disappointed
him, easygoing good-natured boys, average students who
didn't appreciate their privileged lives—Joseph's early years
had been anything but privileged, in a cramped apartment on
the Lower East Side—boyishly predictable in their interests,
showing no unusual skills except for punch ball in the street
and card tricks, their current passion. "Pick a card, Pop," one
or the other would say, and he would do so stiffly, grudgingly.

They would proceed to execute quite extraordinary and baffling feats with the deck for which Joseph could muster no interest, while Gerda, looking on, was suitably amazed. He even found something sinister in such antics, as if they verged on the disreputable.

The boys presented a united front at all times, a separate unit within the family, spending hours together in their room doing God knows what—learning more card tricks, probably; certainly not studying—although if Suzanne wandered in they accepted her willingly, as they would a family pet. Or they would disappear for hours on end, playing ball in the schoolyard, they said if Joseph questioned them. He had given up on them as far as special was concerned. They were decent boys who stayed out of trouble, so he was leaving them to grow up as they would. Now it struck him that it was the girl, whose birth was unplanned and greeted, by him if not by Gerda, with mixed feelings (more responsibility, more expense), who might turn out to gratify his yearnings for something special.

And so he invested his hopes in her, small as she was. Special came to mean more than playing the piano. Special meant school as well. What good was having a gift if you didn't develop the brains to deploy it properly? Suzanne was bright enough, everyone found her charming—she had a natural ingenuous grace—but she didn't put herself forward. Piano lessons were all very well, but she must learn to be more aggressive, to stand up for herself, to compete. Life was a battleground. She had the weapons, but she must train her will to use them.

She did well in school. Her quarterly report cards gave him nothing to reproach her with. Until, in the fourth grade, she presented a report card to him as usual for his signature. Gerda was cleaning up the remains of dinner, and the boys, by then sophomores at Brooklyn College, had gone upstairs ostensibly to study. Joseph was sitting in his shirtsleeves at the small desk in the dining room where he paid the bills. He gave the report card a cursory glance, a small folded four-sided document on stiff paper that attempted to look official. He was reaching for his fountain pen, when he noticed the B+ in geography.

"Why only a B+?" he asked, as if it were a joke, yet not entirely a joke.

"I was absent the day she gave the test. It was when I had the earache."

"And so?"

"And so she said that was a fair grade, considering I missed the test."

"It's not a fair grade. You don't have to accept that. Go back to your teacher," Joseph said, frowning at the world's injustice, "and tell her your father said to give you a makeup test."

"I don't want to. What does it matter? It's not even a final grade, just the middle of the term."

"Do what I tell you," he said firmly. "There's no reason you shouldn't have an A. You need to stand up for your rights. I'm sure you know your geography." He handed the card back to her and turned away to uncap the pen and reach for the top bill on the pile, an envelope, Suzanne noticed as she was turning away, with a tiny picture of a telephone on it.

She avoided arguing with him. His will was as ungainly and immobile as his body. She could be strong, too, in another way: She was able to withdraw and pretend that what was happening was not really happening, just a show she was enacting. In this way, she could do unpleasant things—like many of the actions demanded by school—and get through them with aplomb. The following day she approached Mrs. Gutterman and told her what her father had said about the makeup test. The teacher hesitated, then nodded.

Late in the afternoon, after she had named the mountain ranges of North America, Mrs. Gutterman, a reedy woman in her fifties with gray clothes and wispy blond hair in a precarious pompadour, asked Suzanne to stand up at her seat. As one of the tallest in the class, Suzanne was in the fourth row toward the back of the room.

"All right, Suzanne. We can make this quick. I'll just ask you a few questions."

Not happening, Susanne thought. Just stand and give the answers. The real world is inside, where no one can touch. As the entire class turned to watch, Mrs. Gutterman asked her to name the longest rivers in North and South America, which Suzanne knew, and then the capital cities of several European countries, which she also knew, and then asked her what the prime meridian was, which Suzanne did not know. She remembered it had been explained more than once, but it had puzzled her the first time, and after that she had daydreamed. Now, in the kind of patient, teacherly voice that conceals impatience, Mrs. Gutterman said that the prime meridian was an arbitrary line passing through the town of Greenwich, in Great Britain, at which the earth's longitude is zero. Suzanne still didn't grasp what those words meant, but she did know that if she had memorized them and recited them back, her answer would have been counted as correct.

"So," Mrs. Gutterman concluded, "you can tell your father that B+ was not unfair after all." She paused, then continued with a certain satisfaction. "Tell your father that a B+ is all you deserve." Again she paused, as if reconsidering her words, and added more gently, "And that's not so bad, really. It's a good grade."

That evening Suzanne told her father about the test. "I didn't know what the prime meridian was."

"The prime meridian," he muttered. "Christ, I could have told you that. All right, then, never mind." He picked up his newspaper and slapped its folds into place.

Why didn't he explain it, then, if he knew what it was? He must think it didn't matter, Suzanne thought. He didn't care whether she knew what the prime meridian was. What mattered was whether she could display her knowledge in public.

For her father's sake she didn't repeat the teacher's words. Their asperity was not lost on her, yet she knew they would humiliate Joseph more than they had humiliated her. But if the words struck her only lightly when she was nine, they stayed with her forever, gaining in density, to insinuate themselves whenever her performance fell short of perfection. They were less a mortification, she feared, than a possibly accurate statement of fact: B+ is all you deserve.

But that came later on. Meanwhile, after the memorable day when Suzanne's gift had been discovered, Gerda was quick to spread the word about it, as in the Middle Ages someone might report to the townspeople a sighting of a saint's face on a crumbling wall or cast-off garment, and soon all the neighbors knew. In time Suzanne was taking piano lessons from Mrs. Gardenia, a canasta friend of Selma Gruber across the street, who extolled her mild way with young children. Mrs. Gardenia had short curly white hair fluffed around her head, pink cheeks, and small round wire-rimmed glasses. Her breath smelled of the wintergreen lozenges she liked to suck. She lived and taught in an apartment on Kings Highway, where Gerda accompanied Suzanne every Wednesday afternoon on the bus after kindergarten let out. Suzanne enjoyed the lessons. She liked learning new melodies, and liked reaching up to put her mother's fare in the box on the bus, one dime.

After the bus they walked three blocks to Mrs. Gardenia's tan brick building, where older children played boxball and Hit the Penny out front, then took the elevator to the fourth floor, where Mrs. Gardenia stood waiting at her door, wearing a flowered print dress—Suzanne rarely saw the same dress twice—and black lace-up Oxford shoes, smiling and waving her left hand, adorned with several rings that flashed rainbows in the light.

First thing, Mrs. Gardenia would ask Gerda if she wanted a cup of tea, which she always declined. Then, while Suzanne had her half-hour lesson in the living room, Gerda would sit reading *Redbook* or *Good Housekeeping* at the dining-room table, which was covered with an embroidered cloth, flowers and birds. Mrs. Gardenia had stitched it herself, she told them at the first lesson; it kept her busy in the evenings, and she could do it while she watched her new TV.

The living room was small, crowded with tufted furniture with brass buttons running up the arms, and with knickknacks on shelves, miniature porcelain figurines of farm animals, fringed lampshades, and small scatter rugs on top of larger rugs. A dollhouse room, Suzanne thought, as she stepped carefully so as not to slip on the rugs.

Mrs. Gardenia pulled a chair next to the piano bench and

said, "So, let's hear what we've accomplished this week." She assigned Suzanne scales and exercises from Hanon, which she hated, and every few weeks she would produce a new piece of music, presenting it as a reward. Mrs. Gardenia was lavish with her praise and kindly when she corrected errors in her flutelike voice, sometimes taking Suzanne's hand in hers and arranging the fingers on the keys. Suzanne's hands were still too small to stretch an entire octave.

After the lesson there was a glass of orange juice on a coaster placed on a small table near the piano, and two cookies on a flowered plate next to a white paper napkin folded in a triangle. The cookies changed from week to week; Suzanne liked the shortbread best. She ate her snack while Mrs. Gardenia and her mother chatted about recipes and shopping and mutual acquaintances, Selma Gruber's daughter, for one, who was going out with a law student who drove a flashy car and kept her out till all hours.

Suzanne grew attached to Mrs. Gardenia and her progress was swift. Her hands grew and her fingers gained strength. After the first year and a half there came simplified and abridged versions of Haydn or Mozart sonatas, an occasional waltz. She could hear the music in her head and feel it in her fingers. She even got in the habit of playing her simple pieces on the kitchen tabletop or on her desk at school. When she got into bed, almost unconsciously her fingers played against her palms, repeating phrases over and over. She practiced dutifully a half-hour a day, as Mrs. Gardenia instructed, but after she finished the formal practicing she would amuse herself by picking out popular tunes she heard on the radio Gerda kept in the kitchen, or made up tunes of her own. After another year she was beginning on the Bach Inventions and the easier sections of the French and English Suites, as well as the chromatic fantasies of Kuhlau and a few short pieces by Couperin. But this relaxed idyll changed when she came under the influence of Richard Penzer, the man across the street whom all the mothers warned their girls to avoid.

⌒

All four girls on the block, the little pack of nine-year-olds of which Suzanne was a provisional, half-reluctant member, were collecting money for the March of Dimes. At school they had been given white cans with a slit on the top and, on the sides, a blue-toned photograph of a smiling boy with bangs and missing teeth, sitting in a wheelchair, his hands folded in his lap. He looked like he was waiting for something to happen, maybe waiting for rescue from the chair into which he was strapped and buckled. The money they collected, the girls were told, would be used to help this unfortunate boy and others like him get better. They had polio, the teacher said, maybe from swimming in a public pool; their legs were paralyzed, but they longed to run around as all children do. Nowadays, children were lucky: They had the new vaccine that would keep them from getting polio, and they should be very grateful to Dr. Salk, who had invented it. But some children had gotten sick before there was any vaccine. So the lucky, healthy children must knock on their neighbors' doors and ask them to put coins in the slot to cure the unlucky children.

Suzanne's father hadn't wanted her to go knocking on doors. "I don't like the idea of her begging," he said. "Last year it was to plant trees in Israel, for chrissake."

"This is different. It's not begging," Gerda chided. "It's for charity, for polio. Her friends are going. Let her go with them. She spends too much time alone." He finally agreed, as long as she did her practicing first. Nothing must interfere with the piano. A gift must be cultivated. Joseph anticipated a career for her as a high school music teacher, at the very least. Beyond that, who could say?

Suzanne set out in the early September evening—the days were long and it was still light, an amber, benevolent light— with Eva, Alison, and Paula. Eva was the leader of the group, and the nastiest. Everyone on the block recognized that, and it was a designation she herself acknowledged, one in which she seemed even to take pride. She was the sort of girl who as she grew older would dream up more and more subtle ways to discomfort her friends; meanwhile at the age of nine, she did what was within her limited powers. She tormented her four-year-old brother by hiding his favorite toys and, at bed-time, describing monsters who might visit in the night, from whom any attempt to escape would be futile. Eva's father's dental practice was in the basement of their row house, with a special entrance near the garage for patients. Sometimes she would sneak a book from his office and show the other girls photographs of rotting teeth and pustulating gum sores, or tiny pointed instruments of torture.

Paula and Alison, who were weaker of will and unresource-ful, followed Eva slavishly; she could always think up something to do or someplace to explore, within the bounds of the few blocks they were allowed to travel. Suzanne joined them only occasionally, partly because of her practicing schedule, partly because she disliked Eva's cruelty and the others' stupidity.

But when she was lonely she would seek them out, although Eva, sensing Suzanne's ambivalence, said she came around only when she had nothing better to do, which was true.

The mothers had given them strict instructions for the expedition. They could ring the doorbells of people they knew, which meant nearly everyone in the identical attached brick row houses. If people were in the middle of dinner, they must apologize for disturbing them and leave. They must remain at the doors and not go inside. And if people refused to give money, they must not insist but simply say goodnight and continue on. And be careful climbing over the porch ledges; it was fruitless to tell them not to climb, for that was the common way of going from house to house. Above all, they must not knock on the door of the man who lived in number 23. They'd been warned before about him: Don't get into conversation if he talks to you on the street, and never go into his house if he invites you. None of the girls knew the reason for this restriction; the parents themselves didn't quite understand it. They knew only that Richard Penzer was different from the other neighbors, and in the postwar decade, different was dangerous. His ways were not their ways.

That he lived alone was in itself suspect. Every other house held a married couple with children, and the occasional grandparents. Each house was fronted by a small brick porch, each porch gave onto a flight of steps bordered by shrubs, here and there a hydrangea bush, and each house had its driveway and garage. The driveways of each two neighboring houses were adjacent, so that when the husbands returned from work at the end of the day, cars were lined up in pairs between the houses, as if preparing to dance an automotive quadrille.

Richard Penzer had the requisite porch and stairs, shrubs, driveway and car. But he didn't resemble the other drivers, the husbands in baggy gabardine trousers and wilted shirts, who trudged up the stairs after parking the cars, jackets slung over their shoulders on one finger, a puny stab at the debonair, past the hydrangea bushes, to read the paper while waiting for their dinner. He dressed more carefully, more crisply, and stood up straight and strode more nonchalantly. He was rumored to be some kind of music teacher—this from the Grubers, his next-door neighbors—but he didn't leave early in the morning and return home in the late afternoon. His hours were erratic and unpredictable.

Richard Penzer, who was thirty years old on the evening of the March of Dimes collection, had occasional visits from other young men, and sometimes slightly older men, all of them well dressed, well built, with noticeably erect posture, often but not always carrying black cases—the Grubers said they contained musical instruments; they could hear little concerts through the walls by the men who parked in front of his house and walked up the steps, looking neither left nor right, and then disappeared inside. If it was a single visitor, after a while the two of them, Richard and the guest, might come out and get into one of the cars and drive off. Sometimes Richard Penzer returned quite late at night, and sometimes he and his car, a red Pontiac convertible, were gone for days at a time.

Little else was known about him, barely enough to supply material for gossip. He had moved in two years ago, after the house had stood vacant for several months. The previous occupants had been renting, the Grubers reported, and when the owner died, Richard Penzer, his nephew, inherited it. It was odd, the Grubers agreed with their neighbors, that a young single man who worked in the city ("the city" meant Manhattan), teaching music somewhere, would choose to live on their quiet block, but on the other hand it was an inheritance, rent-free. Most likely he wouldn't stay long; he must be saving money for a move to the city. He wrote music, too, they said, though they weren't sure what kind, and he played the bassoon. From time to time they had to phone him when his practicing continued too far into the night. The bassoon, the Grubers said, was a strange-sounding instrument, deep, low, it was hard to explain the otherworldly mournful feeling it induced. Richard Penzer always apologized after playing too late and stopped immediately; he'd lost track of the time, he'd say. Apart from that he was a good neighbor, but the Grubers' endorsement couldn't stop the general distrust.

Despite his difference, on warm spring and summer evenings he might be seen sitting out on his porch like everyone else, reading the newspaper or chatting with the Grubers next door. He seemed to enjoy talking to their grown and marriageable daughter, Francine, who worked as a secretary at a publishing firm in the city, in the hope of being promoted to editor someday, and at night didn't change into a cotton sundress or jeans, like the other working girls on the block, but remained in her citygoing outfit, a print dress or a suit with high heels and nylons, leafing through magazines on the porch, waiting for a date to pick her up. Lately it had been the same young man for several months, so naturally there was speculation, but the Grubers were noncommittal on the subject.

The four girls were on the Grubers' porch—Mr. Gruber had dropped a few coins in each canister—when Eva suggested they knock on Richard Penzer's door. (Later on, at moments when Eva's behavior was loathsome, Suzanne strove to be grateful for her audacity: If not for Eva, she might not have met Richard, and then her childhood would have been very different.)

"We can see what his house looks like. Maybe it's a torture chamber with chains and stuff. Or maybe he likes to feel up girls. We can see if he tries anything. Nothing can happen with four of us. We can always scream and run away."

Suzanne, who had a well-deserved reputation for naiveté, didn't know what "feeling up" meant, so Eva demonstrated by lunging forward, her hands spread wide to grab at Suzanne's flat chest. Suzanne shrieked and sprang back before Eva could touch her.

"He's all alone in the house," Alison said. "He could have dead bodies in the basement."

"Maybe he was the robber," Paula suggested.

The robbery, an unusual event for the placid street, had occurred a week ago at number 18, home to a young couple with a small boy. When the boy went to wake his parents in the morning, Sam Reichenthal found his wallet gone from the dresser top where he customarily left it. After a thorough search, the only explanation was that a burglar had slipped in through an open casement window on the ground floor that Sam had forgotten to lock, though he denied this. At any rate, the window was found ajar and part of the rug below was bunched up as if the couch had been moved. The intruder must have crept up the stairs and into the bedroom without waking either Sam or Dora and made off with the wallet containing $60. Credit cards, in the mid-1950s, were far from ubiquitous. Life in Brooklyn was benign—even the burglars were mild-mannered.

"People don't rob their neighbors," Suzanne said. "They go out of the neighborhood, where no one knows them." About this she was not naive; she watched *Perry Mason* on TV with her older brothers, who explained the more elusive points of the plot.

One by one, the girls climbed the low brick wall over to Richard Penzer's porch. The front casement windows were covered by shades, so they couldn't peer in. Without waiting for the others to assent, Eva knocked. The door opened promptly and a tall, lanky man appeared, wearing jeans and a black T-shirt, his longish dark hair drooping over his eyes, a slender lit cigar between his fingers. To Suzanne the acrid smell of the cigar was familiar and reassuring; her father smoked them, too, but greener, fatter ones, and gave her their paper gold rings to wear.He left smoldering butts in ashtrays all over the house, which she had learned to stub out.

"Well, good evening. What have we here, a delegation? I've never had the honor before, though I've seen you playing in the street. To what do I owe this visit?"

Eva told him about the March of Dimes and the paralyzed children while Paula and Alison, huddled behind her, giggled at the way he spoke.

"That's very good of you. Why don't you come in while I go and find some change." He held the door wide for them to pass.

No one else had invited them in. They hesitated, looking at Eva, who after a moment strode inside. The others followed.

"Wait here and I'll be right back," he said.

Suzanne gazed around the room. There was a red figured Persian rug on the floor, quite unlike the wall-to-wall beige carpeting of her own living room. There were cylindrical hanging Japanese paper lampshades in different colors, and several huge pillows scattered on the floor. On the wall hung paintings with shapes she couldn't identify—they looked like scribbles, or planets, or freakish fish gliding underwater. One wall was painted dark green; another held a large corkboard with slips of paper pinned to it. In one corner stood a large grand piano, bigger than her own, with music on the rack. Near it, propped up against the wall, was the narrow leather case she had seen Richard Penzer carrying from his car: That must be the bassoon. She had never seen a room like it before.

It wasn't the furnishings alone that made it so different. It was the atmosphere; it was not familial. There was another purpose, another principle, animating the life lived in that room. Everything in it was designed to please just one person, to allow him to carry on just as he wished. It was the clear air of solitude she was recognizing, and also dedication, though she had not yet defined those qualities for herself. She simply felt them, like smelling or tasting something with closed eyes, and though it can't be identified, it elicits a glimmer of recognition.

Richard Penzer returned holding a small bronze bowl full of coins and distributed several in each of their canisters, dropping quarters in one by one with a clinking noise. "I hope this helps your cause. But why not sit down for a moment? I'll bring you some cookies and . . . what do you drink? Juice? Milk?"

Suzanne perched on a straight-backed chair and the other three lined up gingerly on the edge of a navy blue velvet sofa while Richard went back into the kitchen.

"Maybe we should go," whispered Alison. "My mother said—"

"Shh," Eva whispered back. "I want to see what he does next. This is an adventure. He gave us more money than any of the others."

When Richard came back with a tray, Suzanne was sitting at the piano, her hands moving on the keys but making no sound. The music on the rack was by someone she had never heard of, Béla Bartók. Maybe it was a woman—her mother had an old Aunt Bella who lived in the Bronx. Richard Penzer passed around the peanut butter cookies and poured the juice into glasses, then went over to Suzanne. "Do you play?"

"A little. I take lessons."

"Do you want to try it?" As if to encourage her, he sat down beside her and played some arpeggios, then a few notes from Mendelssohn's "Spring Song."

"Oh, I know that," said Suzanne. "But we only have an upright."

"Go ahead, then. Don't be afraid."

"No." She got up from the bench. She wouldn't, not in front of the girls. The music was from another part of her life, her real life that had nothing to do with these girls. They might even laugh at her. It was as if she were two different people, the one who played the piano and the one who went ringing door-bells with them, and the second one was a distorted shadow of the first, a role she had to play because she was a child and that was what children had to do. The piano was something only she could do. Yet here in this room the Two-Parts of her were both asserting themselves, and she didn't know what to do with them, how to reconcile them. This man wasn't like the aunts and uncles her father made her perform for, who didn't really understand the music, merely admired her dexterity, as if she were some sort of acrobat. He was different, he seemed genuinely interested. She had a dim sense that this room and this man came from her future, while the girls, with their petty intrigues and gossip and collection boxes, would soon drift into the past.

"Okay, maybe not right now. But you can come back and try it anytime you want. Just ring the bell," he said, smiling over at her, as if the others had vanished and they two were alone.

"You wouldn't dare," said Alison after they were back out on the porch, nibbling the last of the cookies and climbing over to the next house.

"I might," said Suzanne nonchalantly. "He seemed nice."

"That's because there were four of us," said Eva. "You don't know what he might do alone. We can't tell anyone we went inside. It has to be our secret. Did you see those crazy paintings? I went up to the bathroom on purpose, to look in the bedroom. There's this enormous bed with a purple cover. Lots of books. And more pictures. One of Jesus Christ on a cross with a big hole in his side and blood coming out. It was really gross."

Three days later, in the late afternoon, Suzanne told her mother she was going to Paula's house and rang Richard Penzer's doorbell. He welcomed her as if they were old friends and he'd been expecting her. The bassoon was out of its case, lying on the couch, and a music stand was set up nearby.

"Did you come to try out the piano? Go right ahead." He waved her over. "I have some things to do in the kitchen."

He left her alone in the room with the pictures and the colored lampshades and the bassoon, and she felt at home, as if this were a place that had been waiting for her, like a cottage in the woods in a fairy tale, and she was grateful that she'd finally found it.

⌒

With so many observers on the block, there was no way of keeping her visits to Richard a secret. Gerda scolded her as she had expected and wanted her to promise never to return to number 23. But Suzanne, who felt as excited as if she had discovered a magic kingdom right across the street, allayed her mother's fears by repeating that he was a music teacher, he taught at Hunter College in the city, and no, he never touched her, only helped her with her lessons and played records for her and taught her things; and no, there were never any other people there.

This last was not entirely true. A few times she had come upon a friend of his in the living room—from the doorway she could hear an opera on the phonograph, and she saw the man drinking something amber-colored out of a small glass. Richard had greeted her kindly but asked if she could come back the next day. And twice she had found him with two friends, playing music. One man was at the piano and the other played the violin; Richard was holding his bassoon when he opened the door. He invited her in to listen, but the first time she was shy and backed away. The second time she went in and sat on the couch while they played. She had never heard chamber music before; it was a revelation—had she been familiar with sex, it would have struck her as a new kind of caress. They were playing a Beethoven trio, Richard told her. He was playing the part meant for a cello. She looked puzzled and so he explained what a cello was and said that another day he would teach her about all the instruments in the orchestra. Meanwhile she should simply listen to the way the three instruments played together, like tossing a ball back and forth, or, better still, as if they were having a conversation, asking questions and answering them, or sometimes saying the same thing in their different voices. When they were finished she sat dazzled by what she had heard.

The pianist's name was Arthur and the violinist was called Dan, though at first she was too shy to call them by name. Mostly she called grown-ups, her teachers and her parents' friends, Mr. and Mrs., although she had gotten used to calling Richard by his name. When they were done they played a few parts over slowly to show her how they fit together, and then Arthur let her sit next to him on the piano bench and showed her the music. She even played a few simple measures with the violin and the bassoon, and afterward the three of them clapped. She flushed with pleasure and curtseyed as if she were on a real stage, making them all laugh. This was real, this was the reality she had been looking for. It existed—these men were proof—and she was a part of it.

About a year after she met Richard, Suzanne was summoned by her father to play for Aunt Faye and Uncle Simon, who had dropped in on a Sunday afternoon. They were her favorite aunt and uncle. Faye, her father's sister, was a seamstress with a merry, lilting voice that sounded operatic, flitting rapidly up and down the scale. She was plump and chatty, as lively as her brother was taciturn. Often she brought Suzanne embroidered blouses and once a skirt in a paisley pattern that twirled when she spun around. Uncle Simon could wiggle his ears—though by now she had outgrown her delight in that—and could recite lines of poetry in his faintly British accent. Suzanne loved hearing him come up with his quotations. On their last visit, when her mother and Aunt Faye were discussing what to do about a cousin who was still unmarried at thirty, Uncle Simon cleared his throat dramatically and said, "Full many a rose is born to blush unseen, and waste its fragrance on the desert air." Faye slapped his hand mockingly and said it wasn't over yet for that rose, there was still time. And when Suzanne's father boasted about how well his furniture business was doing—the new housing development a few blocks from the store was a godsend—Uncle Simon muttered, "Put money in thy purse."

Joseph Stellman was immune to his brother-in-law's wit and found his charm negligible, because (as he told Gerda after their visit), Simon could barely make a living as a clerk in a men's haberdashery. "If Faye didn't keep working they'd be up shit creek" was how he put it. "He sits on a stool and reads. The customers have to tap him on the shoulder to get his attention."

When she heard her father's voice calling her from downstairs, Suzanne recoiled. She was in the middle of a Nancy Drew mystery, *The Quest of the Missing Map*, and the plot was at a crucial point: Nancy had found the decisive clue and was about to tell Ned who the villain was and how they would trap him.

"Don't you hear me?" He was halfway up the stairs. "I want Faye and Simon to hear that new piece you learned." Now he was in the doorway. Suzanne looked up, her finger in her place.

"You know the one I mean, with the fancy runs? Is it Bach? Or Beethoven?"

It was a Chopin étude she'd begun working on two weeks ago, the third. Mrs. Gardenia said it was a good place to begin Chopin. "Take it slowly," she said, "one hand at a time, before you try them together. Just do up to here—" she pointed. "That's enough for a start." But Suzanne had played the two hands together on the third day of practicing and gone further than Mrs. Gardenia indicated. The other night her father had stood behind her, listening, then patted her head. "Very nice, very nice." She grew hot with scorn; she hardly knew the piece yet. The dynamics were shaky and she still stumbled over the chromatic chords. He didn't even know what he was hearing.

"I just started that one, Dad. I can't do it right yet."

"It sounded fine to me. Come on, put the book away. You can go back to it later."

She protested, he insisted, until she followed him sullenly down the stairs. He always won. He was still stronger.

She played badly, as she knew she would, even worse than she expected because she was stiff with tension and rage. Her fingers faltered over the runs and botched the chords, even the timing. She stopped at a chord resolution—he'd never know the piece wasn't really over—and, resisting the impulse to end with an infantile bang on the keys, let her hands grip the edge of the bench instead. There was silence. No one could pretend this had been a stellar performance.

"Well, now, that wasn't bad, considering how difficult it is. Chopin, right? One of the études?" Uncle Simon said.

She nodded without looking up. She wouldn't let them see her tears. "I told you," she murmured. "I told you I didn't know it yet."

"All right, all right, let's sit down and have something to eat," said Joseph.

At the table Uncle Simon nudged her and began making up a limerick about Chopin—"There was a composer named Chopin, who wrote études quite hard for the left hand . . ."—but she couldn't bring herself to smile.

As soon as they left, she grabbed her jacket and headed for the door.

"Where are you going?" her mother asked.

"Out." She slammed the door before Gerda could say anything more.

Luckily there were no unfamiliar cars parked in front of Richard's house. Sometimes on weekends his friends came over with their instruments. But today she found him alone, with an opera coming from the radio.

"*Tosca*," he said. "Come on in and sit down. She's just about to throw herself over the balcony, it's only a few more minutes."

To her surprise, she was able to concentrate on the music, and it calmed her. The soprano's voice was powerful and full of grief, but contained, like liquid poured through a channel. Suzanne wasn't sure what the grief was about, but it made her own seem much smaller. Afterward, Richard told her how Tosca had been tricked into thinking the man she loved was dead, and so she jumped off a parapet.

"It's great to watch it onstage," he said. "She jumps and vanishes and you really think the singer is dead. That was Maria

Callas. She's incomparable, of course. What's the matter? You don't look too good."

As she recounted playing the étude so badly, she wept tears of frustration. If she could sing, she would sing like that woman, proclaiming her fury and wretchedness.

"Why didn't you play something else, something you knew? If, as you say, he can't tell one piece from another."

"He wanted that one. I don't know. I didn't think of it. It's like he . . . sort of casts a spell on me. Maybe I wanted it to come out bad, just to show him. I can't play it yet, but I think I made it worse almost on purpose."

"If your father would listen to me I'd tell him to cut it out. But it's all he can do to say hello on the street. Tell me, why does it matter so much? I mean, it's your aunt and uncle. You know them. They know you can play, and even if you couldn't . . . so what if you mess up one time?"

"I don't know. I just can't. When I play for people I have to sound good. It's not just the music. It's as if they're listening to *me*—I mean me the person. If the music is bad, then I'm bad."

"If you think that way, you'll make it all harder. The music is itself—you can't harm it no matter what you do. You're only the interpreter. You do your best. If people are judging you—and you seem to think they always are—all they can judge is that you haven't learned the piece properly yet. It's not your whole identity."

"But it is," she cried. "It's all I have."

"Nonsense," Richard said. "It's not all you have. It may be your best thing, but it's not the only thing, believe me."

She didn't believe him. "And anyway, I get scared when people are listening. I don't know why. I can't do it the way I want, the way I hear it in my head."

"That's not unusual. But you can learn to overcome it, if you really want to play, that is. Meanwhile, if you can't stop your father when he makes you perform, just play something you know well. Something short. And try to remember it's not the end of the world if you're not perfect. You're asking too much of yourself. Christ, you're just a kid. Now, play something for me. Something you love. You'll see how good it sounds and you'll feel better."

She was never shy about playing for Richard. He listened like a professional. When he made suggestions, he didn't seem to be correcting *her*, but rather trying to help get the music out properly. That was what mattered to him. She played the fourteenth Bach Invention, a piece full of wit and verve, and when at the closing chord she looked up at him, he smiled and said, "Brava! What did I tell you?" And she did feel better.

"Did your teacher, Mrs. Flower . . . what's her name again, Mrs. Hyacinth?" He always teased her that way.

"Mrs. Gardenia. You know that."

"All right, Mrs. Gardenia. Did she explain about the staccato at the end of each little phrase? Like this?" He played the first few bars.

"No."

"And remember, the end is marked fortissimo. That's not just loud, but very loud."

"She always says I'm doing fine."

"Well, you are. But look, her cookies aren't going to do anything for you. You need a serious teacher if it's as important to you as you say. Is it?"

"I'm not sure what you mean."

"I mean if you want to make this your life. I think you have the talent, but you need other things, too. The will. You have to want it more than anything else. More than any*one* else. And you have to be aggressive. Do you know what that means?"

"I think so. A fighter. But I'm not."

"Not by nature. You bend too easily, you go along. You're agreeable. But you can learn to be a fighter if it matters enough. Maybe you're too young for me to be talking to you like this. But if you want I can recommend a very good teacher to your parents. You'll have to give up the cookies, though, and he'll be tougher on you than Mrs. Rosebud."

"Oh, stop that. He? A man, then."

"A man. Why, does that matter?"

"I guess not. Would he come to my house?"

"I don't know. You'll have to ask him. Here, I'll write down his name and number. He teaches with me at Hunter, you can tell your mother."

"Okay, thanks." She doubted that her parents would take Richard's advice about anything. Her mother still interrogated her about her visits and needed to be reassured. "We're friends," Suzanne would protest.

"What kind of friends?" Gerda said. "What kind of grown man wants an eleven-year-old girl as a friend? It just doesn't feel right."

She took the slip of paper, but it was two months before she could persuade Gerda to call the man, Reginald Cartelli. Gerda was fond of Mrs. Gardenia and didn't want to hurt her feelings. And wasn't Suzanne making good progress with her?

"Richard says I'd have a better chance of getting into Music and Art if I study with him."

"But that's almost three years away. And it's a public high school. Why should it be so hard to get into?"

"There's a citywide audition. You have to prepare. I don't think Mrs. Gardenia knows anything about it."

"All right, I'll call. But I hate to disappoint her. She's been so sweet."

"Who's more important, Mrs. Gardenia or me?" Maybe that was what Richard meant by being aggressive. Maybe she was learning, at least a little bit.

Mr. Cartelli did not come to her house. Suzanne had to travel to his studio in Brooklyn Heights, where he had two baby grand pianos in the large living room, and only after six months did Gerda allow her to make the subway trip on her own.

A S A BOY, Phil tried hard to break the habit of thinking about his family, his real family, not the aunt and uncle who took him in after the accident. Took him in: That was what their act was called, as if he'd been an abandoned cat crouching in the weeds alongside a road. Remembering, thinking, held so great an allure that it must be avoided. Brooding, his aunt called it when she saw him lying on his bed after school, staring up at nothing.

"You won't do yourself any good by brooding. Better to keep busy. If you haven't got any homework to do, you can help me clean out the fridge."

Brooding meant restaging in his mind scenes from the past as if he were directing a TV sitcom. The four of them around the kitchen table, eating takeout pizza. He placed them all in their proper seats, his father with his back to the kitchen door, his mother facing him, and he and Billy opposite each other, Billy sitting on phone books because he was still small and the table was high. Billy would be performing antics with the strands of melted cheese, twirling them, trying to tie them in knots, his parents scolding but laughing at the same time. Billy, who wouldn't eat the crusts but tossed them onto Phil's plate because, as they all knew, Phil would eat anything, even the dry lukewarm crusts. Then they would clear the table together and his mother would send him and his brother into the dining room to do their homework at the big table, and he would help Billy with any words he couldn't read.

Sometimes he began with the mornings, the lingering warm smell of coffee and toast, the breakfast finished, his father the first to leave, pulling out of the driveway in the Buick, its old gears squeaking, his mother stuffing their lunches into bags and kissing them hurriedly as they ran out to meet the school bus stopped in front of the house. Or Sundays, his large brawny father sitting on the lawn mower, pretending he was riding a horse, entertaining Phil and Billy by zigzagging, making swirly designs in the grass. It was as if by recalling intently, putting in place all the details, even the weather, he could conjure these scenes back into reality. Where did the past go, anyway? It couldn't just disappear, could it? It had happened. It must still exist somewhere in a long chronicle of all the happenings in the world, including those of his own family. If he could somehow revive those scenes, his authentic life, then the life he was living now in his aunt and uncle's somber Brooklyn apartment might vanish like a dream. He would close his eyes and will himself back into his room with the bunk beds, the mess of games and schoolbooks and clothes on the floor, the baseball bat in the corner, the pictures of players on the wall.

The room his aunt and uncle had given him was nothing like what a kid's room should be. It had been a spare room, a den, they called it. "You'll have the den," his aunt said that first night. "You can fix it up later, when we get your things from the house." The bed was a studio couch—they promised to get a real bed very soon, "as soon as we get our bearings," his aunt said—and there was a large leather La-Z-Boy chair and a TV set, a bookshelf with an old set of leather-bound books with gilt titles on the spine that looked like no one had touched them in years. Phil took down one of them to look at, and it made a crinkly sound as he pulled it off the shelf—the cover was stuck to the book next to it. He slid it back quickly. The window looked out onto an airshaft, and the floor was covered with a worn patterned rug whose colors had long since subsided into browns and grays, its fringes in tatters.

His aunt and uncle had gone back to the house in Great Neck, as they promised, a few days after the accident, to get his things and, as they put it, "start clearing things out."

"Are you going to throw everything away?" he asked. "No, no," Uncle Mel said. "Just go through things, see what needs to be done."

Phil begged to go along with them. He wanted to see the rooms, to touch his mother's and father's clothes. He wanted to sit on the living-room couch where he'd watched TV. And there were things of Billy's that he wanted, too. But they wouldn't let him come. They left him with a neighbor.

"But why?" he pleaded. "It's my house. It's my things."

"Don't worry, we'll bring everything that belongs to you," Aunt Marsha said. "It wouldn't be good for you to come. You must try to put that behind you. This is your home now."

He felt the full and despairing helplessness of being nine years old. There was nothing he could do. So, he would never see those things again. And yet they belonged to him, didn't they? If he was the only one left?

Before the accident, he had regarded his aunt and uncle with indifference. They visited occasionally on Sundays, and Aunt

Marsha would ask questions like what was his favorite subject in school, or what sports he liked, and he answered dutifully, bored. She nodded, satisfied that she, too, had done her duty. She was his father's older sister, broad-shouldered and stocky like him, shaped like a cinder block, with short curly very black hair dusted with gray. She had a deep voice like a man's and wore thick glasses and an expression of fixed displeasure, as though what met her eyes failed to meet her standards. Her mouth barely opened when she spoke, and she seldom laughed. She and Uncle Mel had no children. Uncle Mel was mostly gruff and taciturn. But he did like to tell riddles and play games with Phil and Billy, checkers or Mastermind or Battleship. His moves were canny, and he never let them win. "If you can't win the way you planned," he used to tell Phil, "find another way. Don't always stick to the obvious." Other than that, all Phil knew about him was that he was an accountant and he liked horse races. Sometimes on a Sunday visit he would sit down quite close to the TV to watch an important race, and when it was over he usually appeared disgruntled with the outcome. "I hope you didn't have too much riding on that horse," their father would joke, and Uncle Mel shrugged.

"When you're older," he told Phil and Billy, "I'll take you to the track."

But all that was before, when there was no need to think about them. Now that he was in their power, his indifference grew to active dislike. He got the idea that what had happened was somehow their fault, though he knew better. There was no one else to blame, so he fixed on them. And because of his antipathy, the cartons and shopping bags they brought back from the house that afternoon remained unopened. "Brooding won't help," his aunt said, finding him in his room. "You should go out and play ball with the boys on the street. I packed your bat and your glove. They're in there," and she waved at the boxes piled up under the window.

He shook his head. It wasn't his street and those boys weren't his friends. The boys he belonged with were at this very moment continuing their lives on the street that had cast him out, a broad curving street with grassy lawns in front of each house, not like here, the street lined with cars in front of sullen apartment buildings, the ball games—he watched them from the living-room windows—interrupted every few minutes by passing traffic.

"I even packed those things of your brother's you said you wanted. Open the boxes and you'll see. Can I help you?"

He didn't bother shaking his head this time, just waited for her to give up and go away. He was afraid to open the boxes, afraid of what he would feel, what might happen to him when he saw the relics of that life that was over, sucked somewhere into a tunnel of the past.

After a while, during the day he managed to forget intermittently, a few minutes at a time. The neighborhood school was all right, though larger, older, and shabbier than his real school. He had always liked the bustle and purposefulness of school and knew how to ingratiate himself with the teachers. He even began to make friends, though he would never give his aunt the satisfaction of saying so. From his earliest years he had made friends easily; he was gregarious and bright, good at sports, and he was too young and too energetic for wretchedness to engulf him completely.

Still, those first few weeks, at night, as soon as he lay down in bed and after his aunt and uncle had each awkwardly kissed him goodnight, he would obsessively restage his old life, the smell of his mother's hair, like soap and grass, so different from his aunt's, like stale food, the feel of his father's arms hoisting him on his shoulders when he was smaller. Now he could almost carry Billy, at least he was able to stumble around for a few steps before the weight overcame him and he had to toss him onto the bed.

It was Billy, three years younger, whom he thought about even more than his parents, as he lay in bed waiting for sleep. He wasn't used to sleeping alone and could hardly remember the time before Billy shared his room, on the bottom bunk. Although he did carry a vivid memory, fixed as a photograph, of his parents bringing Billy home from the hospital, a package folded in his mother's arms like a loaf of bread wrapped in a blanket. At first he wasn't much fun at all, just a baby Phil couldn't play with and had to be careful to touch gently. But his parents assured him that before long Billy would be walking around and starting to talk, and then Phil would be the big brother; he could teach Billy everything he knew. And they were right. It happened exactly that way. He loved teaching Billy things, and Billy followed Phil around and copied everything he did.

He was made for the role of big brother. It delighted him, satisfying something at once pedagogical and protective in his nature. He even felt that in Billy he was creating something, a boy in his own image, an acolyte, a companion. Someone who would be with him forever, whom he would guide through each new passage in life. They hardly ever fought, as Phil had seen other pairs of brothers do. He had no taste for combat;

not a coward, more of a diplomat, he could usually find better ways than aggression to get what he wanted.

Phil taught Billy to catch a ball and build towers and forts with blocks; he taught him to read before he began school, drawing letters on a blackboard. When Billy started school, Phil picked him up at his classroom door every afternoon to take him to the school bus, and the teachers praised him for being such a fine big brother. He went to bed later than Billy, but sometimes he'd find his brother awake, or he'd make enough noise getting ready for bed to wake him, and then they would whisper and toss the pillows from one bed to another, and sometimes spend the night curled up together in a twist of sheets.

Now Billy had vanished. Out of his life. Phil knew that every living thing had to die sometime, but boys of six did not die. First they had to grow up and get old, which would take a very long time. And anyway, Billy was the younger, so it was not right that he should die first. Phil was supposed to do everything first and then show Billy how. He had no idea what happened after you died, had barely thought about it, so how could Billy possibly manage there, wherever it was, without him? Had it hurt him a lot to die? Phil wondered. The truck crashing into him must have hurt terribly, but what about the dying itself? What had it felt like? He must have been very scared. Phil even felt a twinge of envy: Billy now knew something very important, had done something so important, that he, Phil, knew nothing about. In this matter of death, the roles were reversed and Billy was the knowing one.

And then, weeks after the accident, as he thought all this over, an obvious fact struck him, so obvious that he was surprised it had taken so long to arrive. If he had gone to the shopping center with his family that day, he would be dead, too. He would know what Billy knew. He might even be with him somewhere. He was walking home from school when the thought hit him; he had just parted from two boys who lived in the other direction. He was crossing the street and stopped in the middle, shuddering. A taxi honked and braked and he ran quickly to the other side. For an instant he felt how lucky he was that he hadn't gone to the shopping center. He'd had a narrow escape. He, of all of them, was the lucky one.

And then immediately came the opposite wish—that he *had* gone with them. At least they all would have been together and he would not be condemned to living in the dismal apartment with his aunt and uncle. He was sure his parents wouldn't have wanted that fate for him. Or maybe—and this thought was even worse—things would have turned out differently had he gone. He might have asked for some new game he saw in a shop window, or an ice cream, and then they would have left the parking lot later and never been anywhere near that truck. He might have saved them had he gone. Yes, the whole thing might be his fault, for refusing to go.

A fresh wave of grief broke over him, mingled with guilt and remorse. Again he would sink weeping into sleep, his mind a swirl of memories and regrets. This phase lasted longer; it never really ended, but it was subdued, and at home in the apartment he grew quieter and more sullen as he reviewed the events of that day, as fresh as if they had happened an hour ago.

His parents were taking Billy to get a pair of sneakers, and they had other errands, too, things for the house, a new garbage can, a toaster because their present one burned the toast no matter what the setting. None of this was of any interest to Phil. He begged to be allowed to stay home alone: He was old enough, nine and a half, really closer to ten, he reminded them; he had things to do. He was constructing a fort, a complicated affair of wooden blocks and metal parts, wires, bolts, and nuts he'd picked up at the town dump, to be populated by toy soldiers in battle dress. Finally his parents had consented, but he must not open the door to anyone. So when the police came knocking, he refused to open the door until the policeman said that he must. They wouldn't say why they'd come, but they asked the names of his closest relatives and he told them about Aunt Marsha and Uncle Mel in Brooklyn. He didn't know their phone number, but he gave them the address book beside the telephone.

While one policeman made the call in the kitchen, speaking so softly that Phil couldn't make anything out, the other one, husky and young with a blond crew cut, his gun firm and impressive in its holster and his club wobbling against his leg, stayed in the living room, asking Phil silly questions about what baseball team he rooted for. All Phil wanted to know was what had happened, why they were in the house, and when his parents and Billy would return. Had they done something bad and gotten arrested? His father had gotten a speeding ticket only a few months ago. Phil even wondered if the police could possibly be there for him. Last fall he and three friends had sneaked a few Kit Kats from the Walgreens in the shopping center, but that was so long ago—the store couldn't suddenly have found them missing, could they? Could you go to jail for something like that? They had also written bad words in the boys' room in school, but there was no way anyone could know who did that. Anyway, the cop didn't mention any of that, didn't ask any questions the way they did on TV. In fact, he acted very friendly.

Not until an hour and a half later, when his aunt and uncle appeared, was he given the news—though by then he already understood that this was not about candy bars, that something was very wrong.

Phil sat down on the couch, as his aunt told him to do. Aunt Marsha was trembling and weepy, and Uncle Mel was more grim and gray-faced than usual. Something had happened to his parents and Billy, but it was as if his mind stopped before a concrete wall and couldn't think past it. Later he was amazed that he hadn't understood right away. It must have been because his parents' death was inconceivable. He knew a boy at school whose father had died of cancer after an operation and months of treatment, and one whose mother had drowned while swimming at Montauk. But the idea that his entire family could be gone all at once, when only a few hours ago the house had been filled with their presence, their voices, was beyond his imagining.

The cops retreated to the kitchen just as his aunt began. "We have some very sad news." She took off her thick glasses and wiped her eyes, which were red and brimming with tears. Twice she started to speak, but covered her face and couldn't continue. "You tell him, Mel. I just can't."

By that time he was pretty sure he knew. But it was Uncle Mel who finally cleared his throat noisily—Phil was repulsed by the sound of the phlegm rattling around—and in his grainy voice announced that Phil's parents and brother had been in an accident on the Long Island Expressway, barely ten minutes from home. "It was a truck. A semi," he said. "A pileup. I'm sorry, young fellow." He patted Phil's shoulder clumsily. "Rotten luck."

"So, where are they? Are they in the hospital?"

There were no euphemisms for death. It took Mel several faltering tries to bring it out, and it seemed to Philip later, remembering, that during his uncle's faltering tries he was willfully refusing to understand what Mel could not bring himself to say. He wanted just a few more seconds of ignorance before he had to allow the truth to enter.

He couldn't reply. He couldn't even cry, at least not then. He sat stiff and still, baffled. A few hours ago everything was ordinary, even dull. It was late summer; most of his friends from the neighborhood were still away at camp. He'd been at camp, too, for three weeks, and returned to the quiet of fading August, the parched lawns, the streets nearly empty of the usual clusters of kids on bikes. He didn't mind too much. School would start soon, everyone would be home, and there would be plenty to do. He'd been content building the fort, placing his soldiers in strategic positions. Now everything was changed.

"But where will I go?" As soon as the words were out, he knew it was the wrong thing to say. He hadn't meant to say that—it just came out. He had so many questions, he didn't know what to ask first. He wanted to see his parents and Billy, but he was afraid to ask. He didn't even know where they were, where they took dead people. Not the hospital, if they were dead already. The police station?

"You'll come home with us," Aunt Marsha said, and put

her arms around him tentatively, as if she didn't know how to touch anyone. The arms felt heavy and he wanted to shake them off, but he didn't; finally she removed them.

He'd been in their apartment twice before but had no memory of it. Now, he hated it the instant Uncle Mel unlocked the door and they stepped inside. The furniture was dark and heavy, the shades drawn, so that the sun wouldn't fade the couch, his aunt said. In the front hall stood an enormous grandfather clock with a pendulum that never stopped, and it let out a little *ping* every fifteen minutes. Phil hated the trembly little *ping*, which never failed to surprise him. He peered into the large bedroom and smelled a musty stale odor. His aunt and uncle's huge bed was covered with a green chenille spread, and opposite the bed was a TV set. The venetian blinds were closed.

"Why do I have to stay here?" he said when they showed him the room with the leather La-Z-Boy. "Why can't I go to my cousins in Boston?" His mother's sister lived there. He didn't know the cousins well, they were older, but anything would be better than this.

"This is closer to where you grew up. Your aunt has three children already and they're barely getting by. I called her this afternoon. She'll come down to see you tomorrow, and for the . . . for the funerals, of course. You can visit them sometimes, but you'll stay with us."

"I can stay with my friend Danny. He's my best friend. I sleep over there all the time. I bet his parents would let me. They like me. I can call and ask. Then I can go to the same school." His voice was rising in despair.

"You can call your friend tomorrow, certainly. Maybe he'll

visit you. But you'll live here. We have no one. You can be our boy."

"I'm not your boy. I don't want to be your boy." He began to cry.

Aunt Marsha didn't know how to soothe him. She cried along with him. "Look, Philly," Uncle Mel said. He never liked to be called Philly. It sounded too much like Billy; it made them sound like twins, and they weren't. He was the bigger one. "Look, this is really hard, we know. But this is how it's going to be, so the best thing is to start to get used to it."

After that he protested no further. He had no recourse. He was a child, and children were helpless. But he would grow up, and then he would be free of them. He would grow up fast and show them he could manage without them.

They didn't like him, he could tell. When he sat silently at meals, eating the unfamiliar heavy foods, the soups and roasts that lay in his stomach like wads of damp cardboard, his aunt would urge him to speak. How do you like school? How is your teacher? Are you making friends? He was unable to muster any replies. But if now and then his misery lifted and he jabbered at length about some enthusiasm, as he used to do with his real family, the science experiment that had produced a terrible smell and made the whole class roar and hold their noses, or the movie about camels, or his spectacular feat on the climbing bars in the gym, they stared glumly as if waiting for him to come to an end. It was no fun telling them anything. They'd just nod and say, That's good, that's fine, and do you want some more potatoes? After dinner he sulked and helped clear up, then went off to his room and closed the door.

When his aunt visited the school on Open School Night, she got a good report about him. She told him so. "Your teacher says you're a good student, Philip. And a friendly, lively boy. Those were her exact words. So why aren't you a friendly, lively boy around the house? Can you explain that?"

As he got older he trained himself to stop reconstructing his former life. His aunt was right. It did no good. It was over, beyond anyone's power to bring back. Instead he looked to the future and began planning his escape. As soon as he reached sixteen he could quit school, hitch rides across the country, camp out in the woods and forage for food, like a boy he'd read about in a book. He could get odd jobs, maybe work on a construction gang. A new apartment building was going up across the street from his school. From the classroom windows he could watch the men, and at lunch hour he snuck out for a closer look. The men maneuvered cranes and derricks, piled dirt and hauled beams, and some sat on seats high above the ground, manipulating the machinery; others sprawled on the sidewalk, wearing their hard hats, eating hero sandwiches, and making jokes, calling out to the girls passing by. Or he could start his own rock band, like Buddy Holly. He was just a kid when he started out. Phil's parents had one of his records and sometimes danced to it in the living room while Phil and Billy watched and laughed.

Phil loved all kinds of music, and his aunt found him a teacher so he could continue the piano lessons he'd started two years ago. He didn't like this new teacher as much as the one back at his real house, but still he practiced diligently. For a rock band, though, he'd have to learn to play the guitar. If his aunt and uncle ever asked what he wanted for his birthday, he'd say a guitar. He could learn on his own, or take classes after hours at school. With his band he could tour all over in a bus painted with crazy colors and pictures. He'd seen one parked on Flatbush Avenue, with wild hues and shapes—bizarre animals climbing over each other, impossible flowers and ripples and stars. He could drive a bus just like that. Uncle Mel had promised to teach him to drive as soon as he was old enough to get a permit.

Sometimes at night, while his aunt watched TV, he played games with his uncle. Mel taught him to play chess, and by the time he was thirteen Phil became so adept that once in a while he even won. Uncle Mel loved to discuss what he called strategies, and he carefully explained what the word meant. When the game was over he would go back over each move and explain his strategy. "You see, when you moved your queen there—and that was a pretty smart move, by the way—I couldn't get my bishop where I had planned, and my knight was unprotected. So I had to find another way to cut you off. There's more than one way to skin a cat, know what I mean? If the obvious way doesn't work, look for something else. Be ready to change your plans. That'll do you in business, too." Then he launched into stories about his successful clients, how they had revised their plans to make products people would want. They couldn't always reveal their plans or their procedures openly or totally—of course not. No one would survive in business if they never cut a few corners here or there. The crucial advice, Phil remembered always: The main thing was to achieve your goal by whatever means, and for that you needed a strategy. More than one. A main strategy and then a backup. Or two.

WHEN SHE WAS thirteen, Suzanne found herself bringing Richard the very same complaint about her father's demands that she had two years ago. Only this time she thought she'd handled things far more cleverly.

Once again she'd been reading on her bed on a Sunday afternoon—past Nancy Drew now and on to Jane Austen's *Sense and Sensibility*—when she heard his pebbly voice calling her from downstairs. They had visitors; she'd heard the door open a while ago and the usual trilled greetings. So it was going to be the same thing all over again. She'd thought it was finished, this summoning her to entertain when guests turned up. He'd stopped after the fiasco with Aunt Faye and Uncle Simon, with only a couple of relapses. But now she was definitely too old. She was tall, almost as tall as her father; she wore grown-up clothes and her long sleek hair fell down her back. Men on the street looked at her as if she were a real woman. And her father still treated her like a circus act. It made her feel sick, a tightness in her throat, the threat of an avalanche in her gut. She wouldn't answer.

He kept shouting and finally came clomping up the stairs and knocked on the door—this brief warning a small deference to her age—then too quickly entered, undoing the value of the gesture. "What's the matter with you? Are you deaf?"

"I was asleep."

"Well, wake up. The Woodsteins are here. You know they love to hear you play. And they brought Mr. Woodstein's sister and her husband from Philadelphia. They're staying in New York for a week."

His shirtsleeves were rolled up, revealing his thick hairy arms. He was glancing around the room with a proprietary air, like an animal surveying his territory, Suzanne thought. It was her room. She didn't want his gaze taking in her things, the books on the bed, the lipsticks on the dresser, the photos of famous musicians she'd cut out of magazines and stuck on the mirror the way other girls hung up photos of movie stars.

"I really don't feel like it, Dad. I'm tired."

"What's this nonsense? You know you enjoy it once you get started. I can see it in your face. Comb your hair and come down. We'll be waiting."

This, she vowed, would be the last time.

She greeted the Woodsteins politely—it wasn't their fault, after all. The couple from Philadelphia, introduced as Mr. and Mrs. Newman, were short and stout, so alike in their plump placidity that they might have been sister and brother. They were overdressed for a Sunday afternoon visit, Mr. Newman in a checked sports jacket and maroon slacks, and Mrs. Newman in a tight green wraparound dress from which her pudgy knees protruded, the nylon stockings straining over the flesh. Mr. Newman was bald except for a reddish-gray fringe, but Mrs. Newman had hair enough for both of them, a halo of gold curls sprayed to a fine metallic finish. They sat docilely on the cream-colored couch that always reminded Suzanne of an angel food cake, their faces stiff with eager anticipation.

"We love music," Mrs. Newman said. "We tune in to the classical station all the time. It would be such a treat to hear you. If you don't mind, of course."

"I'm used to it by now," Suzanne mumbled. Her father cast her a sour look as she slouched to the piano. Gerda was off in the kitchen, preparing the snacks that would follow the music. Suzanne imagined she must have left the room on purpose: Gerda knew how much she hated being displayed. If her brothers had still been at home, they might have managed to distract the guests—in the past they had saved Suzanne more than once. But they had moved out and gotten an apartment together in Park Slope after college, and she saw them rarely.

"Well, what kind of music do you like? I mean, like what composers?" She wanted to find out if the Newmans knew anything at all or just cared for the novelty of the experience, like watching a dancing elephant. It didn't really matter whether the elephant did a waltz or a tango. The Woodsteins, she had already ascertained, knew nothing.

"Oh, you choose. We love everything," said Mrs. Newman, crossing her legs at the ankles and leaning back.

Suzanne played a simple gavotte from one of the Bach English Suites, choosing it almost perversely as the least she could possibly offer and might get away with. But it was not enough of a showpiece; by the hesitant way the guests clapped and exclaimed yet remained sitting expectantly, she could tell it would not suffice. They considered it a species of appetizer.

"Would you like to hear something I made up?" she asked.

"Oh, don't tell me you compose music, too?" said Mrs. Newman. "That is so fabulous. Yes, please, let's hear it."

She played the opening of a Rachmaninoff prelude. Mr. Cartelli had said she might be ready for a few of the preludes in Opus 23. She had just begun studying the eleventh, which was difficult, though Mr. Cartelli said the others were even harder. She played what she could remember of the opening, then began skipping the harder parts, interpolating passages, inventing transitions, then repeating the beginning. She was rather pleased with the collage she was constructing; Rachmaninoff himself might be amused. Every now and then she glanced in the guests' direction, but clearly there was no danger. They sat rapt.

"Amazing," they said, when she finished with a barrage of chords. "What a gift!" And so on.

"What did I tell you?" her father cried. "Is that something or is that something?"

"Thank you," Suzanne said, and made off for the kitchen to get a glass of water. What a fool he was. He didn't even recognize the piece she'd been practicing for weeks.

"Did you tell them you made that up?" Gerda said in a low but tense voice. She was arranging pastries on a platter, and the kitchen smelled of powdered sugar.

"Whatever you heard, that's what I told them."

"You didn't make that up. It's the Tchaikovsky? Or no, wait, it's the new Rachmaninoff he gave you last month."

"Well, great, at least someone around here listens." She grabbed a cream puff from the platter and bit into it. Gerda slapped her hand lightly for spoiling the design of the pastries and rearranged them to hide the empty space.

"You mustn't do that. It's wrong. Utterly wrong. I'm surprised at you."

"It's more wrong that he still makes me perform, just for his fat ego. This is the last time."

"Two wrongs don't make a right." One of Gerda's favorite axioms.

"They'll never know the difference. Neither will he. So what does it matter? I was just entertaining myself. Aren't I allowed to have any fun out of all this?"

"Of course it matters. You certainly don't need me to explain why. It's stealing and it's lying. And about something you love, or claim to love. Don't ever do that again."

"I'm going out," she said.

Richard's car was in his driveway, her reward for ingenuity. She was embarrassed to be bringing him the same old complaint, afraid of wearing out his patience. But this time was different. He was always suggesting that she think of new ways to approach problems that arose in music, so why shouldn't that advice apply here, too? He might even find what she'd done today a step toward aggression, in a way. She was coming closer to the world he lived in, the world that was complex and real, the world where cleverness could defeat ignorance, where people took music seriously, not like the Newmans, who didn't even know what they were hearing.

If only he didn't have visitors. His friends often dropped in on Sundays, men who sat in the living room smoking and drinking beer or wine, listening to recordings of operas, comparing notes and gossip about the singers. From their talk she had the impression they must know the singers intimately, but when she mentioned this to Richard he laughed and said it was just music-world gossip. Some of his friends worked behind the scenes at the Met or the smaller opera companies, or elsewhere in the music world—at magazines, in arts management, or staging performances. They picked up information and spread it around. It was a small world, he said.

"I thought *this* was the small world." Suzanne had waved vaguely toward the window facing the street.

"I know what you mean. I meant in another sense, though. An in-groupy sense. Kind of like high school."

Now when she rang the bell he appeared at the door with the bassoon in his hand. Behind him she saw a man sitting on the couch, holding a cigarette and leafing through a magazine.

"Oh, I'm sorry. It's a bad time. I'm interrupting."

"No, no, it's okay," said Richard. "Come on in. Suzanne, I don't think you've ever met my good friend Greg."

She still wasn't accustomed to calling adults by their first names, and so she blushed and stumbled over the name as she said hello. She wasn't used to shaking hands, either, and offered hers limply while he grasped it firmly. Greg appeared older than Richard, with fine lines around his eyes and graying hair, but he was lean and athletic-looking in blue jeans and a dark red pullover. Almost like an actor, or the host of a TV news show, the sort of man her mother would call distinguished if she saw him on TV, though Suzanne wasn't quite sure what distinguished really meant. It had something to do with being "well turned out," as her father would say, someone you would pick out in a crowd as special or different, more aware of the impression he was making.

"What is it?" Richard asked. "You look like something's the matter."

"Oh, nothing much. Same old thing, really. Well, not exactly. Something different happened. But I can tell you about it another time."

Greg rose, holding his magazine—a copy of *Opera News*, she could see now—and headed toward the kitchen as if he were quite at home. "That's all right. I'll get myself a cup of coffee. Nice meeting you, Suzanne."

"I'm sorry I barged in like this, Richard."

"It's okay. What happened?"

"I just did something . . . I don't know . . . I thought it was a brilliant idea when I did it, but now I'm wondering. Maybe it was a bad thing. I can't tell."

"Well, how bad?" He waved her to a chair and set the bassoon down. "Murder? Blackmail? Kidnapping? You'd know right away that those were bad. No ambiguity there."

Already her mood was lifting just by being in his presence, in his living room. She laughed. "Kidnapping might not always be so bad. I wish someone would kidnap me. Why don't you kidnap me?"

"I wouldn't have any place to hide you, for one thing. You wouldn't want to stay down in the basement. There're sometimes water bugs. Anyway, your parents probably think I've already kidnapped you in spirit. So, what did you do?"

She told him. She had a faint hope that he might find her little trick clever, though hope was waning as the sense of reality claimed her, as it always did in Richard's living room, along with the sense of pleasure. What she wanted most was a word from him that would erase the image of Gerda's stern face. But nothing like that came. He didn't even smile.

"What made you do that?"

"Oh, you know. Because I'm so sick of my father making me out to be some sort of freak of nature. It makes me wish I was ordinary. Who asked to have talent, anyway?" But that was not true, she knew even as she said it. She didn't want to be like Eva or Alison or Paula, who had nothing special. She wanted to be herself, but free. Like Richard. "I wanted to see if I could get away with it, I guess. Amuse myself."

"Surely you can think of better ways to make him stop. Talk to him. Tell him how you feel."

"Are you kidding? He knows how I feel, but he insists. And I just can't . . . you know, resist. Anyhow, the point is, it worked. No one noticed. That's how dumb they are."

"You sound like an obnoxious little snob. Their intelligence is not the point. Do I really need to explain to you why what you did is wrong? Claiming someone else's work as your own? It's stealing."

It was what Gerda had said, and it sounded just as bad coming from Richard. Maybe worse.

"The music is still there," she protested. "It hasn't disappeared like when someone steals a painting from a museum. Anyone can still play it or listen to it anytime. And it made those people happy to hear it. It made me feel happy to do it. What's so wrong about that? Everyone's happy and no one is hurt." She was convincing herself once more of the cleverness of what she had done. It was as if a dialogue were going on in her head, like a TV courtroom drama. She was the defense attorney who had just made a shrewd argument. But Richard would be the ultimate judge.

"Come on, Suzanne, don't be disingenuous."

"What does that mean?"

"It means pretending to be more simple-minded than you are. You know very well why it's wrong."

There was no answer to this court's pronouncement.

"I thought you might find it funny," she murmured. She could smell the coffee from the kitchen, a rich luscious smell. Her mother said she was too young to drink coffee. All she allowed her was tea, which Suzanne found insipid. The house was so quiet, she could hear Greg turning the pages of his magazine.

"You must have known I wouldn't find it funny. I can't encourage that kind of joke—it wouldn't be right. You came to confess."

"You mean like you're my priest?"

"Okay, this time I absolve you. But you mustn't ever do it again. And you've got to do an extra hour of chromatic scales to atone. That's what priests do—they make people say extra prayers. Those will be your prayers."

"Big deal," she scoffed.

"Seriously, don't try that again, Suzanne. If you get into Music and Art and pull anything like that, it could get you into a lot of trouble."

"You sound just like my mother."

"And why not? Your mother isn't always mistaken. Tell me, aside from feeling exploited, what is it you dislike so much about playing for people?"

"Being forced is what I dislike. And besides, it makes me feel sick to my stomach. I get hot and cold and my fingers turn to jelly. The people who listen might not know the difference, but I know, and I hate the feeling. It's like my hands are out of control."

"That's not so uncommon. It's plain stage fright, and lots of musicians suffer from stage fright to one degree or another. Ask Tom Cartelli. Maybe he can help you. How are you getting on with him, by the way?"

"Fine. He's a great teacher. He doesn't say much and he's not very friendly, but I've gotten used to that. He can say one little thing, or change the position of my hands in a tiny way, and it makes such a huge difference. But no cookies, of course. He's definitely not the cookies type."

"No, not at all. Meanwhile, since you've already performed today, would you like to hear Greg? He's a very good pianist, teaches at Mannes. I'll ask him to do something for you that you haven't heard, by Poulenc. I love Poulenc. You should hear more twentieth-century music. He did a terrific trio for oboe, bassoon, and piano, but unfortunately we don't have an oboist on the premises. Greg?" he called into the kitchen. "Come and give Suzanne a treat."

"Could I have a cup of coffee, too?" she asked. "It smells so good."

"I think we could manage that. Two treats, then. Greg?" he called again.

B Y THE TIME he was a sophomore in high school, Philip had made himself known to teachers, students, and staff, a rangy, sandy-haired figure loping down the halls on his various errands, waving to friends as he passed, always busy, always ready to take on more. He was in charge of the instruments for the junior orchestra, seeing that they were kept in good condition and got put away properly. He was the secretary of the student government and kept meticulous minutes of the bimonthly meetings, spiced by a playful but never nasty wit directed at the self-importance of his fellow officers. He sorted press releases and discount ticket offers for Miss Hirsch, the assistant principal, and kept her bulletin board of concerts and museum exhibits up to date, sometimes adding reviews he cut out of newspapers and magazines.

Philip himself had been surprised that the coveted High School of Music and Art had accepted him, so he could hardly blame Aunt Marsha and Uncle Mel for their astonished faces. He'd kept up his piano lessons, not only because he loved the power of making music, but because they were a reminder of his old life, one of the few tangible reminders. He remembered how his mother had encouraged him, and when he was in good form he imagined he was playing for her. Wouldn't she be thrilled to hear how much better he played now! Still, he didn't overestimate his modest gifts. When he came home and announced the news in the kitchen—"I got in!"—they were startled into silence. And then of course Marsha and Mel said the expected things: You see, you did better than you thought at the auditions, what a great opportunity, now make the most of it. They'd gotten accustomed to his changing moods by then, as he had grown used to their oblique modes of expressing affection. He knew they wanted the best for him, not that his knowing endeared them to Phil. The three lived by a shaky entente, compounded, like all agreements between incompatible parties, of pragmatism, apprehension, and self-interest.

Rearing a child hadn't changed Mel and Marsha very much, at least visibly, but Phil, growing up in their gloom, had cultivated a persona of affability and competence. At school he presented himself as the kind of clever, unpretentious boy who inspired trust in teachers and classmates alike: good-looking but not distractingly so, with an undistinguished but well-proportioned face enlivened by keen gray-green eyes and a disarming smile. He dressed neatly in crisp chinos (he had learned to iron them himself) and clean shirts, avoiding the shabby look some of the boys had begun to affect. ("Why are your friends trying to look like hoboes?" Uncle Mel once asked. "Their clothes look like they slept in them.") He was talkative but never overbearing—from living with his aunt and uncle he'd learned when it was politic to hold his tongue. With friends he was even-tempered, funny, though never a clown. With teachers he was dependable and efficient: polite without being obsequious, shrewd without being disrespectful. He got good grades but wasn't arrogant or overconfident, as many of the bright kids were. Not enormously talented musically, it was generally agreed, but he certainly worked hard. Not many of the music students were serious about professional careers. Those who were preferred to go to the High School of Performing Arts. The teachers at Music and Art were content to create an audience of talented amateurs and intelligent listeners—anything beyond that was extra. They all could see that a boy like Phil would do well in whatever career he chose. When he said he would do something, it got done.

Now in his junior year, he spent two periods a week after classes assisting Mr. Sadler, the chairman of the math department, marking test papers, entering grades, filing, copying exams on the new copier in the main office. Besides his promptness and efficiency, he was an amiable boy and Mr. Sadler was immensely pleased with him. Philip Markon, Mr. Sadler would say if anyone asked about him, "Philip Markon could run General Motors. And I wouldn't be surprised if that's what he ends up doing."

The work in Mr. Sadler's office was not demanding. It left Phil plenty of time to look around, check into files, and gather information. Information was always useful, even if you didn't yet know what for. Just knowing the lay of the land is good, Uncle Mel had taught him. Mel was full of practical tips learned from business experience and succinctly expressed. Wherever you end up, Mel told him, before Phil knew what high school he'd be attending, get to know people and find out all you can. On the night before classes at Music and Art began, Mel took him aside and said, "You're a good student. You'll do fine. You don't have to be the best piano player there—just keep your eyes open. And I don't mean only in class. Get in the habit of noticing everything around you. You never know what might come in handy."

Phil nodded soberly. He'd reached the same conclusions on his own years ago, when he accepted that his life with his aunt and uncle was not a bad dream from which he would soon awaken, but reality in one of its unlovely shapes. He understood instinctively that while he couldn't yet change his circumstances, he could study them thoroughly. His method as a young boy was not to snoop through papers or drawers, as he later learned to do, but to watch and listen. From his aunt and uncle he had learned much about the strategies two disappointed people could use to undermine each other and, once in a while, surprisingly, to offer comfort. He wondered what their lives would be like without him, the intruder who disrupted their grim calm. After a while he came to feel that their fretting over him, especially his aunt's, gave them an activity and a focus. Without him there might be nothing, or whatever dull ambience there'd been before he arrived. His aunt had said he'd be their boy, and she had honored that intention. He wasn't a boy they had wanted or even a boy they could love, but they took him as theirs, he had to grant them that. Before he reached high school he vowed he would never endure a life of disappointment, never end up dreary and bitter at what the world had not given him. The world gave nothing secure— he knew that. You had to take what you could and hold on tight.

Whenever Mr. Sadler was out of the office, Phil explored. He found the principal's evaluations of all the teachers in the math department, as well as all of their CVs. Most had gone to local colleges, one to Harvard; a few had worked in business, and one, to his surprise, had had a brief acting career. The majority had taught all their lives, progressing upward from lesser schools to this highly desirable one. Mr. Sadler himself had once taught at City College, only a few blocks away. What might have caused his retreat to the high school level? Philip wondered, and intended to find out. He came upon records of the grades given to classes over the last several years, and copies of past algebra, geometry, and trigonometry exams. Of course, no teacher would be foolish enough to use the same exams every term, but certain key problems were sure to recur in one form or another. After all, the subject matter in algebra and trigonometry wouldn't change over the years as it might in history or social studies.

Philip himself did not require any extra help with tests. He had a natural facility for math and he kept up with the homework. Besides his genial manner, it was his excellent grades in trigonometry, a subject that could defeat even the brightest students, that had made Mr. Sadler notice him. But a handful of friends and acquaintances occasionally faltered and were grateful for some assistance. Phil was willing to offer that if anyone approached him. Not often, of course. The last thing he wanted was for word to get around. He wasn't running some sort of scam, just helping out a few friends. He didn't ask anything in return. His reward was simply the feeling that he could help others in need, and frankly, the tests were awfully hard: After all, the students at Music and Art had been chosen for their talent and couldn't be expected to be math wizards as well. Why drag down their averages and make it harder for them to get into college, when they would never need the math anyway? There was no harm done. Most important, he didn't give out answers, just likely questions. His friends still had to supply the answers on their own, though Phil might point them in the right direction, as any friend would do. Didn't people study together all the time, helping each other out?

One November afternoon Mr. Sadler walked into the office, silent on his gum-soled shoes, and startled Phil by clapping him on the shoulder. "How's it going, Phil? Everything under control here?"

He'd been entering the grades on the advanced algebra mid-term, a course for seniors. Two guys he'd met on the basketball court in the gym had asked, a bit sheepishly, if he couldn't raise them by a few points; they knew they'd done miserably, and with college applications in the offing . . . Phil didn't feel a great deal of sympathy. Advanced algebra was an elective, not a requirement. He hadn't taken it yet himself, but Mr. Sadler provided him with the proofs and correct answers so he could grade the papers. If the seniors didn't think they could handle it, they shouldn't have taken it. There were plenty of gut courses to make the final year an easy one. He wasn't even sure if the senior grades would be issued in time for the transcripts sent to colleges—he made a mental note to find out. But none of that was really his concern. The thrill—and he was frankly aware that there was a thrill—came from doing what he did, regardless of the circumstances or merits of each case.

"Fine, I'm almost done. Just another two minutes." He'd been pondering whether it was safe to give Bobby Foreman, a bass player, an 85 rather than the 75 he had earned. If Mr. Sadler gave the papers back without looking at them, which often happened, it was quite safe. Phil could simply enter the higher grade in the book. But if Mr. Sadler went over the papers, then

Phil would have to alter Bobby's work, a greater risk than he cared to take.

The teacher pulled up a chair and sat down near him. He often liked to have a chat. Maybe he was lonely, Phil thought. He'd come to regard these chats as part of his job, and reminded himself that he was earning extracurricular credit for them. He set the test papers aside.

"So, where are you thinking of applying to college, Phil?" Mr. Sadler's hairy fingers played restlessly with a pencil. Phil knew he smoked—he was probably dying for a cigarette.

"Well, the applications are still a couple of years away, so I'm not sure. Juilliard, maybe, but it's a long shot. Or there's always City. My aunt and uncle can't afford to send me out of town. Wherever I go I'll need financial aid."

"City's a good idea. What about other colleges in New York? NYU, Columbia? Columbia has an excellent business school, by the way."

"But they're not known for music, are they?"

"On the contrary, Columbia has a fine music department, very innovative. Though I suppose it's more musicology than practical experience or performance. Anyway, it's a good idea to have a wide choice. You know, just in case." He was beginning to sound like Uncle Mel, Phil thought, with his strategies. "Juilliard is extremely competitive, as I'm sure you know. People apply from all over the country, the world, even. And you're very good in math. Science, too, I understand from Mr. Peterson. Do you have any idea what you want to do, I mean career-wise?"

Mr. Sadler was speaking quite slowly, as if he were planning his words in advance. Again Phil was reminded of Uncle Mel, struggling to explain his parents' death. That same deliberate tone, like treading gingerly, walking a tightrope, though Mr. Sadler's manner was much smoother than Uncle Mel's, and his voice was sharp and crisp, not grainy.

"I really don't know yet. Definitely something connected to music." He was about to mention the band he hoped to get into shape in the next few months. He had a trumpeter and drummer lined up, and they needed to find a good guitarist, maybe a banjo or uke, then see if they could get a practice room or use the cafeteria after school. But he changed his mind; he didn't want to hear his plans addressed in that same cautious tone.

"Music, of course. I understand that. There are lots of ways to work in the music business, you know. People don't realize it's not just performers. There's artists' management, public relations, even entertainment law. That's something to think about. Writing reviews, criticism. Sound engineering—so many new technologies are in the works, they're going to transform the music business as we know it. What I mean is, consider all your options. I have a friend in the admissions office at Columbia. I could have a word with him when the time comes. Of course, it's no guarantee of anything, you understand. Who knows, you might win a state scholarship if you do well on the test. That would cover a good part of the tuition."

"Well, sure, any help I can get . . . I'd really appreciate that. Thanks."

"Okay, I'm off now. When you finish entering the grades, leave the papers in the right-hand drawer and I'll return them first thing tomorrow. Be sure to lock up."

Alone again, Philip entered a grade of 85 for Bobby Foreman. He raised Freddy Bocelli, the other senior, a few points as well. Mr. Sadler wouldn't bother looking at the test papers again. Who the hell did the old fruitcake think he was, anyway? What could a math teacher know about who would get into Juilliard?

He locked up and went to the practice room he had reserved for four thirty. He was working on a Bach fugue from *The Well-Tempered Clavier*. The fugues eluded him: Four voices in counterpoint made for a struggle, and he tried the piece over and over, more and more slowly. He'd get it eventually, he always did, but it took so great an effort. There were students who could sight-read those fugues and make them sound halfway decent the first time. Each time he paused he could hear the faint sounds of others practicing in the nearby rooms.

Who was he kidding, anyway? He didn't stand a chance of getting into Juilliard. The best he could ever be was a gifted amateur. A knowledgeable one—he excelled in the music history courses and had a good ear besides. He knew how the music ought to sound. Occasionally he wrote reviews of concerts for the school paper, and the faculty advisor had praised them. But a performer, never. He didn't have it. He could end up in an office, arranging tours and concerts for Bobby Foreman and the others, the ones practicing in the rooms around him.

All the while he worked doggedly on the fugue, but by the time the hour was up he had made up his mind to apply to the schools Mr. Sadler had suggested. If the old guy could wangle him a scholarship, he wouldn't refuse. It wasn't giving up. The other was a dream he'd never really believed in. This was just being practical.

TO ESCAPE the packs of students clattering down the hall between classes, Suzanne turned around to face the bulletin board outside the secretary's office. Maybe if she moved very close she might magically dissolve into the bulletin board, become two-dimensional, a paper cutout. Or even more miraculously, someone who'd seen her in a class would notice her and speak to her. There were times when her old childhood anguish about being real overcame her, times she wished she had never come here and gone instead to the local high school with Eva and Alison and the other girls from the neighborhood. But Richard and her piano teacher, Mr. Cartelli, even her parents, had said how wonderful it was that she'd passed the auditions and been accepted at the High School of Music and Art. She must take the opportunity, even though, her mother added, it meant that long subway ride from Brooklyn alone every day. Gerda had offered to come with her the first day, but Suzanne refused in horror.

Everything about the school was better than what she'd known before, more colorful, more intense, high on a hill overlooking miles of city streets—the very air felt charged. She'd learned more French in one week than she had in a year in junior high. Except that no one knew who she was. To be known: It was what she craved. It was her second week of high school, and still she was anonymous, invisible amid strangers. She was not used to anonymity; at home, on her street, she had come to take her reputation for granted. She was the lively, sweet-natured girl with the special gift that would someday bring her a special life that the others, the ordinary ones, couldn't hope for. The reputation could be a burden, an embarrassment, yet now she missed it. Here, if she didn't turn up her absence would barely be noticed.

And she had looked forward so much to the new school. The prospect of escape—in Brooklyn, Manhattan seemed like another country—and of finding new friends had helped through the long hot summer, a summer the kids on the block had inaugurated with a trip to Coney Island. Knowing she would very soon be in a new world had gotten Suzanne through that dreadful evening when she was crowded into a car in the Cyclone roller coaster with the fattest boy on the block, Arnie Perchusky.

It had been a humid June night, school would be over in two days, and the dreaded Regents Exams were finished. She had the whole summer to practice. Mr. Cartelli had set her to work on a Brahms early sonata, and Richard said she must start learning some twentieth-century music as well—Bartók, Stravinsky, Satie. . . . She dreamed daily of the future, of the miracle of being accepted at Juilliard when the time came, of someday playing on a grand stage—but she was superstitiously afraid to extend her fantasies that far. Meanwhile, she practiced fervently to make them come true.

She was lonely, but leaning against the parked cars on the street with the girls and boys from the neighborhood didn't relieve her loneliness, merely screened it; still, the warm nights drew her outside with a hope shadowed by hopelessness. So when the group decided to borrow enough cars to drive to Coney Island—several of the local boys were old enough to have driver's licenses—she went along. The Cyclone was nightmarish, the fat boy beside her an opaque stranger. Everything about the excursion made her swear to forget this part of her life, nearly over. When the awful ride was finished she and the boy slunk apart, he too perhaps dreaming of a future in which he would be thin, an athlete maybe. Suzanne was certain she would leave, one day for good.

And now here she was, again feeling alien. The worst moment of the day was lunch in the cafeteria, carrying her tray and heavy book bag, gazing straight ahead, trying to appear casual as she moved through the aisles, looking for an empty table. She could usually find one near the edge of the room, and once she was seated and peering around, her fingers unconsciously marking a Bach Invention on the tabletop, she noticed a few others like herself, alone and reading, or pretending to read, while they ate. Why couldn't the solitary ones approach one another? You're alone and I'm alone, so why not sit together? But that wasn't the way things were done, not in high school, at any rate, perhaps not anywhere. No one wanted their humiliation exposed.

As the students jostled behind her in the hall, she made a show of studying the notices pinned to the bulletin board, then began reading them in earnest. One offered free tickets to a Sunday matinee concert at Carnegie Hall. Suzanne had never been to Carnegie Hall. Richard had taken her twice to recitals at Brooklyn College—her parents had let her go, provided he escorted her to her front door immediately afterward—but never to anything in Manhattan. Why not? She plucked up her courage and stepped into the office. Trying to keep her voice firm, she inquired about the tickets.

"Sure, and you can have two if you like," the secretary said brightly. "Maybe you want to bring a friend."

"No, one is fine. Are they really free?"

"Of course." The secretary had two spots of rouge on her cheeks and gray ringlets, and on her smooth empty desk stood a cut-glass vase with a single flower. She reminded Suzanne of Mrs. Gardenia, and like Mrs. Gardenia, she smiled too much. "Are you a freshman?"

"Yes."

"Well, you're in luck. They don't often give away something as good as this. Rudolf Serkin. I'd go myself, but I've got to take care of my grandchildren. Here you are." She handed her the ticket. "Enjoy it. And keep checking the bulletin board. You never know what might turn up."

Suzanne tucked the precious ticket in her wallet. She could tell her parents it was a required assignment. Her mother still fussed about the subway and warned her every morning to be careful. Careful of what, she didn't say.

She arrived twenty minutes early on Sunday afternoon and ambled up and down Fifty-seventh Street, though it was hardly suitable for ambling. The rattling, incessant traffic made the manhole covers rumble; trucks and taxis blared; caravans of green buses slogged along. Next door to Carnegie Hall was the Russian Tea Room, with a gleaming gold samovar in the window, flanked by reproductions of ancient icons. Peering inside, she glimpsed velvet curtains and waiters dressed in embroi-

dered tunics. Farther down the block was an enormous bookstore, and beyond that, a Bickford's cafeteria where solitary
people sat over cups of coffee, looking dejected and aimless,
reading newspapers or staring into space.

Back inside the lobby a crowd had gathered, women with
faces caked in makeup, moving gingerly in high heels, draped
in furs though the weather was still mild in September, and
gray-haired, clean-shaven men in dark suits. She felt shabby in
her nondescript gray jacket and Cuban heels. No one else was
alone.

She edged her way through the crowd toward a woman
taking tickets, who directed her up a flight of dingy stairs with
dingy, pale green walls. The staircase continued endlessly, round
and round. After several flights she showed her ticket again and
was told to keep climbing. As the stairs continued, the crowd
thinned out and she stopped counting. At last, when there
were no more steps, she was handed a program and directed
to a seat in the center of a row, fortunately not yet filled, so she
didn't have to step over too many people.

The hall was immense, a fairy-tale palace, its luscious cream-
colored walls and ceiling adorned with elaborate curlicued
carvings. High up were suspended magnificent chandeliers
with glittery crystals that stirred faintly in the air currents.
Everywhere was red velvet and a heady scent of opulence. On
the stage hung a heavy crimson curtain, and on each side were
the box seats with their red plush chairs. She had never been
in such a huge theater before. Years ago, when she was a tiny
girl, her parents had taken her to see *Peter Pan* and, a few
years later, *The Sound of Music*, but those theaters were not as
large or glamorous, as richly garnished and decorated, as here,

and her parents had flanked her like bodyguards. Here she was alone. Not lonely anymore in the crowd. Yet she was trembling at the newness of it all, as if something would be required of her. There was nothing she need do, she reminded herself. Only sit still and wait, look and listen.

In the orchestra below were rows and rows of heads, many of them gray-haired. If she squinted, the heads looked like marbles lined up on a Chinese checkerboard. Looking down made her dizzy, like the Cyclone in Coney Island a few short months ago, sitting with Arnie Perchusky. That had been dreadful, the sickening pitch downward and the tremulous ascent, but here the dizziness was almost pleasant, like the time last May when she got tipsy at her cousin Sandra's wedding. Uncle Simon brought her a glass of champagne that she drank too quickly, as if it were soda; she felt a frothing deep inside that excited her, as if something uncontrollable, unpredictable, was about to happen. She giggled, and when Uncle Simon escorted her onto the dance floor, she moved as if she were floating, almost levitating. When the dance was over her mother knew right away something was different. "What did you give her?" she asked Simon accusingly. "She's barely fifteen." But Gerda's voice was amused, too, almost flirtatious. She must have drunk some herself, Suzanne thought. "Time for her to have a little fun," Simon said with a wink. "You make her work too hard."

She studied the program. The pianist would be playing Beethoven's *Waldstein* Sonata, the Bach C-minor Toccata, the first set of Schubert's Impromptus, and, to close, Brahms's Variations and Fugue on a Theme by Handel. The *Waldstein* was a happy coincidence; she had just begun studying it with Mr. Cartelli. So far she had worked on only the first two movements. Mr. Cartelli had told her to get the first movement up to speed and in the second, to use the pedal more sparingly. He didn't praise her often; he was sober and demanding and not given to conversation, a change from Mrs. Gardenia and her chatter, but they had grown to understand each other. He'd said at first that he rarely took students so young—Suzanne was ten when they began—but after hearing her play he relented, warning that if she was serious, she must follow his instructions to the letter and practice at least two hours a day.

A middle-aged couple sat down on her right and smiled. The woman had stiff sprayed blond hair and purple lipstick and wore a black tailored suit and a print blouse with a big bow at the neck. The man was bulky and had trouble squeezing himself into the seat. He kept squirming and adjusting his body; Suzanne was glad he wasn't beside her.

"Are you by yourself?" the woman asked.

Suzanne nodded.

"Well, you must love music. Isn't that nice?" she said to her husband. "A girl who loves music so much that she comes on a Sunday afternoon. It's very high up, but don't let that worry you. In Carnegie Hall you can hear everything perfectly, down to the last note, even up here. We have a subscription to the whole series."

Suzanne nodded again. She didn't know if you were supposed to talk to your neighbors at a concert, the way you would at a party or a wedding. Luckily the woman opened her program and so Suzanne could continue reading about the pianist, Rudolf Serkin. He was from Czechoslovakia and had been a child prodigy, had played all over the world and won prizes. She wondered how much he'd practiced in his youth. Probably hours and hours each day.

When all the seats were filled, the hall very gradually grew still, as if the audience understood it was time, that something momentous was about to happen. The curtain parted to show an enormous black grand piano in the center, on a gleaming wood floor. The piano and the floor caught the light from the chandeliers and shimmered. When the hall was utterly silent, a small gray-haired man in a black cutaway and shiny shoes appeared from the wings. Suzanne was too far away to see his face, but she noticed his deft movements and the way he inclined his head slightly, acknowledging the audience. He sat down and adjusted the stool by turning a knob below. Then he raised his hands over the keys.

The woman was right. She could hear every note; they emerged from his fingers like clear crystals. Yet she barely recognized the *Waldstein* Sonata: How could these be the same notes she struggled with? They had motion and coherence and shape, motion above all. The repeated triads of the opening, which she couldn't manage to make sense of, became a hammering, insistent demand. The first movement climbed compulsively, as if the music were being pursued, chased by more music, each phrase impatient to assert itself and rush on. She tried to follow along with her fingers on her knee, but he went too fast. She needed all her concentration simply to listen.

The music was being made right this minute by his skimming hands, which looked, at so far a distance, like pale fleet fish glimpsed underwater. The notes had been written down centuries ago, and now they were rising from the instrument as if they were brand new. Mr. Cartelli had tried to tell her something like that. The composer hears something in his head, he said, and writes it down, but it lies there inert until someone rouses it, and then it's as alive as the day it was written. Do you understand? The notes were more than a technical challenge to be mastered, a series of difficulties that should result in a beautiful sound. They were a dream of the ear, and playing them was giving that dream sound and texture, the dream of a dead man passed on to living listeners.

During the intermission, while the people around her made their way down the aisles, she stayed in her seat. Where could she go? There was no one to talk to. What if she didn't get back to her seat in time and had to climb over the entire row of people? She studied the program, read about the lives of the composers and the music, but was too distracted to grasp any meaning. She couldn't wait for the small man to appear again, to pass the dream along.

She listened to the rest of the program, especially the gorgeous Schubert Impromptus, in rapture and despair: I could never play like that. And then she thought, I will. She would practice even harder, longer hours, until she could do what this man, this Rudolf Serkin, was doing. He was not a B+. He was beyond all ordinary ratings.

When it was over, he rose slowly, as if exhausted, and came to the center of the stage to accept the clamor of applause. He looked diminished, shrunken into his black suit, the magic gone from his person yet still hovering in the air around him. He disappeared into the wings, but the audience kept clapping. He returned, a bit more briskly, as if in that one instant he had gathered his strength, and bowed again and again. They wouldn't stop clapping. Even from so far away she could see him smile. The applause made him happy, happier than he could show. All at once everyone was standing up, clapping for the small man, and he, in the bright light below, seemed to grow larger. All those people were thinking of nothing but him, and their applause made him occupy more space in the world. There was no doubt that he was real, no chance that he would shrink away. The more they admired him, the larger he became, the more firmly rooted.

Suzanne's eyes filled with tears. She realized, with shame, that the glory showered on him moved her even more than the music had moved her. It was the music that should matter. And yet it was as if his gift, his performance, were merely the preliminaries needed to achieve the praise. The glory. He was drenched in the brightness of the world's love. Wrapped in glory.

She would show them. She had a gift, too. She would do nothing but practice for the rest of her life, for that reward. She would do the chromatic scales in reverse, the triads and fifths and sevenths, the arpeggios Mr. Cartelli believed in like an article of faith. She would harden her will; she would do whatever was necessary to have that.

Again and again he disappeared into the wings, but they wouldn't stop calling him back, and now he appeared weary, even impatient. He had had enough, all that he needed. And still there was more.

The woman standing next to Suzanne turned to her excitedly. "Now, wasn't that fantastic? Isn't he just a genius? It's like that every time!" All Suzanne could do was nod. If she tried to speak, she might burst into tears. This was too enormous to speak about. All the people in the hall would be thinking about him long after he left the stage; days later they would be remembering the music, remembering him. Every single person in the huge hall knew his name. How many people? Thousands, maybe. The woman next to her waved good-bye and turned away, and Suzanne rubbed her fists against her eyes so no one would see her tears. She would have that. She must. What else was there worth having?

⌒

It took longer to go down the stairs than up, the crowd was so dense. But Suzanne barely felt the press of bodies against her. The image of Rudolf Serkin, bathed in light, bowing again and again, remained with her, and she could still hear the closing bars of the *Waldstein* as if they were rising from the piano behind him. When someone tapped her on the shoulder, she almost tripped.

"Hi. Aren't you in my French class?" It was a tall boy with longish straight hair, sandy brown shading into blond, and he was dressed for the occasion in a dark sports jacket. He was gazing down at her as if they were old friends.

"I don't know. Am I?"

"Third period? Mr. DeLuca?"

"I guess so." So she'd been noticed, though she'd never noticed him before.

"I always sit far back. But I've seen you up front. You're a freshman, aren't you?"

She laughed. "How could you tell? I don't carry a sign."

"I haven't seen you around, and you have that look, kind of dazed, you know. Oh, I don't mean it in any bad way, you just look like you're finding your way around. It *is* confusing, so much going on, so many people. You must have had French before, to be in intermediate."

"I had it in junior high. It seems like an eternity ago."

"I know what you mean. Are you here by yourself?"

She nodded.

"Me too. I like to get away on weekends. I live with my aunt and uncle, and they're a drag. And I love to listen to music, especially people who play the way I'll never come near playing. Frankly, I don't know how I got accepted in the first place. Anyway, so, what did you think of this?"

What did she think? How could she possibly say what it meant to her without telling her whole life story? "It was fantastic," she said lamely. "He's amazing." She wanted to say that it was her first time in Carnegie Hall, but she held back—it would sound so naive, and this boy had such a knowing air.

"Yeah, well, Serkin is always amazing. I never heard him in person before, though, only on records. So, you play the piano?"

They had reached the lobby at last and stood awkwardly in the center, the crowds pushing past them toward the exit.

"Yes. But at school, as the second instrument, they assigned me the violin. I don't know why. I'm still learning how to hold it. I can't seem to get that right." She smiled again. "What about you?"

"Piano, too. I got assigned to trumpet. But at the end of last year I did get into the second orchestra—they probably don't have enough trumpet players. Do you want to stop somewhere for a coffee or something?"

Was he actually asking her out? He wanted to spend more time with her. "I don't know. I mean, yes, I would, but I ought to call my mother and tell her I'll be late. She always worries when I go to the city alone, like God knows what might befall me."

"Befall you? Ha! I like that. There's a phone booth on the corner. You can call from there. Where do you live?"

"Brooklyn."

"Me too. We can ride home together on the subway. My name is Philip, by the way. What's yours?"

Before she quite realized how it happened, they had become a couple. Despite her good looks—she had become unusually pretty, she could see for herself: the sleek long hair, the perfect skin, the long eyelashes and large eyes she had just learned to outline with a dark pencil (nasty Eva had some uses)—she had never had a boyfriend before. She hadn't wanted a boyfriend before, at least not any of the boys she knew in school. The ones who approached her were not the ones she wanted, and she brushed them off as not worth her time.

She dreamed of older, sophisticated boys, closer to men, the kinds of boys she would never find in her neighborhood. Still, observing other girls, the flashy girls, she wondered how it came about, how the terms of the pairing were negotiated. Was it a tacit arrangement, something you drifted into, or were there open declarations, as in the movies and on TV? And now it was happening to her, practically overnight. At school she went from being the mysterious-looking pretty girl no one knew, the girl who walked alone from class to class, avoiding meeting people's eyes, to a girl who was attached, and to someone clearly important. Phil knew everyone, it seemed. Even the teachers paused to greet him in the hallways. And he introduced her to everyone, forthrightly, like someone he was proud to be with. They sat together in French class; in the cafeteria, whichever of them arrived first would save an extra seat, and quickly their table would fill up with friends.

And because everyone recognized that they were a couple, she found herself, in between classes or after school, standing in the midst of a clump of kids, chattering, giggling, gossiping. It was a marvel to her, how simply being attached to a boy, a boy everyone knew, could give her this instant status.

What she wondered at, above all, was why he had chosen her when he could have anyone he wanted, any of the popular girls who waved to everyone who passed. It wasn't only his lightweight, understated charm; he was good-looking, too, with his long thin face and regular features and odd gray-green eyes, intelligent eyes that always seemed to be assessing what was before them. With so many advantages, he still wanted her. She knew her own advantages: Besides being pretty, she had begun to dress carefully, in the style taken up by girls who wanted to be seen as arty or bohemian, a word they liked but whose meaning they were not entirely clear about, either geographically or culturally. Dark tights, turtlenecks, long flowery skirts, long hair, dangling earrings. She would often add something distinctive, colored tights or a looping scarf or oddly shaped beads she bought in Greenwich Village. But her looks alone couldn't explain it. There were plenty of attractive girls. The only special thing about her was her talent, and she didn't think that was something that would matter to a boy like Phil. Though she might be mistaken. At the very start, before they were firmly joined, he had begged her to play for him in one of the practice rooms and had seemed genuinely awed.

"Do you realize how good you are?" he said, and the gray-green eyes shone and seemed to penetrate her.

"I don't know. There may be plenty of others like me."

"Oh, no. You're special. Believe me, I've heard a lot." Special: the same word her father used, but in Phil's voice it lost its grating edge. And then he kissed her with his tongue in her mouth and he wanted to go even further, but she wouldn't. It was too sudden, and especially not in the small practice room where anyone might walk in. He didn't pressure her. She asked him to play something and he refused. "No, not after that. Some other time."

In the first few weeks she strained to be bright and entertaining, as if she might bore him. But very soon her pride put a stop to that. If he didn't like her as she was, well, then, forget it. What was the value of having a boyfriend if you had to work to keep him? No, she would be only what she was, and that would have to do. Let it last as long as it could. She had never known this kind of pleasure, a true friend her own age, someone who cared about the same things and wanted the same things, someone to whom she was not peculiar or eccentric for wanting those things.

For he was a true friend. It was much more than kissing in the back rows of dark movie theaters, or holding hands on a bench in Washington Square Park, or going to parties—she'd never known there were so many parties on the weekends—where they could find secluded places to explore each other, up to the point where Suzanne said no. It was the talking, the exchange of confidences, that thrilled her.

Often they rode home together on the subway. It was a long ride and Phil lived three stops past hers, but if they were in the middle of a conversation he got off and walked her to her street. They talked about everything in their lives. She told him about her family, how her father pressured her relentlessly and—what made it worse—ignorantly about her music, how ever since her talent was discovered she had become a prized possession he could show off for his own gratification. She even told him about the mortifying fiasco years ago when she played so badly for Uncle Simon and Aunt Faye, a scene that even now brought her a shudder of disgust. Phil thought she took it too seriously; he was sympathetic, but clearly to him it was a minor family incident, almost comic. She didn't tell him about the visit of the Woodsteins and the Newmans from Philadelphia, when she claimed the Rachmaninoff prelude as her own. Richard was the only person who would ever know about that.

She even told him about Richard and what he meant to her, how she would probably not be at Music and Art right now without his encouragement. It almost seemed a betrayal of something precious to talk about Richard to Phil, and yet it was so important a part of her life, she felt he couldn't really know her without knowing about Richard. She described his house and his paintings, his friends and his music, how until now he had been the only person who truly understood her. And had given her her first cup of coffee, which she had been addicted to ever since. She caught a shadow of jealousy pass over Phil's face, and that shadow gave her a surprising flicker of delight. Of course, there was no competing with Richard, he was in a class by himself, but she couldn't explain that.

He told her about living with his aunt and uncle, the gloomy apartment, the heavy meals eaten in near silence, except when he attempted to break it with an account of some school antic, and afterward the silence took over again. Their gloom was like a spreading stain he was determined not to allow to reach him; he must outrun it whenever it threatened to catch up. He did this by going to all the free concerts and staying late at school, getting involved in anything that would keep him out of the house. His aunt and uncle didn't even like him, he said. Perhaps they thought that having a boy of their own would cheer them up (with a chill, he remembered his aunt saying, "You'll be our boy," but he didn't repeat that to Suzanne). Having a boy had not helped them. If anything, he had made them gloomier.

Suzanne found it incredible that they didn't like him. At school everyone liked him; he could get along with anyone, never got angry or sullen or ruffled. Nonetheless, he said, his aunt and uncle thought he was worthless; he could do nothing to their satisfaction. But he would show them, and very soon.

He told her about the accident on the Long Island Expressway that had killed his parents and his younger brother, and that would have killed him, too, except he had been stubborn and refused to go. To this day he didn't know if he had made the right decision. At this Suzanne gasped. Even in her lowest moments she would never have preferred to be dead. Thoughts like that were in a realm beyond her boundaries. He showed her a photograph of his real family, a black-and-white snapshot he carried in his wallet: the four of them on the lawn in front of their house in Great Neck. His parents looked young and happy; his mother was slim and girlish, with her hair in a ponytail, wearing shorts and a T-shirt (so different from chunky Gerda, who wore housedresses); his mother had her arm around Phil and his brother. His father was tall and lanky like Phil, with lots of thick dark hair, and he towered above the others. Phil and Billy were making funny faces for the camera. The photo was taken just a few months before the accident. He couldn't remember who took it, probably a neighbor. He tucked it back in his wallet and she saw tears in his eyes, but he quickly blinked them away. ·

They talked about their aspirations. In those they were very much alike. Maybe that was what had drawn him to her, Suzanne thought. Maybe ambition could sense itself in another. They would both be very successful and show everyone, Suzanne because she must—ambition was by now too deeply rooted in her to dig out—and Phil because his aunt and uncle expected so little of him. It was essential to prove them wrong. He wasn't yet sure what he would do. He had drive and determination in abundance but wasn't enough of a musician to perform. He would do something in the field, though, maybe sound engineering, something that required skill and memory, a good ear and good hands. But he trusted that she would have a great career as a performer. He would help her get over her hesitations. He would love helping her. He liked helping people, he said, but didn't add that he liked the powerful feeling it gave him. Nor did he tell her about the grades he altered in Mr. Sadler's records. For now all he could do was get her into the classes she wanted, or get her tickets to concerts not yet posted on the bulletin board, but later on, he could do more.

It didn't take Gerda long to catch on that there was a boyfriend, and when she did she insisted on meeting him. So one day when Phil walked her home from the subway, Suzanne invited him in. She had trepidations—he would find her house so dull—but it was better to do it on the spur of the moment than make a plan and suffer anxiety in advance. What she would have preferred was to bring Phil to Richard's house. She would do that one day. Sitting in Richard's living room with Richard being his nonchalant, wise, wry self—that was the setting in which she would like Phil to see her.

Gerda was taken by surprise in the kitchen, wearing her apron and rolling out dough for a piecrust. But she quickly removed the apron and assumed her most gracious manner, happily doing nothing to embarrass Suzanne, such as interrogating Phil about his family or fussing over him. She asked only where he lived (Brooklyn was reassuring), what instrument he played, and how he liked Music and Art. As for Phil, Suzanne, not long after, came to understand his behavior with her mother as a performance; he had so many roles at his command. He concocted a blend of deference, courtesy, and innocence—how had he known this would be the perfect approach? He must have a gift for sizing people up instantly, getting their number, as her father would say.

Gerda gave him seven-layer cake and milk, making a little joke about how thin he was, and Phil accepted a second slice with just the right degree of appreciation, admiring but not fulsome. Suzanne said little but watched each of them playing their role so well, awed by their natural adaptation, a talent she lacked. She could be only the one self, which vacillated unpredictably between talkative exuberance and shy reserve—the moods overtook her haphazardly, beyond her control.

When he finished his cake, Phil took his empty plate and

glass to the sink, thanked Gerda, and said he wished he could stay longer but he had to get home—he had a history test in the morning.

"He seems like a really nice boy," Gerda said the moment the door closed after him. "Very polite. But you might have given me some warning."

"He walked me home and it just seemed like a good time. You kept saying you wanted to meet him." She took a slice of cake. She'd been too nervous to eat while Phil was there.

"So, what about his parents? What does his father do?"

Here it was, inevitably, but at least Gerda had restrained herself until he left.

"His father had a business in Great Neck. Sporting equipment, I think. But both his parents were killed in a car crash when he was nine. So he came to Brooklyn to live with his aunt and uncle. The uncle is an accountant."

"Oh, the poor boy. But does he have any brothers or sisters?"

"He had a younger brother, but he was in the accident, too. I'm going upstairs. I have homework."

Once Phil was in her life, the trudge up the hill to the subway each morning, past the stationery store and the movie theater, the Chinese restaurant, the soda fountain, the butcher, and the cafeteria, was no longer a path heading to anomie, but a harmless route to the place where she belonged. By her junior year she was known less as Phil's girlfriend than as one of the most gifted students in the class. It was taken for granted that she would apply to Juilliard and that she would be accepted, maybe even awarded a scholarship. Life was never easy for Suzanne— she was not built for ease—but for a while it was good.

⌒

Philip was a year ahead of Suzanne in school, and in the spring of her junior year, he was already preparing to go to Columbia, where he had a substantial scholarship. That March Elena arrived. From the Soviet Union, though it seemed from out of nowhere. One day she wasn't there, the next day she was, so different from the others that everyone was immediately whispering about her, except for the few girls who actually tried talking to her. They reported that she spoke an odd form of English—fluent, more or less grammatical, but with so thick an accent that it was hard to understand her. She was tall and thin, her hair very long and blond, fairy-tale golden, and she wore it coiled and piled on top of her head like a much older woman.

In every way she was unlike the other girls. It wasn't only the wary, canny expression on her face, but also her clothing. She wore skirts and jackets in drab colors, gray-green or black, too heavy for the season, and her skirts were too long—the others were already in miniskirts. Her shoes were brown, more like boots with laces. "Someone ought to set her straight," murmured Jennifer, one of the more fashionable girls. "Take her down to the Village and get her put together. Or even an Army-Navy store. It's amazing what you can find there." She couldn't be called out of style, exactly, because people were wearing all sorts of odd, patched-together getups. But Elena's clothes were too ridiculous.

The way she asked directions was noticed, too, for she had little hesitation in seeking help. She wasn't the least bit shy, they decided, just aloof. She asked as if she didn't care what they thought of her and her strange accent, or as if she weren't in a high school but in an office building or some government bureaucracy. "Can you advise me, please, where would be the gymnasium?" or "Where is located the office of the assistant principal, please?" As if she had learned the phrases from a book, but not the right way to string them together. And that extraordinary accent in that low, very adult voice.

Some found her a figure of comedy and snickered, not always behind her back. Other students were intrigued, found her exotic, and wanted to get to know her, as if it would be an honor. But they were put off by her manner: stuck-up, they called it, as Suzanne had occasionally been called as a child by the girls on her block. Meaning, Elena didn't seem sufficiently grateful for their tentative approaches. They expected her to be humble, and she was not humble. She behaved as though school were a place where she turned up daily because it was required of her. She didn't realize how privileged she was to be attending this special school to which the others had worked so hard to be admitted.

With all that, they were curious. There were few foreign students, and none from the Soviet Union. Who was she, and how come she had suddenly appeared among them in the middle of the term? It was Philip, with his sources of information and access to file drawers, who found out the facts. Having gotten what advantage he could from Mr. Sadler of the math department, who'd kept his promise about dropping a word to his friend in the Columbia admissions office, Philip now spent his free periods working in the principal's office and was chummy with the principal's secretary, who was bored and enjoyed a bit of gossip.

It was a romantic story. Elena's mother, who was widowed young, was a Russian–English interpreter, often assigned to visiting dignitaries who came through Leningrad. (That might account for Elena's odd English, Phil suggested; she'd probably learned it from a book, with her mother's help, but hadn't had much chance to speak. In the middle of the Cold War, English probably wasn't a high priority in the schools.) The mother was assigned to translate for a famous American cellist on tour in the Soviet Union; fortunately, some cultural exchanges still survived, despite the icy political relations. The cellist, also a widower, fell in love with his interpreter, married her, and brought her and Elena back to the States. Elena hadn't taken his name, Phil noted, which showed a sort of modesty—she wasn't trying to profit from his renown. Her fellow students would have recognized it right away. Though no doubt the connection helped her get into Music and Art so quickly.

Not that she couldn't have been admitted on merit alone. Back in the Soviet Union she'd been a child prodigy at the piano. Her mother was eager at the chance to leave—who wouldn't want to get out of there? Phil said—and thought her daughter's opportunities would be better in the United States. As the story spread through the school, Elena came to be regarded with awe, which made the others keep their distance. She walked through the halls alone and sometimes could be seen chatting with the teachers, especially with Mr. Shukov, the history teacher, who spoke Russian; they would make extravagant gestures while uttering their harsh, unintelligible phrases. An aura of untouchability was cast onto her, compounded of remoteness and vague resentment, a resentment she had done nothing to earn except own the facts of her life.

Phil and Suzanne were carrying their trays through the cafeteria, looking for a good seat, when he spied Elena alone at a table for four, eating a bowl of soup and reading, or pretending to read, a battered, hardcover book. They were too far away for Suzanne to see if the book was in English or Russian.

"Let's go sit with her," Phil said.

"You think so? She looks like she doesn't want to be disturbed."

"Of course she does. I bet she wishes people would come over and talk to her. She's new. We ought to help her out. Come on." He led the way, and Suzanne had no choice but to follow.

"Is it okay if we join you?" he asked in his most winning manner, while Suzanne, slightly behind him, smiled tentatively and stole a glance at the book. It was in Russian.

"Yes, please, of course," Elena said, and put the book away. As she smiled Suzanne noticed that her bottom teeth were crooked. Now that she was here with a rich stepfather, she would surely have them fixed.

After that opening moment they all relaxed. Elena was quite ready to talk, not stuck-up at all, though it was something of a struggle to understand her. Even she herself laughed at the mispronunciations Phil and Suzanne discreetly pointed out. But how she'd improved since she'd first arrived a month ago! They should have heard her then!

And so they became friends. Philip possessed the magic touch: Whoever he befriended was rescued from foundering in the chill waters of anonymity and attained the gilded shores of popularity. As it had happened with Suzanne, so it happened with Elena. The other girls, and, soon after, the boys, clustered around her. They didn't call her aloof anymore; she was simply, well, different. She seemed older, as if she had endured more of life, or at least more of life that was notable. She was willing to answer their questions about the Soviet Union but didn't play on their sympathies or exploit the exoticism of deprivation. Certainly life there was harder; things taken for granted here were not so easy to come by. But of course they knew all that, didn't they? She smiled as she spoke. Of course they read the papers. The people, however, were not the monsters represented in the Western press.

Her new friends nodded knowingly, but few of them actually did read the papers. They knew about the Cold War, but it had been going on for so long—since before they were born— that it was accepted as an immutable global fact, nothing that touched their lives. Even the Cuban missile crisis of a few years ago had largely evaporated in the mists of adolescence.

They asked her about the famous cellist Paul Manning, now her stepfather, and life in his Park Avenue apartment. He was wonderfully kind, she said, and really not all that rich, at least by American standards. "At home we were required to share our apartment with another family, so this feels like . . ." She searched for a word. "Luxury," Phil supplied. "Yes, that is right. Luxury." The other family were boorish people who drank all the time and kept the TV on incessantly and left their dirty dishes in the sink.

Her stepfather was unpretentious and spent most of his time practicing, preparing for concerts. She was happy above all for her mother, who had worked so hard to make ends meet and now could finally rest. There was even a maid who cleaned the apartment, something they'd never dreamed of.

When they asked how she liked being here she smiled ruefully, though not with condescension. She was so self-absorbed,

Suzanne would soon discover, that it would not occur to her to condescend: These Americans were not yet real enough to merit condescension, though they would become so soon enough. She hadn't been unhappy, Elena said, despite the living conditions. She wasn't at home that much; she had her friends. And she would have gone to the Moscow Conservatory, a peerless place, the pinnacle of achievement for music students. "Like the Bolshoi school for a dancer," she said. But she was here and she would make the best of it—that was her way. "It is good here. It is excellent school and teachers are good to me. And not for long. Later I will hope to go to Juilliard, almost like Moscow Conservatory." That was probably settled already, Suzanne thought; very likely she'd be spared the ordeal of applications and auditions.

It was Chekhov's stories Elena had been reading, Suzanne found out when she asked, and she immediately took a collection out of the library and read the stories late at night in bed. They reminded her of Elena, wry yet accepting, with a kind of melancholy good cheer.

Things changed after that first day in the cafeteria. Philip wanted them to have lunch with Elena every day. He shifted into performance mode, Suzanne noted, as he had with her mother, only this was quite a different performance. He tried to impress Elena, amuse her, give her advice about school and about the city—a one-man tourist agency. Elena was a fine audience: She laughed at his anecdotes about the teachers; she listened to his advice about what to see and where to go.

"Have you been to the Metropolitan Museum yet? You must go. They have a great Impressionist collection." Suzanne was surprised. He'd never mentioned the Metropolitan Museum to her; she didn't know he had any interest in art. "And the Museum of Natural History is a lot of fun, too, if you like dinosaurs and whales and Indians."

One day he suggested a ride on the Staten Island ferry. "It just costs a nickel, and it's a great view of the skyline."

"What do you do there on that island?" Elena asked.

"Nothing." He laughed. "That's part of it. There's not much there. You just stay on the boat and ride back and look at the skyline. We'll do it one of these Sundays. Maybe next week." He turned to Suzanne—he was sitting between them. "Okay? We've never tried that."

On Friday afternoons Suzanne went straight from school to Greenwich Village for her lesson with Cynthia Wells, a young pianist and Juilliard graduate Richard had recommended when Mr. Cartelli retired the year before. On the other days, if Phil wasn't staying late to take care of the instruments or paste up the student paper (he'd arranged for an interview with Elena, "Russian Prodigy Lands at Music and Art"), he and Suzanne would take the subway to Brooklyn together. Now he began leaving her notes saying he had to stay in the principal's office or work an extra hour in the practice room. On one of those days when she received a note, she saw him leaving school with Elena, his arm around her shoulder.

She grasped that it was ending as abruptly, though not as unaccountably, as it had begun. That he had many facets she knew, but he had never seemed duplicitous—in fact, she'd thought him too transparent in his eagerness to please, to help, to be appreciated. Probably Elena appreciated him more explicitly than she did, or he found her more deserving of his help.

Jennifer murmured advice in the girls' locker room. "It hasn't gone very far yet. You can still get him back. Keep him, I mean, if you play your cards right."

"What 'cards'?'" Suzanne said. "I'm not playing any card game. And I don't want to keep him. Why should I, if that's what he's like?"

Jennifer looked at her, incredulous at the naive question. "That is very immature. Think about it before you do or say anything rash."

There was nothing to think about. She scrawled a note saying good-bye in the briefest possible way and slipped it into the pocket of the jacket hanging from the back of Phil's chair, wrapped around his keys so he'd be sure to find it. At the end of the day she left through a side exit in case he was waiting for her in front, trying to make it up. The term had only a few weeks left—already the trees were in lush bloom and the classroom windows were wide open, with the scent of honeysuckle wafting in—and during those few weeks she never spoke to Phil or Elena again. Each of them tried several times to stop her in the hall or in the cafeteria, but she walked past as if she didn't recognize them. She found a sealed envelope slipped into her school bag and on the front, in capital letters, PLEASE LET ME EXPLAIN. She tore it up without opening it and tossed the pieces in a trash can in the subway station.

It wasn't easy to maintain her pose of calm indifference, but she managed by force of will. By force of anger. Except for Fridays with Cynthia, she went straight home, her face stiff on the subway as she studied the textbooks she liked the least, trigonometry and chemistry, memorizing formulas for the coming Regents Exams. Once she got home she dashed upstairs to weep into her pillow, and she refused Gerda's attempts at consolation.

It had been almost three years. She'd been so sure of him. He had told her he loved her. He had promised her things and had fulfilled his promises, gotten her free passes to concerts and rock clubs in the Village, where he had contacts. He'd even told her she kept him sane, that without her the miseries of home and his lost family would overwhelm him. She had never believed that; he'd been fine before they started. He would always be fine. That was his fate and his nature. She liked thinking in large terms like those.

When she thought of the things they had done together—once in the principal's office after everyone had left for the day, and a few times in her own bedroom on a Sunday afternoon, when her parents had driven out to New Jersey to visit relatives—she blushed with shame. She hadn't wanted to do it; it was so hugely forbidden. And what if she got pregnant? But Phil persuaded her. They were getting too old to be fooling around like kids; they'd been together so long. He'd use protection. She'd been afraid to face her parents after the first time, as if it were written on her face. Gerda surely would know—she had uncanny instincts. But facing them proved easier than she anticipated, and Gerda didn't seem to notice any difference. At sixteen, nearly seventeen, Suzanne decided she could never be sure of anyone again. She would always be on her guard for hints of betrayal.

For a while Suzanne's plight was the talk of the junior-class girls, most of them siding with her. Although Elena had her defenders, too: You've got to take what you can get, some of the girls declared. All's fair in love and war. As for Phil: Boys do that, they're fickle, they don't know what they want. Fortunately for Suzanne, who shrank from notoriety, the affair was soon overshadowed by a plagiarism case. One of the girls in her circle of the popular, Helene, was discovered to have plagiarized a paper on Jean-Jacques Rousseau for a class in modern European cultural thought. That sort of cheating was almost unheard of at Music and Art, or at least almost never surfaced, and Helene was the new topic of conversation, also with her supporters and detractors. Rumors flew, of how she had been discovered—it happened that the teacher had recently read the book she'd cribbed from—how she had been sent to the principal and lectured. "And the worst part of it, Helene," her teacher had allegedly said, "is that it was so unnecessary. You could have written an excellent paper on your own. You probably didn't even save much time. What on earth possessed you, such a good student?"

In public Suzanne sympathized with Helene. She truly felt sorry for her, knowing how painful it was to be the topic of whispered conversation. Privately she was shocked, even offended, at what Helene had done. This wasn't some childish prank with no consequences to speak of, as when she herself had passed off a Rachmaninoff prelude as her own work, and anyway, that was four years ago—she certainly wouldn't repeat it today. No, this was serious; this was school. There was one's permanent record to think of, and moreover it was shamefully dishonest. But Helene's troubles, for Suzanne, were only a minor distraction. Always foremost in her mind was Philip and his betrayal.

Friday afternoons were a relief, because of her lesson with Cynthia. It was a busy time. Suzanne had to prepare for the end-of-term recital required of all juniors and seniors. She'd chosen a Haydn sonata that had looked simple at first glance but showed its subtleties the more she worked on it; she was also required to do a chamber piece, and together with a violinist and cellist was practicing the first of the two Mendelssohn piano trios. It would never do to break down in front of Cynthia, so exasperatingly serene, so sophisticated, so reasonable. Lessons with Cynthia meant only work and more work.

Cynthia was twenty-seven but seemed to Suzanne much older, with her own apartment, her grown-up clothes: She never wore jeans but dressed for lessons as if she were going to the theater. She was starting to play in recitals in small venues and was destined for success, Suzanne could tell. Certain people were, like Phil, and perhaps Elena. It had nothing to do with talent. Such people moved in the world as if it were theirs to manipulate, not hesitant or apprehensive. Cynthia was glamorous, though not beautiful. Striking, rather, with her prominent features, her dark hair cut short like a boy's, and her heavy jewelry, necklaces and glinting earrings, but no bracelets or rings on her large hands, which could stretch two notes past an octave. She asked Suzanne nothing personal and told nothing about herself, except to explain once in a while how she had mastered a difficult passage. Suzanne had no idea whether she had a boyfriend or lover—she lived alone, that was clear—but if she did, she would never let herself be dropped. She would do the dropping. "You might find her cold," Richard had said when he first suggested her, "but don't be put off by that. She's an excellent teacher and really a kind soul at heart, only she doesn't like to show it."

"Why not?"

"Oh, you know, some people are afraid of being hurt. Of getting attached."

Something about the way he spoke—too self-consciously offhand—made her think they had been a couple. They'd make a good pair: Cynthia's chill and Richard's warmth, her sleekness and his nonchalance. Suzanne couldn't imagine Cynthia hesitant about anything. Certainly she was no one Suzanne could confide in, except as her feelings emerged through her playing. When she pounded out Chopin's twelfth étude or the passionate Brahms *Intermezzo* from Op. 118, she felt all her rage going into the music. Cynthia liked that. "I heard real passion there," she said. "That's fine. That's how it should be. Only don't get carried away. Remember, passion with control. You want to move your listeners to feel emotion, not to be overwhelmed by it yourself. Just because people call it the *Revolutionary* Étude doesn't mean you should be in attack mode."

At those moments, when they felt close purely through music, Suzanne would have liked to ask Cynthia how she recovered from love affairs—for surely she must have had many—but Cynthia, unlike Richard, did not encourage such liberties.

⌒

Suzanne found a job working as a music counselor in a summer camp far enough from home that she needn't visit on weekends, and there, on neutral territory, she made friends easily. There was an older boy, also a counselor, pursuing her, whom she liked well enough, and with a nonchalance quite new to her, she didn't need much persuasion to sleep with him, sneaking out to his bunk while his roommate was on kitchen duty after dinner. He seemed impressed by her experience and her responses, and she let him think it was his own appeal. In reality, and this surprised her, when the boy moved inside her, it wasn't Phil she envisioned, but rather Richard. At first she tried guiltily to banish those fantasies, then after a while gave up and indulged them; they worked so well. This continued all summer, a colorful backdrop to the daily duties, yet she was relieved to know the boy was from Seattle so they wouldn't be seeing each other again. Parting was not hard.

She felt as if she, too, had learned to play roles the way Phil did, and, for all she knew, everyone else as well. She had met people from all over the East Coast and unearthed a bolder Suzanne from a repertoire she hadn't known she possessed. She returned for her senior year feeling grown-up. And Phil was gone, off to Columbia, she heard; now she was ready to see what else the world had to offer. This fall she would apply to Juilliard—the auditions would be dreadful, but she believed she'd get in—and then her true life would begin. What she had now only with Richard and Cynthia would spread and fill the rest of her days.

She found solace in visiting Richard and in playing for him. Aside from her family, he was the only listener who didn't make her feel queasy with anxiety, the stage fright that dogged her more and more the older she grew. He was her one true friend, the one person with whom she could show her real self.

"You are the genuine article," he said one evening. She'd hardly come in when he said, "Play something for me. Nothing fancy, just something to settle me. It's been a long day." Without a word, she sat down and played one of the intermezzi Brahms wrote for Clara Schumann.

"You are the genuine article." He said it as if he hadn't been totally sure before but now there was no doubt. She swiveled on the piano bench to look at him sprawled on the couch, his forgotten cigarette smoldering in an ashtray. He was smiling broadly, with satisfaction, and she smiled back. His hair was unruly and he needed a shave and he wore an old black sweatshirt she'd seen dozens of times, and yet he managed a casual elegance. He looked all at once beautiful to her. She felt something stirring in the air between them, and she longed to get up and touch him. She had turned seventeen over the summer and felt that her childhood—so prolonged—was at last over.

She didn't go over to touch him. She sat on the bench staring for so long that he finally asked, "What's the matter?"

"Nothing. Or at least nothing I could talk about."

"Try. Is it anything at school? The teachers?"

She shook her head.

"I know you broke up with your boyfriend last spring. Is it still that? Is he really worth months of pining?" He had just the hint of a smile, as if he were afraid to sound mocking.

She'd never gotten around to introducing Philip to Richard. Maybe she knew he wasn't worth it, that he didn't deserve Richard, he was a lower order of being. Her own thought startled her—exactly the kind of bigotry she scorned in others.

"No, it's not him anymore. I'm over him." She hoped that was true. Her feelings were such a tangle that she couldn't tell whom or what she wanted. But she wanted something. And she had to speak, though she was shivering with embarrassment. Children were powerless, but adults could claim the world. Certain adults. Why shouldn't she be one of them?

"It's you," she began, then paused while he waited, looking

puzzled. "We've known each other such a long time. You've done so much for me. But you still think of me as a child, don't you?"

He grinned as he would at a child. "No. You're a woman of the world now. Especially after a summer of staging musical comedies. I wish I'd seen them. I bet you were a fantastic director. I think you have a touch of the martinet, beneath your charming good manners and appealing nature."

"Oh, stop teasing. That is the worst. Don't you think I have feelings?"

"I know very well you have feelings. I'm sorry. I didn't mean to hurt you. But I really don't get it. Tell me what's on your mind."

"How can you not get it? All right. It's you. I mean, you and me." She stared at him helplessly, willing him to read her mind.

It was a while before he spoke. He sat looking down at the patterned rug at his feet. "Oh. Oh, I see. I am so, so sorry. I never meant to give you the impression . . ." He spread his arms out as if to encompass the room, as if to indicate the obvious, then got up and paced to the window and back.

"It's not simply that I'm so much older. I won't even use that. But . . . you didn't know, after all this time, after all the people you've met here?" He stopped and faced her squarely. "You are a very innocent girl indeed. Look, you've met Greg here so many times. You mean to say it never occurred to you . . . ?"

Something inside her, a vital organ, seemed to drop into free fall, leaving her weak. Whispers, rumors, nasty words she'd heard at school flickered through her mind. "A fruitcake, that's what he is," Philip had once said about Mr. Sadler. "I can tell by the way he looks at me." She knew what he meant, but had never given a thought to Mr. Sadler.

How on earth could I have been so stupid? she thought. She had a flash of anger at her parents as well. Why hadn't they told her? They must know. Everyone must know. That must be why they treated him with such distance, such suspicion. Of course. She flushed with shame. It was bad enough to have declared herself as she did, but to someone who didn't even like women, in that way, at least. She'd been prepared for him to say he was too old, she must put away that sweet but impractical idea, they would forget all about it and go back to being good friends. She had almost hoped he would say that; it would forestall the complication and entanglement, yet leave her with a grief to harbor, sad but tender, grief like a secret, soothing companion. But this! There was nothing soothing about this.

She couldn't account for what she said next. "I always thought there was something between you and Cynthia."

"Well, yes, there was, briefly." He looked away and his eyes closed for an instant, as if recalling a specific memory. "Can't you understand? I'm not that . . . what shall I say? Exclusive. Sexual choices are complicated, Suzanne. Cynthia and I shared a lot. One thing leads to another. It just happened."

"But not with me."

"No, not with you. Use your head. I'm more than twice your age. I'm a teacher. You're a student. It would be wrong. I'd be justifying your parents' bad opinion, doing exactly what they always feared."

"But don't they know?"

"I don't know who knows what. I try not to pay attention. It's not easy. I've no wish to make it any harder."

"I've got to go now." She stood up and moved toward the door.

"Hold on. Don't run away. That's what you always do when there's something you don't want to face. Remember when you were a kid, with your parents? Or after your father made you perform? You'd dash out like a pianist rushing offstage and come here. You can't always walk out of a room or a situation you don't like. I'll make you a cup of coffee."

She remembered the heavy yellow ceramic mugs from which she had drunk so many cups of coffee; they felt like a part of her childhood she must leave behind. "I'd rather have a glass of wine." She thought he might object, but he opened a bottle of red and poured some for both of them. "What's wrong with walking out on a situation you don't like?" she asked. That was exactly what she had done with Philip, never spoken another word to him after she saw him walking with his arm around Elena. It hadn't occurred to her that there was a better way.

"Everything is wrong with that. Look what's happened here. You've learned something you didn't know before. That's always a good thing, at any age. When I met you, I was an adult, and I learned I could get really excited about the talent of a young child. That was something I hadn't known before. I'd always worked with older students, but you had some kind of uncanny instinct about music I'd never seen in so young a kid. So I followed it. That's all I meant. That we became friends meanwhile was a bonus. I never meant it to bring you any pain."

She sat back down on the piano bench and hid her face in her hands. "I'm so embarrassed. I can't believe how stupid I've been. How blind. How can I ever live in the world if I can't see what's right in front of me?"

"Just sit here awhile and calm down. Don't flee—that's the

main thing. Now you'll start looking at the world more closely. There is a world out there, you know. It's not all in your head." He drank half of his wine. "Talk to me."

"What's there to talk about now?"

"Plenty. Does this change how you feel about me? I mean, now that you know. Do you feel deceived?"

"No, I don't think you ever tried to deceive me. And about the other, you know, what you are, your life, that doesn't matter to me. Oh, I'm saying it all wrong. I don't mean I don't care about your life. I mean you're the same to me as ever. But I'm not the same. And here I was thinking . . ."

"Suzanne, you're not in love with me. You just want to be in love with someone. You suffered over the boyfriend, so naturally you look to someone you trust, who's never betrayed you. And I never would. But that's not being in love. It's being grateful, and comfortable, and all sorts of good things."

"How do you know who I'm in love with or not? You talk like you know everything. You're the only person who . . ." She drank and wept.

"I've been the only one for some things. And I can still be. But you'll have plenty of others. You'll see. You're just at the beginning—"

"Oh, stop. At least stop being so banal. That's what I liked about you, that you weren't as banal as everyone else." She'd wanted to say "loved," not "liked," but the word wouldn't come out.

"Okay." He was silent for a while, smoking. "My parents didn't speak to me for a long time. I'm an only child. I was their hope for more family, grandchildren, the real deal. But that was the lesser part of it. They couldn't bear the idea of my . . . life.

What I did. They found it disgusting. As many people do. It was hard. Terrible, in fact."

"And now?" she asked.

"Now they need me. They're old and not well. They need help, and I guess a queer son can do that as well as anyone else. If not for that, they might still not be speaking to me. Oh, unless some of my compositions get played or the opera I'm working on gets produced. That would make them happy. They'd think maybe it was all part of the artistic temperament."

"How do you stand it?" It struck her how narrow her world was, how minuscule her conception of human behavior, human suffering. She'd felt the same jolt—this sense of enlargement, of enlightenment—when Philip told her about the death of his family. Once again she glimpsed how little she knew of the world outside her head, what people endured in that world. Would she ever know that breadth of pain? She both dreaded it and longed for it, curiosity vying with fear.

Part 2

SUZANNE AND ELENA were the only pianists in the senior class who were selected for a final audition at Juilliard, which surprised no one. On a blustery, rainy morning, they were ushered into a small room by a pole-shaped woman behaving like an official guard, who waved them to chairs facing each other and told them to wait until they were called. There was nothing in the room but a half dozen plastic chairs, a water cooler, and a scratched, dented old desk, its top bare. This was the closest the two girls had been in nearly a year. To avoid Elena, Suzanne stared at the plain wooden door to the studio where the auditions would be held, as if behind it were a gallery of torture instruments. With her fingers on her knees, she practiced the pieces she had prepared.

Although not precisely torture, the auditions were a trial: The applicants were instructed to prepare a Beethoven sonata; a major Romantic work, meaning Chopin, Brahms, Liszt, or Schumann; an étude by Chopin, Scriabin, or Rachmaninoff; a Bach prelude and fugue, and a twentieth-century work. Cynthia, who had not only been through the process herself but later served on the admissions committee, was full of advice. "Don't try to impress them with something flashy, just do a substantial thing well. Forget Scriabin, stick to Chopin; you're good at that. And we'll pick a difficult Bach prelude so they can see your fingers fly. Remember, the whole thing is only about fifteen or twenty minutes. You're not going to have a chance to play everything; you've just got to be prepared. They'll stop you when they've heard enough of one piece and tell you to go on to the next, so don't be surprised at that. Look them in the eye when you first go in. Don't give them the girlish charm— act like an adult." And so on.

"So, what are you going to play?" asked Elena abruptly. She was wrapped tightly in a large nubby shawl, something she must have brought from Russia, Suzanne thought. The room was chilly. Elena had cut her golden hair last year; no longer wound in the old-fashioned coils, it was stylishly layered with wisps straying over her eyes. Every so often she brushed them away with a careless gesture. She had had her teeth fixed, as Suzanne had foreseen, and now they were perfect, her smile like a toothpaste ad. Suzanne's dark hair was swept up in a beehive, and she wore a dark suit that her mother had helped her pick out, with stockings and heels. In her school clothes she looked younger than her age, and she hoped the suit would give her an air of maturity, of readiness for serious study.

Elena's voice startled her.

"Come on, Suzanne, it's silly not to talk. I mean, after all, here we are, going through the same thing. We're both scared shitless. It's better to talk."

Elena's English was almost perfect now, too, not only barely accented but full of colloquialisms. A quick learner, Suzanne thought.

Suzanne recited her list of selections. For the Beethoven sonata she'd chosen the *Waldstein*, hoping the memory of

Rudolf Serkin would sustain her; for the major Romantic work she would do the first Chopin ballade; then a Liszt étude; the D-minor Bach prelude and fugue; and, for the essential twentieth-century piece, a movement from Prokofiev's third *War Sonata*. Elena's choices, when she answered in turn, sounded impressive. Rather than the sober *Waldstein*, she'd picked the showier *Appassionata*. For her étude she was doing one by Scriabin, notoriously difficult. And the modern work was by Hindemith, whose work Suzanne barely knew: one of the interludes and fugues.

It didn't matter, she told herself; this kind of thinking was so petty. Elena was sure to get in no matter what she played, because of her stepfather. Although she was good enough on her own—no one could deny that.

"You have more variety," Elena said. "Mine is too pretentious. Like I'm trying too hard."

"Well, it's too late now to worry. They've seen hundreds of people go through this. They're used to every type." Suzanne turned away again, but there was nothing on the walls to look at, as if the room were deliberately unadorned to keep the students fixed on their fear.

They would be playing for four teachers, two of them legendary. One was the imperious Marina Kabalevsky, not only a renowned teacher but a dynamo of activity who at sixty-nine had begun a brilliant concert career, and also Joseph Bloch, less flamboyant but equally august, who had taught the history of the piano repertory to every pianist who passed through Juilliard.

"Suzanne, can't we behave like adults now? I only went out with him for a month or so. We didn't ever really get . . . you know, close. Philip Markon!" The rhythms of Elena's speech had taken on a curt New York dismissiveness. The way she uttered his name and grimaced made Philip sound too trivial to bother about. "Anyhow, it was finished a year ago. I'm sorry. I would have been glad to give him back to you"—she giggled, as if she realized she was discussing Phil as if he were a package—"but you wouldn't even look at me or speak."

"I didn't want him back by that point. He never even said a word to me about it. Just started not showing up."

"He tried. He said you wouldn't listen."

Suzanne shrugged. "I hardly even remember anymore. Honestly, I never think about it. When I was a camp counselor last summer, I met someone I liked a lot better."

"Well, good. But still, I'm sorry for the way it happened. I shouldn't have done it. I didn't really understand he was seeing you, I mean, in that way, you know, exclusively. But I knew very soon that it wouldn't last long. He was so superficial. That's what my mother said the first time he came over. He tried to impress her, talking about the concerts he'd been to and the museums and so on, like he was a precocious intellectual, and after he left she said he was all surface and just showing off. Pretty soon I realized she was right."

Could it be? Did that charm and fluency on tap, that ready competence, mean superficiality? Surely his grief over his lost family, his resolve to escape from his aunt and uncle's grim depression, weren't superficial.

Her own mother had been impressed with Phil, and Gerda's instincts were usually good. What a bright boy, she called him. A really cultured boy. Elena's mother must be far more worldly, a woman who could see right through people. That was another expression Suzanne's father liked to use: I could see right through him, he sometimes said of business acquaintances. While she and Gerda were innocents, deluded by surfaces. Even Richard had called her an innocent, that mortifying night when . . . she couldn't bear to think of it, even now. What made her an innocent? Was there something missing in her? Why didn't she see what others saw?

"That doesn't seem totally fair. I think he's more than surface."

"Okay, maybe superficial isn't quite right. I know he suffered, losing his family and all. And he was very smart and could do a lot of things. But there was something not quite . . . like he wasn't totally what he pretended to be. Like the surface was hiding something. Or maybe nothing—maybe surface was all there was. Anyway, it's ancient history now. What does it matter? Can't we be friends?"

"All right, we can try," Suzanne said. Elena was right. It was history. Before it had happened, they'd liked each other. Elena might be the only person she knew at Juilliard—assuming she passed the audition. They could help each other, although Elena never seemed to need much help.

"It's going to be so great. These are the real musicians," Elena said breathlessly. "I used to hear about them back home. And they'll be teaching us. It's fantastic. Did you know that just last week Madame Kabalevsky had this fabulous concert with the New York Philharmonic? She played the Schumann Concerto in A Minor, the same piece she played when she graduated from the Moscow Conservatory. She's in her eighties now and still going strong. I was there, I mean last week, not sixty years ago," she added, laughing, the teeth flashing. "It was totally amazing."

"You were actually there?" Suzanne had read about the concert in the paper, but as something that might have taken place on the other side of the globe. To her it was a dream world she might hope to enter after years of work, while Elena was already in it.

"Paul got complimentary tickets." Paul was her stepfather, the cellist. "The audience went wild. I heard Horowitz say it's all in her phrasing and her tone, that those are the most important things for a pianist. Anyway, you know how everyone says she's such a scary teacher, so strict and demanding, she taught Van Cliburn and all sorts of people? But she's really very nice. Not arrogant at all."

"You know her?" Suzanne whispered.

"Not well, no. But she's come over a few times, like after concerts. There are always these parties, sometimes at our house. I've barely said more than hello, but I could tell she's not as tough as they say. All her old students loved her. You just have to get used to her."

Clearly there was no need for Elena to be "scared shitless" about the audition, thought Suzanne. For her it was more of a formality, an opportunity to show off.

☊

The curriculum they began in September was even more rigorous than it sounded in the catalog. Professor Bloch's required course in the history of the piano repertory—a hallowed tradition for decades—was only the beginning. The former director, William Schuman, had left a few years ago to become the president of the brand-new Lincoln Center, but during his tenure he instituted changes that made the course of study more demanding: programs combining history, theory, and music literature in order to produce what he regarded as educated musicians rather than highly trained technicians. Then there were language classes, as well as group and master classes where students would play for each other and learn how to offer critiques. But the core of the program for the piano students was the teacher they were assigned to study with once a week for the entire four years.

Suzanne would be in the care of the formidable Mme. Kabalevsky, who had gazed at her soberly, with an assessing eye, during her audition. Everyone knew her story. She was an older cousin of the well-known Dmitri Kabalevsky, a major figure in the Soviet world as both a composer and a teacher, who eventually joined the Communist Party and held official posts. Marina Kabalevsky, meanwhile, left at the time of the revolution with her family. Before that, though, she won the coveted gold medal at her graduation from the Moscow Conservatory and married a fellow student, a tenor who went on to sing in the Mariinsky Opera. He was the performer while she remained the helpmeet, teaching and of course attending all of his performances. He was most celebrated for the role of Lensky in *Eugene Onegin*. After the Russian Revolution they lived in various European cities and eventually came to New York to join the faculty of Juilliard, then called the Institute of Musical Art. Mme. Kabalevsky continued teaching there after her husband's death in 1950, and shortly gave in to her colleagues' urgings that she play in public, making a spectacular debut at sixty-nine. Twelve years later, she was still performing and teaching, a tall, regal woman with short gray hair, a composed, determined face, and piercing eyes. Suzanne was terrified.

"You should be flattered that you were assigned to her," Elena said. "It means they think you have real potential." This did not make her any less tense when she knocked on Mme. Kabalevsky's door for the first time.

She greeted Suzanne kindly, and with no preliminaries sent her over to the piano. "I remember you from the auditions. You did well on the Chopin, and also the Bach prelude and fugue. So now show me something different. Let me see what else you can do."

Suzanne, who had not spoken, fumbled with the opening of a simple Mozart sonata, and Mme. Kabalevsky stopped her immediately.

"You can do better than that. I see you're afraid of me. That's the trouble—my reputation follows me and it scares you. You can't play the piano if the fingers are tense—the most essential thing is to relax. The greatest pianists have the most relaxed touch, they caress the keys, they don't batter them. Remember that." She paused as if for a response, so Suzanne nodded. "Now, we must get one thing straight if we are to stay together: You must not be afraid of me." She smiled mischievously, aware of the absurdity of issuing such a command, and Suzanne had to smile back despite herself.

"I'll try." She noted that unlike Elena, Mme. Kabalevsky had made no effort to lose her thick accent. Of course, she was in her thirties when she came here. And it did contribute to her uniqueness.

"Trying isn't enough. Just make up your mind and do it.

Whatever I say to you doesn't matter personally. I like you. I'll like you more and more as time goes on. I get attached to my students, especially the good ones. When I criticize your playing, it's about the music. All right? You will not be afraid? You will relax? Pretend you are in your home, playing for yourself. Or your mother. You have a mother who appreciates your playing?"

She nodded again.

"All right, there's no one home but you and your mother, and she's in the kitchen. You're alone."

Strangely enough, her command worked. Suzanne willed herself to rout her fear, and very soon she was thriving during the strenuous lessons. Maybe under Mme. Kabalevsky's care, her stage fright, which had grown worse, not better, since childhood, would disappear, like adolescent acne or leg cramps. Maybe Mme. Kabalevsky would work a miracle; there was a touch of the sorceress about her. After a few months, when they knew each other better and Suzanne felt more free to speak, she asked, "How come they didn't assign Elena to you? I would think since you're both Russian, you'd be a good match . . ."

Mme. Kabalevsky didn't answer for a moment, and Suzanne feared she'd gone too far. Then the teacher said, "It would be too easy for her. Too comfortable. We can't make things comfortable. Obstacles are good."

Elena had been assigned to the stern and unsmiling Mr. Mitchell, who seemed unmoved by her élan and was attempting to restrain her tendencies toward excessive romanticism and the too-liberal use of rubato.

It wasn't long before Suzanne and Elena were best friends.

The perspicacious Mme. Kabalevsky noticed this and took to calling them Snow White and Rose Red, Elena with her blond hair and fair skin and Suzanne darker, more sultry-looking. The famous teacher greeted them in the halls this way, as if they were semimythical creatures out of a story. "Snow White and Rose Red with talent," Mme. Kabalevsky would say, smiling, and then walk on.

Once, Elena had the nerve to stop her and ask what the story was. "Oh, it doesn't signify. An old tale of the Grimms'. Two sisters take care of a bear who turns out to be a prince. And then one marries him."

"Which one?" Elena asked.

"I think Snow White," and Mme. Kabalevsky went on her way.

"You can have the bear," Elena said. "I don't plan to marry anyone."

"And who says I do?" Suzanne retorted.

Elena was the closest friend Suzanne had ever had, apart from Philip. Her confidence and enthusiasm were contagious; everything seemed brighter in her presence, brighter and more manageable. Suzanne never troubled to wonder—as she had with Philip—why Elena had chosen her. She knew. It had to do with each one's tacitly recognizing not only the talent of the other, but the enormous ambition, what the music meant to them and what their success would mean—though they were still too young to make a clear distinction between the two. What Philip's companionship had accomplished in high school, Elena's did at Juilliard: It quickly felt like home. They compared notes on what they were studying, they listened to each other play and gave advice, they played pieces for four hands, and they agreed they were among the most promising students, although there were a few, like Emanuel Ax or Misha Dichter or Garrick Ohlsson, who might be as good or better. Together they sat in the student lounge and took part in the talk, the endless talk about teachers, technique, and music-world gossip.

The students would gather in clumps in the lounge late in the day, their instrument cases at their feet, scores sticking out of tote bags, the plastic tables covered with cardboard coffee mugs and crumpled napkins, cigarettes burning in ashtrays. Some were recovering after a grueling session with a teacher, others waiting their turn in the practice rooms, which stayed open until ten. They gossiped about the teachers' eccentricities—who used too much aftershave and who needed a complete makeover—and methods: the motherly encouraging ones and the coolly distant, the patient and the impatient, those who praised too much or never, those who might be alcoholic or homosexual, or who were rivals, or the few who came on to students, male or female . . .

The pianists, especially those in their first year, compared the teachers' contradictory demands and instructions. Frank Wallace's teacher was always urging more pedal, he reported: "She says the piano is not naturally a legato instrument. You have to make it sound like one. And don't wear shoes with thick soles— you have to really feel the pedal under your feet." Frank was the only black student in the class, a southern boy from Georgia with astounding technique, so his comments were given special attention. But according to Steve Henderson, a corn-fed boy from Nebraska who looked more like a football player than a musician, his teacher advised just the opposite: "Too much pedal blurs the sound and makes it murky. That's his mantra. Try for a clean, crisp sound. Crisp, he snaps his fingers. Use the pedal only when you absolutely must. Learn to stretch your fingers instead."

Or the teachers differed on the best way to practice. A few demanded their students do scales and arpeggios and chromatics before playing any real music, while Elena's Professor Mitchell said to forget the exercises. "He says we can get all the technique we need from Bach or Chopin or Liszt. Ruth Laredo never practiced an exercise in her life. Or so he claims." One required that they play each hand slowly and separately before trying them together, while another found that a waste of time. "Just sit down and sight-read it up to speed. Any decent pianist should know how to sight-read. If you can't, then practice it until you can," said Rose Chen's teacher, Professor Brent. Still another teacher thought that good natural sight-reading— always considered an enviable gift—could be a mixed blessing: "It makes the learning too easy, he says. You're in danger of a superficial interpretation." Tanya Borowitz's teacher was even against practicing slowly, which they had all been taught to do as children. "He says once we can read it through, we should practice it faster than it's supposed to be, so when you do it at the correct tempo it feels easier." Some wanted them to read through the score first and analyze it, before even trying it on the piano.

A few insisted that the wrists be held high, with the fingers forming an arc over the keys, while others preferred the hands held lower, but Simon Valenti's teacher, the venerable Adele Marcus, said it didn't matter how they held their hands—whatever was comfortable, as long as the sound was right. "Look at Glenn Gould, those flat hands. Gould says you don't play the piano with your fingers, but with your mind. And that low chair he uses! You know he cuts several inches off the legs of his chairs? But she said I better not try that here." And some teachers didn't mind what fingering they used, so long as it was comfortable, while others seemed personally miffed if they ignored the composer's fingering notations—why would he have included them if they weren't important?

How were they to figure all this out? Suzanne, who dropped in to see Richard whenever she could find time, asked him about the confusing advice. He agreed with Adele Marcus that any technique was fine as long as the music sounded beautiful and faithful. As they all grew more experienced, they would naturally find the methods that suited them best. Meanwhile, he said, they should do what their teachers asked.

Given the degree of talent and the magnitude of the burgeoning egos assembled in one building, the atmosphere at school was less rawly competitive than might be expected. Perhaps the love of music, such a benign passion, tempered the sharp edges of rivalry. But after the gossip and complaints and talk of the music itself, much of the chatter in the lounge was about what became known jokingly as "the tree falling in the forest," code words for their own yearnings and doubts and ambitions. "The tree falling in the forest" meant, if it turned out that you spent your life accompanying singers and teaching students, or, even more extreme, as a stockbroker or a travel agent (not unheard of among the graduates), playing alone evenings and weekends in your living room, what did your devotion to music mean then? What reality did your playing have if no one ever heard it, like the tree falling in the forest? Could you still call yourself a musician?

"Of course you can," said Simon Valenti, a strapping boy from the Bronx with Italian immigrant parents. "That's not even a valid question. It's not the audience that matters. It's the music, the feeling it gives you, the sound you strive for. For yourself, for the composer. That's enough."

"You say so now," said Elena. "But would you still think that if you kept trying and no one wanted to hear you? Would you still be so idealistic?"

"Sure. There'd always be someone who wanted to hear. My family. My students," said Simon. "I'm not saying I wouldn't enjoy playing in Carnegie Hall—maybe even the same season as you, Elena. But if I couldn't, I'd still be happy to have a life with music. I just want to be with the piano, to feel it and touch it. It's almost like a love relationship—I miss it if I don't stroke it every day."

"I feel exactly that way," Suzanne broke in. She loved the instrument itself, she said, beyond the music she could coax from it. She loved the look and the feel of it; it was a friend, even a lover. When she said "lover," a giggle rippled through the group—it wasn't a word they used or heard very often.

Despite the purity of Simon's argument, and however modest the students appeared, almost all of them privately nursed fantasies of standing onstage in a few years, taking their bows to rousing applause. Only a few honestly felt otherwise. Tanya Borowitz, the timid freckled redhead from New Hampshire, who had memorized the Goldberg Variations when she was still in high school, said at the outset, "I'm going to teach. I can't go out there onstage. They were always making me do it in high school, and each time I almost passed out from fright. It was no fun at all. The rewards aren't worth the stress." The others nodded sympathetically—it made for that much less competition.

Only a few were bold enough to openly claim their future. Elena was one. "I plan to succeed, and I don't see why most of us shouldn't make it. We're here, after all. If we're good enough and work hard and cultivate the right connections, plus a little bit of luck . . ."

They started laughing as her list grew longer. "Is that all?" Rose Chen asked. "Would there be enough stages to accommodate all of us?"

Though Elena never flaunted her connections, everyone knew she wouldn't hesitate to use them. Who would? Not that she isn't really good, they whispered among themselves, but it can't hurt to have Horowitz and Serkin—yes, the very Rudolf Serkin Suzanne had heard at her first real concert—coming over for dinner every now and then.

Suzanne listened intently to these conversations, and when she spoke it was with a fervor that she regretted immediately. It embarrassed her to show how ambitious she was, like confessing to some shameful flaw. Yet she was glad to know she wasn't the only one driven by relentless need. In Brooklyn, from earliest childhood, she'd been regarded as the prodigy. She was used to moving through the neighborhood with her reputation on her sleeve, like an insignia by which people could recognize her. But her classmates here had been hometown wonders, too. The collective fervor in the room was like a cloud that sustained them on a magic carpet.

Tanya's mother was a writer. Or called herself a writer. She'd published a novel twenty years ago and nothing since but a few stories in obscure magazines. She worked as a paralegal in a law firm and wrote for two hours every night, Tanya said. She did it for the pleasure of writing itself. She believed in it like a religion, like someone going to Mass every morning.

"But does she still try to publish?" asked Jason Shaw, a skinny violinist who already, as a freshman, had been selected for one of the school's two orchestras.

"I'm not sure. She doesn't talk about it, though she does still have an agent she's in touch with. But publication isn't the whole point. That's what she says, anyway. You don't work for fame. You work for the process itself, for the product."

"Ugh, don't call it a product," said Elena. "That makes it sound like canned soup or toasters. It's art."

Art. The two times Suzanne had used that word at home, her father had snorted and even her brothers, visiting for Sunday dinner, smirked. They wanted her to be a musician, but they didn't like the changes her training would bring. She must remain the agreeable girl who never did anything questionable or "out of line"—her father's expression. And avoid pretentious words like "art."

"That may be okay for a writer," said Peter Jackson, a native New Yorker who was studying the clarinet. "My father's an actor. He's been in commercials and a lot of off-Broadway shows. But he can't make a living acting. He has a day job in the gift shop at the Met. I feel sorry for him, always going to auditions, always waiting for the callback. You can't act alone in a room, the way you can play music or write. There's not even any tree to fall in the forest with an actor. You need the stage and the audience in order to do your thing. As a matter of fact, you can't do too much alone with a clarinet, either—there's not much solo stuff. But at least I can get work in an orchestra."

"For pianists, too," said Elena, "it's either solo performing or accompanying or teaching."

"That's not so," said Simon. "There are chamber groups. Look at the Beaux Arts trio, or the Istomin-Stern-Rose Trio. Those are terrific pianists. I wouldn't complain if I could be in a group like that."

Some nights, in a coffee shop near school, Suzanne and Elena and a few of the other pianists—Rose, Tanya, Simon—would play a game where they each made up reviews of their debut recitals, striving to outdo each other in extravagant, fulsome praise. Their creations inevitably ended up in parody and raucous laughter. "Maybe we should try the worst possible reviews for a change," Elena suggested, but Suzanne was against that. "You never know—they might come true."

In her fourth month at school, a notice posted all through the corridors announced that the great pianist Anthony Dawson was coming to give a master class. The class would be a major event, held in the largest auditorium and publicized in local papers; the public was invited to attend. Rumors flew, speculating on which fourth-year students would be selected to play for him.

Dawson's visit was scheduled for two o'clock on a bright November day. By one thirty the piano students had already found seats toward the front, and the rest of the student body—instrumentalists, singers, dancers—was not far behind them. The first few rows were reserved for faculty and for the three students who would be playing. They sat stiff and silent as if frozen; Suzanne, with her usual jumble of emotions, envied them and pitied them, and was glad she wasn't one of them. She looked around: The auditorium was filled, and about a third of the crowd weren't students—amateur musicians, most likely, or local music lovers come to see and hear the great Anthony Dawson.

Just as the audience was growing restless, Dawson entered at the back, escorted by Mme. Kabalevsky and Mr. Hofmann. Heads turned; the teachers rose to greet him. "Did you ever meet him?" Suzanne whispered to Elena, beside her.

"No," she replied, "and even if I had, I'd never walk over with all the faculty surrounding him. That would be very bad form."

Finally the greetings were over and the teachers settled into the front row seats. The first to play was Amit Mukherjee, who had come all the way from Calcutta and was among the school stars; everyone predicted a brilliant career for him. He played Beethoven's Piano Sonata no. 26, *Les Adieux*, one of the most difficult. After the first movement he paused and glanced at Dawson, who waved him to continue. Amit had the mannerisms of famous pianists Suzanne had seen: a swaying of the shoulders, a shaking of the head, too artificial, overconfident.

Dawson let him play to the end of the piece. This might bode well or ill. Suzanne thought his playing lacked the poignancy and delicacy the music required, and she waited curiously to see what Anthony Dawson would say. Amit finished with a flourish and turned to face the audience with a look of satisfaction. But in a few moments, he seemed to shrink in his elegant clothes.

"We can see that technically you're quite the wizard," Dawson began.

"Uh-oh," Elena murmured.

This was not a good sign. Dawson went on to praise Amit's facility and mastery of the notes, the pedaling, the phrasing. "But your presentation was a little hard, don't you think? By hard, I mean heavy. Brusque. Crisp."

"He's one of the tough ones," whispered Elena. "I went to a few of his master classes while we were still in high school—sometimes I cut class to go. He may be right, but he's harsh. I'm glad it's not me sitting up there."

Finally Dawson sat down and played a section of the opening. As he began, the audience stirred, as if gathering its attention, and indeed the music was transformed, with nuances and a tenderness that had been submerged before.

He asked Amit to repeat the second half of the final movement. While Dawson played Amit had stood to one side, holding himself very straight, and now, as he took the seat again, he nodded and smiled at the famous pianist. He had collected himself; this, too, was part of his performance. To Suzanne's surprise, he played with far greater delicacy and warmth of expression: In ten minutes, in exchange for his pride, he had learned how to give life to the sonata. Not a bad exchange, she thought. It wasn't that Anthony Dawson was unkind. Rather, he was intimidatingly cordial, dauntingly thorough.

The next student, Pete O'Brien, was a boy from Queens who had already won a minor contest and given a few local recitals. He did not have Amit's irritating mannerisms, but rather approached the piano like a gladiator seeking to conquer it. He played Brahms's B-minor Rhapsody. Whether it was nerves or whether he was not as wonderful as reputed, his playing was noticeably forced. Effortful. Suzanne could feel his effort in her fingers, it was so tactile.

He was lowering his head to begin a new passage, when Dawson spoke from his seat in the front row. "Just one moment," and he stepped up to the stage, holding the score. "Well, that was fine," he said kindly. "That was well done. You've worked hard, obviously. Just a few things to point out." And there followed ten minutes of close, unsparing criticism. "You must give the notes their full value," he said. "Just because they're played presto doesn't mean you can slide over them." Then he talked about the various forms of staccato: Secco staccato, he explained, was not the same as staccato. And then about shading and nuances, playing a couple of bars here and there to illustrate. And on it went, while Pete, in a dark suit and tie for the occasion, seemed to shrink exactly as Amit had done. Anthony Dawson played a section from the opening, and again all the shades in the music became brighter.

There was a short break after Pete finished, so short that the audience was advised not to leave their seats—just long enough for Dawson to "catch his breath," as Professor Hofmann said. While Elena chatted with the person on her right, Suzanne spent the few minutes wondering how she could possibly withstand such public criticism. Under Mme. Kabalevsky she had gained courage and learned self-control. She could tolerate the biweekly critiques held for the students fairly well; the listeners were her teachers, her classmates, her peers. She knew she was one of the outstanding pianists and that others knew it, too; in this tight milieu, reputations were quick to develop. But nothing could thicken her skin; every critical word still seeped into her pores. Elena was just the opposite. Suzanne had seen it in class. She took in the comments, nodded, and forged ahead. She never appeared wounded—she had an impervious surface. Elena had no trouble distinguishing between her performance and herself.

If she were to play for a pianist like Dawson in two years, if she were ever to play for an audience at all, she must find a way to get over her fear. Her friends all bemoaned their anxiety, but Suzanne's terror, she knew, was different. It would not permit the life she had dreamed of since childhood. Watching the master class, she couldn't deny that any longer.

The last to play was Laura Duvenek, also a star student with great expectations. She was a narrow reed of a girl, unprepossessing in looks, with stringy blond hair, and unlike the boy students, she hadn't bothered to dress for the occasion but wore a drab everyday shirt and skirt with shoes that were down at the heel. She'd have to get someone to fix her up before she appeared on a New York stage, Suzanne thought. But it was evident from the start of Haydn's Sonata in E Flat Major, one of the simpler ones, that she was the most accomplished of the three. Dawson stopped her only once, in the first movement, the allegro. He suddenly leaped from his seat and onto the stage. "No, wait, stop right there. You're losing the shading, the nuance. It's those triplets. They're much too slow." He was excited; he practically shoved her from the bench and played the passage with the triplets, and at his quicker pace they were entirely new, brilliant, rousing. He got up and waved her to the chair.

"Now you. Do what I did."

Laura did not seem disconcerted in the least, or troubled

by the several hundred people focused on her. She played the passage again, and the triplets at the rapid speed took on the luster that had been missing. She stopped and looked up at him, without the slightest hesitation. "Like that?" she asked.

"Yes. Precisely like that," he said, smiling, and returned to his seat. She played the rest of the sonata uninterrupted, and Anthony Dawson returned to the stage and praised her as he had not praised the others. The audience applauded, but Laura seemed indifferent to anything but Dawson's words. If only I could be like that, Suzanne thought. But not look like that, she added quickly, in case any nameless gods of music students could hear her prayer.

⌒

What with the headiness of Juilliard, her new friends and teachers, that old affair with Philip shrank to almost nothing. A childhood incident. She had a couple of brief flings with fellow students—Simon, for one—but they all knew it wasn't serious; it was recreation, a relief from the weight of their studies, and less intense than the studies. She barely thought of Philip at all; the grief he had caused her dissipated. She and Elena never mentioned his name. He was not even history, for history is remembered and recorded. He was obliterated.

After a year of commuting up to Morningside Heights an hour twice a day on the subway—such a waste of precious time—Suzanne persuaded her parents to let her live close to school. She found a room for rent in an airy apartment facing the Hudson River, belonging to the widow of a Juilliard professor. Mrs. Campbell was mild and unobtrusive and spent most of her time painting watercolors of Riverside Park scenes and volunteering in the local church's preschool program. She liked having a music student in the apartment and charged a low rent, which she made even lower when Suzanne agreed to take on some errands and household tasks. Best of all, she had a grand piano in the living room and said Suzanne could use it whenever she wished, so she didn't have to worry about signing up for practice rooms—there were never enough. Suzanne was content with her simple room—narrow bed, desk, bookcase, and chair—and she hung bright Dufy prints on the walls. She was even more content with school, despite its occasional terrors. Her turn in the master classes with visiting pianists had not yet come, but it would; there was no evading it. Still, she would remember those years at school and in Mrs. Campbell's apartment as the happiest of her life: There was work she loved and did well, and despite her fears, extravagant hope.

"I'm as good as most of them," she told Richard breathlessly on the phone. She had so much to do, was always in a rush. "I'm probably one of the best. There are a couple of guys who are really good, and also this one girl, this Russian, the one I met back in high school. She's the one who took my boyfriend, I told you about that. But now we're close friends. She might be slightly better than me. But a tiny bit on the splashy side."

"It's not a competition, you know," he answered. "Or shouldn't be. You're there to study. In the Olympics there's only one gold medal. But there's room for all different kinds of pianists. If you're any good, and you know you are, you'll do fine."

He was wrong, she thought. He was the one sounding innocent now. Of course it was a competition. Getting into Music and Art had been a competition, playing in front of

three stone-faced teachers, each taking notes on a clipboard—
she could remember the scratching of their pens—and then
another competition to get into Juilliard. The halls here were
lined with bulletin boards posting notices of contests. Everyone talked about the contests—how they ranked in importance
and prestige, which they should enter and when they would be
ready, which recent graduates or even the few current students
had won and were already embarking on recitals. Winning a
major or even lesser contest assured you of a year or so of bookings, not to mention the goodwill, however transient, of eager
managers and a welcoming public. You had to win something,
no matter how obscure, or at the very least be a runner-up,
to get started. The competition never let up. Didn't Richard
know that? B+ was not good enough.

Her final year was the most pressured. She, along with many
others, was preparing to enter the contests. There were so
many, she could hardly keep track of them. She dreaded the
auditions, but Mme. Kabalevsky insisted she try, if only for the
experience. She said if Suzanne could overcome her stage fright,
she would be sure to win sooner or later. And with all that, Juilliard was in the midst of a major move, three miles downtown
to Lincoln Center: There were the disruptions of instruments
being crated and loaded onto vans, of cartons of files stacked
in the hallways, and the students' anxiety about what the new
quarters would be like. Suzanne and her friends were glad they
would be completing their studies in the slightly seedy but
appealing neighborhood uptown, adjacent to Columbia University and Riverside Park, where in all seasons they loved to
walk, watching the river and the passing boats. In winter some-

times the ships stayed in the same place for days, clogged by ice floes, and in summer small pleasure crafts, sailboats, even sailfish, would skim by, and the occasional kayak.

Juilliard's home in Lincoln Center was above a huge stone plaza, relieved only by the fountain in the center. It was surrounded by buildings housing a theater, the opera, and the ballet, and the faculty all welcomed this. But the upperclassmen were dubious. "Slick," Elena called it, over and over, her word of greatest opprobrium, and Suzanne tended to agree with her. "We'll be the last living relics of the good old days," Simon Valenti said, putting his arm around Suzanne; she couldn't tell whether it was nostalgic camaraderie or if he hoped to resume the very brief affair they'd had early on. She hoped it wasn't the latter. She had succumbed in a moment of lassitude. He was very attractive, she had to admit, with his long lanky body and shock of black hair almost like an Indian's; when she got bored it had taken several weeks to extricate herself.

"No, there'll always be the teachers," Elena said, glancing at the two of them with slightly raised eyebrows. "Madame Kabalevsky will be here forever, and so will Mr. Schell and Adele Marcus and most of the others."

Elena won the Tchaikovsky Competition right before she graduated. And though they were still good friends and she tried not to be envious, Suzanne couldn't help thinking, Always a few steps ahead. Everything came easily to her. Not only a new high school, but a new country. A new language. She sailed through it all as if a benevolent breeze were propelling her. It would probably be that way forever, Suzanne thought. She might as well get used to it.

During her first few years out of school, Suzanne remained in Mrs. Campbell's apartment and took odd jobs accompanying singers, playing for dance classes, teaching—anything that could bring in some money. Meanwhile, she returned to studying with Cynthia and occasionally took a lesson with Mme. Kabalevsky, to prepare for still more contests. For two of them she had to make a hasty trip abroad, so short and so marred by anxiety that she hardly felt she'd been away. Her stage fright interfered with the auditions. She would start out brilliantly, and the judges would straighten up and scrutinize her, sometimes making notes. But after a few moments the loathsome panic would grip her, and no matter how hard she tried to control it, using the mind games Mr. Cartelli and Cynthia had taught, it would get the better of her, so that by the end she was trembling and struggling to stay in control. Even so, she played remarkably well, but never as splendidly as the first few minutes had promised.

Then finally she did win one, three years after she graduated from Juilliard, not the most distinguished but still a respected one, the Busoni Competition in Bolzano, Italy, which Alfred Brendel had won in its first year. The panel of judges this time was wiser than most. As in so many contests in the arts, often the winner was of the satisfies-all-and-delights-none variety— it was a risk to choose an erratic, unpredictable unknown. But this time Suzanne had managed to dazzle the judges enough to make her a topic of prolonged discussion. Nothing mediocre about her, the notable pianist Aida Rinaldo said—she's either brilliant or paralyzed by fright. I'd go for that one over ordinary competence any day. It happened that La Rinaldo, as she was known, had suffered from stage fright as well and had undergone a series of treatments, from Rolfing to hypnosis to psychoanalysis, in order to overcome her fear. Her insistence won the others over. "We have enough decent pianists all over the place," she said. "Let's take a chance on someone special. If she doesn't work out, I'll take the blame."

Now, thought Suzanne, maybe the life of her fantasies would begin. The concert in Bolzano flew by like a dream. And as in her dreams, she played well, buoyed up by having been chosen and by the kindness of La Rinaldo, who befriended her.

⌒

Cynthia was in the habit of giving parties. It wasn't only because she enjoyed seeing her apartment crowded with well-dressed people. Each party was a triumph over the shabbiness she had grown up in and would never reveal to anyone by word or deed or furnishing. Even more important, she wanted her best students to get used to being out in the world, meeting people, making connections. Sad but true, she told them: Success was not simply a matter of playing well. It had to do with whom you knew and how you behaved and how eager you appeared; all these things she had discovered and mastered through arduous experience. Suzanne was smart enough to know those truths, but perhaps not aggressive enough to act on them. She must be helped. Cynthia felt a special sympathy for Suzanne, not only because of her talent and ambition—the ambitious recognize each other as if by a secret code—but because her own background was not too different: as provincial as Suzanne's, only poorer.

It was inevitable, then, that after Suzanne won first prize in the Busoni Competition, Cynthia would give a congratulatory party. "Invite anyone you like, everyone you know," she said, "and I'll do the same. This is really a big moment."

Suzanne hadn't realized Cynthia's apartment could hold so many people. The party was similar to the ones she'd been to before: the women shiny, polished, colorful, the men a trifle less sleek, freer to appear eccentric, and everyone holding glasses and negotiating minuscule hors d'oeuvres passed around by a couple of first-year Juilliard students. Only this time the crowd was larger and she couldn't retreat to a quiet corner with a few friends. She was the guest of honor. Everyone wanted to meet her. Cynthia kept bringing people over; Suzanne tried to keep track of their names and who they were, but very quickly it was all a muddle. "Don't worry," Cynthia whispered. "You can't remember them all. We'll go over it later. Meanwhile, just act pleased and excited. Treat everyone well—you can't always tell by appearances who's important."

She had no chance to talk to her own guests: Elena, who was, naturally, making the most of the occasion, the others from Juilliard, and aspiring musicians she'd met since. During a rare instant when she was on her own, in between introductions, came a tap on the shoulder. She turned around. Her first response was one of puzzled familiarity—she almost couldn't place him. He was smiling broadly, looking older, totally grownup in a well-tailored suit, utterly changed from the lanky boy in neatly pressed chinos. But she wasn't completely sure until he spoke her name; then she knew the voice instantly.

"Suzanne! You're so gorgeous and elegant! Not that you weren't before, but this!" Philip let his eyes wander appraisingly over the narrow black silk dress, then grasped her shoulders and bent to kiss her lightly on the lips before she could pull away. "Tell me how you are."

She wanted to turn and run, but she was too old for that now. And where could she run in this crowd? Anyhow, he would follow her or find her later. There was no escape.

"I'm fine." She couldn't help the tone of insinuation in her voice, almost accusatory. These days he didn't cross her mind for weeks at a time, yet here was that bitterness rising again, like an acrid taste. For God's sake, let him not talk about the past.

"Is it possible you're still angry? I can see you are. For chrissake, Suzanne, we're not in high school anymore. I'm sorry. I was an idiot boy."

She smiled unwillingly. The words were satisfying, as if indeed she were still in high school. "You were. You lout." It came out sounding flirtatious, though she hadn't meant it to.

"I agree. Let's make believe we've never met. I just saw you across a crowded room. Who's that girl? I asked myself. I've got to meet her. And congratulate her. It's great news! I can't say I'm surprised. I always knew you had it in you. Now all sorts of doors will start opening. Oh, but no, I can't say that— we're pretending we've never met."

"Don't we know each other too well for that?"

"No, you don't know me at all anymore. I've changed. I've developed depth and substance," he declared with an ironic smile. "Are you still working with Cynthia? I remember you started in high school."

"Yes. I stopped when I was at Juilliard—Madame Kabalevsky was as much as I could handle, and after that I went back. She's been awfully good to me. How do you know her?"

"I know everybody. Remember? I always did. I've been

working as a recording engineer with RCA for four years now, ever since I graduated from the business school. Still learning, but I get to do a lot on my own, tapes, song demos, presentations for new artists, even film scores. I started working for them as an intern while I was still at Columbia and found out I had a knack for it. Editing, especially. Tape and razor are almost all you need. And an ear, of course. I've recorded Cynthia's recitals."

"Really? She never mentioned that." But why should she? Suzanne thought. Cynthia never confided about her life.

"Oh, yes, a Brahms piano trio and also the *Dumky* with Kinsky and Paul Manning—you know, Elena's stepfather. I'm starting my own business on the side too. Artists' management. I haven't lured Cynthia yet, but I have a few promising beginners and I'm pretty good at getting them gigs. I don't mind doing the small stuff, and it leads to bigger things if you have patience. One client recommends another, and so it goes."

He was still the same, she thought, the boy who knew everyone, was competent at everything. Making his accomplishments known, yet somehow not boastful, rather matter-of-fact. The boy who would always need to prove himself. She didn't know how long he might have gone on, if she hadn't been tapped on the shoulder again. This time it was Richard.

"Suzanne! I congratulated you on the phone, but that's not enough for something like this!" He embraced her in a huge hug. "This is the most wonderful news. It was bound to happen. I want to hear all about it, every note. We'll have lunch. But I'm sorry, I didn't mean to interrupt."

"No, not at all." She introduced them. "Philip, this is Richard Penzer, the composer and friend of my youth. I wouldn't be standing here if not for him. And Richard, you must have heard me talk about Philip Markon? Well, you might not remember, why should you? The boy who ditched me in high school for the glamorous Russian? Who is somewhere on the premises, by the way."

"Ah, the teen heartbreaker." Richard shook hands with a brief, reserved laugh, as if he still harbored a touch of resentment on Suzanne's part.

"I see I'll never live it down. It was my biggest mistake," Philip replied. "Of course I've heard about you. Suzanne used to talk about you as if you were a god. And now the reviewers do, too. I saw *David and Jonathan*. It was marvelous."

Richard nodded, like one grown accustomed to praise. *David and Jonathan*, his opera based on the biblical tale, had recently played in an East Side hall to rave reviews. After so long, he'd been discovered. Next season it would be produced at the New York City Opera, though, as he told Suzanne when it happened, "These discoveries are always a joke. I've been here all along. They act as if I sprang yesterday from the head of Zeus. But now at least I can get anything I want produced, for as long as it lasts. I've got a drawer full of scores I worked on, back in Brooklyn and before."

"The god and the devil," Suzanne said, "brought face-to-face." The silliness of the words made it all right. The residue of sour gall she'd buried for so long evaporated, and she looked at Philip with a fresh eye. He did seem to have more substance. Seeing him side by side with Richard made him more acceptable—as if their occupying the same room, the same world, at least to the extent of being at the same party, legitimized him. And he knew Richard's work—another point in his favor. He couldn't be all surface.

Suddenly Elena was beside her, draped in a flowing coral dress that hung low on her hips. She gave Philip a perfunctory greeting, a hug so light it barely merited the name. "Sweetheart," she said to Suzanne, "you're the belle of the ball. You're not only talented, but you look fantastic and you've got all the best men." Before Suzanne could speak, she turned to Richard. "You must be Richard Penzer. I know you're an old friend of Suzanne's. She's spoken so much about you. In fact, she's made you sound superhuman."

"Richard," Suzanne interrupted, "this is Elena Semonyova, my friend from Juilliard. A wonderful pianist, as I've told you before."

They shook hands. Suzanne's heart filled with an unaccustomed gladness. She was surrounded by her three closest friends—why not count Philip, in the spirit of generosity, of deference to the past? Well, at least the people who had most believed in her and encouraged her. Who knew her. She was lucky indeed. Looking at them, one by one, as they carried on the ordinary party chatter, she felt blessed, wrapped in warmth that would carry her into the future.

She forced herself to stop daydreaming and pay attention. Richard and Elena were engaged in lively banter, dropping the names of composers and performers she hadn't heard of, and now Philip was speaking to a beautiful older woman in red who'd just appeared and embraced him. For a moment she felt left out. But she brushed that feeling aside: It was the foolishness of the old, childish Suzanne. Philip no longer mattered, and it was wonderful seeing Richard and Elena together, all because of her.

Then abruptly the perfect little grouping was over. Someone sidled up to talk to Richard, who gave her a quick kiss good-bye and moved off; he'd call during the week to make a date. Elena drifted in his direction. Cynthia brought two more guests to meet her, a flute player from the Metropolitan Opera orchestra and an administrator of a downtown performance space, and Suzanne kept up her enthusiasm as best she could. She knew Philip must be nearby, watching, waiting for his opportunity.

When the party thinned out and she'd thanked Cynthia, it seemed natural that they should leave together. Philip was hungry and suggested a pizza. She agreed that though the alcohol had been plentiful, the food had been rather scanty. Just the opposite of the way it had been when they were growing up.

And so it began again. Only this time it didn't start with tentative fumblings in the back of movie theaters. After the pizza she went with him to his apartment in the Village, to his bed, which would eventually become her apartment and her bed. Even as a boy he had had an instinct for making love, and as a man he was even better, the kind of good lover who seemed almost trained for the role, or perhaps just very experienced: slow and attentive, lavish with words as well as gestures, and despite the touch of deliberation in his moves, he was effective. He was generous by nature. Suzanne didn't tell him that none of the few men she'd known before him had made her feel as glorious as he did. She held something back. Perhaps the small residue of bile had not dissipated entirely.

It became an affair. Affairs had not yet been replaced by the more antiseptic "relationships," and she liked whispering the word to herself, breathy with sophistication. A good affair. Good times, good sex, good feelings. Her first really serious one, after several that had sputtered out for lack of oxygen. Plenty to talk about. With Philip you never lacked for conversation. The slight leftover resentment, aged like a Chinese egg, only added spice and vinegar to their lovemaking: Suzanne played a game of resisting, and Philip liked using his powers of persuasion, even if it was only pretending.

There were moments, later on, when she believed it should have remained an affair, should have run its course like the rest. Serve as experience. There might have been more like it, who knew for how long, until she subsided into marriage. Or not.

⌒

In the midst of the good affair, Suzanne's father suffered a fatal collapse, briefcase in hand, while walking from his car to the furniture store, right in front of the newsstand where he bought his daily *New York Times*. Uncannily, this manner of death was what Gerda had warned Joseph of so often and so emphatically that the children, when they were young, used to snicker at her words. "If you keep driving yourself that way, you'll drop dead of a heart attack," she'd say when he went to the store on weekends to check on the employees, or sat up late at the dining-room table, poring over orders and receipts and catalogs.

"You want this house, don't you?" he'd answer. "You want Suzanne to be able to study. That won't happen by itself." The boys' expenses were not taxing; they had gone to Brooklyn College under protest and gotten through with minimum effort. Neither one had wanted to join him in the business. Fred took a low-level job in an insurance company and Gary worked in a stationery business, neither of which position could give their father much gratification.

Now Gerda's predictions were confirmed. Suzanne had always imagined that at his death, which she'd seen as far off, she would feel relief: The burden of continuing to prove herself "special" and bring glory to the family would drop away. She would never stop craving success, but maybe the density of the craving—her own now, not his—would weigh less heavily on her. She could live the way others lived. She didn't really know how others lived, what they felt inside, but envisioned it as a kind of serene drifting through the days, something she had never known. Whatever her life would feel like, it would be minus her father's urgings, forever at her back like a gust of wind even though she no longer lived at home or saw him often. He was there behind her, stalking.

At the funeral she was too preoccupied with trying to comfort her mother to feel her own grief. Philip was there, of course, being unobtrusively helpful, being kind to Gerda, who was even fonder of him now than she had been long ago. After all, now he was a grown man with a growing business. He remained at the house throughout the day, helping them receive visitors, making coffee and conversation, joining forces with Suzanne's brothers to fetch chairs and carry platters of food the neighbors had brought. As if he were part of the family, Suzanne thought, and she both appreciated this and resented it. He was digging in too deep, establishing himself as a fixture in her life. Sex and good times and friendship were one thing, but this—her family, the Brooklyn house, her complex feelings about her father—came from another part of her life she didn't want invaded. In fact, she preferred to shut it up behind closed doors.

Afterward, her grief at Joseph's death was overshadowed by simmering anger. For all the pride her father took in her, he hadn't really known her. Her talent had stood between them like a screen. Maybe they wouldn't have known each other in any event; he wasn't a man given to intimacy. He was all bluster, all display; whatever was inside remained heavily veiled.

Joseph had chosen to be cremated, and Gerda hated the idea. Not only did it seem alien—no one she knew had ever been cremated; it seemed to her a primitive and disreputable rite. Moreover, she told Suzanne, she had read in the paper just a few months ago about a crematorium somewhere in Pennsylvania that was discovered to have sold bodies to some weird illegal operation, a cult, she couldn't remember what, and given the bereaved families the ashes of animals instead. Or maybe only a small part of the ashes they were entitled to.

"Come on, Mom, that sounds too crazy to be true," Suzanne said. The three of them, she, Gerda, and Phil, were sitting around the kitchen table, drinking coffee late at night after all the visitors and Suzanne's brothers and their wives had left. It seemed accepted, tacitly, that Phil would spend the night. She certainly wouldn't make any pretext of having him sleep in her brothers' old room.

"But I read about it in the *New York Times*."

"Remember what Dad used to say? Don't believe everything you read in the papers? Anyhow, that was in Pennsylvania, and the place we're using is in New York."

"Maybe they all do that. How do you know?"

"I don't think you need to worry about that, Gerda," Philip said.

Suzanne shrugged. "Does it really make any difference?"

"What do you mean?" Gerda retorted. "Whether we get his ashes or some stray dog's? You don't think it makes any difference?"

"Ashes are ashes, Mom. It's not the real person. It's just symbolic. And if you never know what you've got on the shelf . . ."

"You're just saying that to upset me. Phil," Gerda appealed to him, "don't you think it matters? Whether I have the real ashes or not? Tell me—you've known loss. Wouldn't it matter to you?"

"My parents and brother were buried, so I don't know how I'd feel about ashes," he said. "But I can see your point. On the other hand, they are mostly symbolic, as Suzanne says. . . . It's what you feel in your heart that matters. But anyway, I doubt you're in any danger. Since that article appeared—I saw it, by the way, really shocking—all the places are going to be very scrupulous for the next few months."

Gerda listened carefully but still looked doubtful.

"Look, we have to follow his instructions," said Suzanne, getting up to load the dishwasher. "I'll take care of the whole thing tomorrow and you won't have to think about it. Meanwhile, I could use some sleep."

"You'll have to keep them then, the remains, I mean. I'm not keeping anything on a shelf that isn't authentically him." Gerda started toward the stairs.

"Not remains. Cremains, they're called," Suzanne corrected.

"Don't get funny with me now," and her mother turned and shook her head as if to throw off a buzzing hornet.

She didn't feel the expected relief after his death. If anything, the "drive" her father had spoken of so vehemently was even stronger, as if with him so vastly unreachable, she had to go to even greater lengths to prove herself, like shouting to someone way out of range. His ambitions had lodged in her, wormed their way in like a parasite, a toxic substance; they were his immortality, which she carried within her. He had bequeathed it to her.

She handled the arrangements and became the possessor of a cardboard box holding a plastic bag of ashes—sifted, as the crematorium advised; that way there would be no large chunks of bone. The contents of the bag that arrived in the mail were surprising in their whiteness and fineness; they resembled the small mounds of plaster the workmen had left each day when their house was painted, just before she moved to Mrs. Campbell's apartment. Despite her mother's doubts, she trusted that the ashes were her father's, and she didn't know what to do with them. Joseph had never specified. "Burn me up!" was all he'd ever said on the subject. So she stashed the box in a corner of the closet, behind her shoes. Of course, she would never tell Mrs. Campbell what was back there, and felt faintly guilty about harboring the box. One of these days she'd think of a good place to scatter the ashes. Maybe on a beach out in Brooklyn where they'd mingle with the sand. Or she could go down to the Hudson River during one of her afternoon walks and dump them in. On weekends she took long walks through Riverside Park, staring out at the river and the ships. It was hard to get right down to the river without crossing the highway. Meanwhile, the ashes remained in the closet, and when she finally agreed to move into Philip's apartment in Greenwich Village, she took them with her.

And soon after that it was more than an affair. Indeed, the opposite of an affair. He asked, he implored; he said it had been fated since high school; he gave his best performances and she couldn't find the will to resist. She was agreeable, as Richard had told her long ago; she went along. She married him. There were no good reasons to resist, and he had been so kind all through this stressful time. She wasn't sure she was in love; the only time she had been in love was with Richard, and even about that she had her doubts. But there was no one she liked better. Philip was so familiar that there could not be the succulent delight of discovery. She did love sleeping with him, though, loved it more than she had expected or known was possible. She gasped with pleasure, she moaned, she felt what women were supposed to feel, didn't she?

Only sometimes when they made love she had a sense that something was wrong. She couldn't say quite what, but it expressed itself as a petulant voice in her head that contradicted her words and acts. Like the voice when she was a young child, insinuating that maybe she wasn't quite real. That old voice had quieted, but this one seemed a more mature version of it, a menacing voice that wanted to undercut her pleasures. She believed the words she murmured to him, the words that said she was happy, that said what she liked or what she wanted.

But the voice inside whispered, Are you really happy? Is this really it? And on the sheets her restless hands would be playing phrases from Schubert or Liszt, difficult phrases.

Philip did everything to please her. (And why wouldn't he? the voice whispered. He wants you.) There would be ease in a life with him, emotional ease, an ease that would leave her free to face the difficulties of work. He knew her, that was the main thing, and what she craved was to be known, in every sense. He knew her talents and he knew her ambitions; now he knew her body. He liked to look at every part—there was no hiding anything from him. While he looked, he spun elaborate fantasies of how he would help her move ahead, but to him they weren't fantasies. She tried not to let herself be influenced by these, but they worked on her cravings like fairy tales on susceptible children. What more did she want? She wanted the doubting voice to cease. She married him despite the voice, and she trained her ears to shut it out.

As both Philip and Mme. Kabalevsky had predicted, a number of small gigs resulted from the contest Suzanne won. A few came from people she'd met at Cynthia's party, and others were arranged by Philip, who had become, tacitly, her manager, even before they decided to marry. She had never sought a manager, didn't need one yet, she thought, despite Elena's urgings. Elena, who had been taken on by her stepfather's manager, was busy touring in the Midwest, but she prodded Suzanne regularly by phone.

The gigs were in local halls in Westchester and Rockland Counties or Long Island, small towns in Connecticut and Rhode Island. Never mind small, it was a start, Phil said. It got her name around. Richard agreed: Play wherever they're willing to have you. That's what a professional does. It would be good for her, Richard said, to get used to the traveling, the unfamiliar instruments and settings, to learn all she could. Suzanne played better in these places than she expected, or rather, her nagging stage fright was more manageable. Along with her talent, she had a streak of condescension born less of snobbery than of naiveté. Such places were too reminiscent of her own origins to be more than mildly threatening. They were not the kinds of places that figured in her dreams; still, out of pride, she always tried to give her best.

She got excellent reviews in local papers, her name got around, and after a few months, through his growing connections, Philip arranged a recital at a good hall downtown, part of New York University, where he had friends in the music department. With that one "under her belt," as he put it, there would be many more, he assured her.

On Philip's advice, she rehearsed in the hall twice, so that the place would feel familiar. It was larger than most of the others she'd played in. By the time the Thursday evening arrived, she knew its high ceilings, the severe cream-colored walls with Doric columns in low relief, the rows of maroon plush seats, slightly canted, the balcony. She arrived early and sat in a small dressing room with Philip, suffering the agonies of anticipation. So it was a relief at last to be called by the stage manager.

Despite her visits, she'd never seen the hall lit for a performance. As she entered from the wings, the lights assaulting her eyes were so bright that for an instant she saw nothing but bursts of color like fireworks, low to the ground. She paused, blinked, then moved toward the large dark object in the center of the flaring colors: the piano. The floorboards beneath her feet, waxed to a high sheen, shimmered faintly as if in a mirage, their parallel lines appearing to bend. Lining the rim of the stage were more balloons of color; it took her an instant to grasp that they were flowers in large pots. Hydrangeas, like the ones leading up to the row houses on her childhood block.

Her instinct was to turn and run, but she did what she knew she must—this was what she had worked for all these years. At center stage, slightly in front of the piano, she bowed. Philip and Cynthia had told her she must also smile, but she couldn't force it. How could you smile out into darkness, at people you couldn't even see? The only way she knew they were there was the clatter of applause. As her eyes adjusted to the light, blobs of heads appeared, patches of bright clothing here and there, but no clear faces.

She couldn't see them, but they were all watching her. Why couldn't she be happily in the audience, too, looking forward to someone's playing music? Why must she be the chosen one, the sacrifice? As they watched her, her dress, a long navy blue evening sheath, simple, sleeveless, with a V-neck, suddenly seemed all wrong, both too fancy and too austere. Her shoes, high heels with a T-strap, were wrong, too. She might trip and fall. But what nonsense was she thinking? Surely Rudolf Serkin didn't think about the fit of his suit or the color of his tie when he went onstage. Or, who knows, maybe he did. Never mind. She must focus on the music. You must know the music so well, Mme. Kabalevsky said, that you don't need to think about it. And yet you must think of nothing else. But those pieces of advice were contradictory, weren't they?

As the coughing and fussing of the audience ceased and Suzanne turned to sit down, she was startled by footsteps behind her. It was the page-turner, a student dressed in black, modest and unobtrusive. The girl glided to her seat to the left of the piano bench. Suzanne had met her before, had seen her backstage a moment ago, and yet her presence onstage felt like a burden. As a student, she herself had been a page-turner on occasion: She remembered well the pleasure of sitting onstage, so close to the music, but knowing the audience was not think-ing of her, barely noticed her. Had her presence disturbed the pianists? That had never occurred to her. It had been a combination of full exposure and extreme solitude, hiding in plain sight, which suited her. Perhaps she should have remained a page-turner.

She must stop these idiotic thoughts and begin. Nothing but the music. She flexed her fingers and placed her hands over the keys. Don't rush, Cynthia said. Take your time. They'll wait. But not indefinitely. Not as long as Suzanne would have liked to wait. She played the opening notes of the Mozart Sonata no. 13. She had learned it as a child with Mr. Cartelli, and for a few moments a cheerful nostalgia infused her playing with warmth. The first few bars went fine, but as she moved into a ritardando, which contained a faint hint of the slow movement to come, she couldn't recall any of the notes ahead. The score was up on the rack, there was no real danger, but it would be distracting to have to read from the music. Never mind, the notes will come as their time comes. And so they did. They were in her fingers.

As she was nearing the end of the first movement, something felt wrong in her body. A shudder went through her, then a clutch at her chest and stomach muscles, as if a clamp were gripping them. Panic, her faithful companion. It would spread, she knew from experience. Already her hands were losing warmth. She couldn't remember what was ahead from one measure to the next, but her hands managed to keep going— good hands, they even understood the phrasing and tonalities. But now she was in the second movement, andante cantabile; could the hands alone convey the singing tone that was needed? Because her mind, which dictated the tone, seemed to have floated upward like a balloon, propelled by puffs of panic.

All she could do was let her hands continue as best they could, while she hovered above the keyboard. If only she could stop and flee. Disappear. But there was no stopping now. She had to go on.

She tried to use the old trick that had helped her through bad moments in high school and earlier, when her father had forced her to play for guests. This isn't really happening, she would say. It's not even a dream, just something you must wait out, do mindlessly, and soon it will drift away like smoke. It's not happening, while her fingers continued to play the notes and the lights blazed overhead and the scent of the flowers wafted from the footlights, and every so often the page-turner reached out to flip the page, each flip bringing her closer to the end of what was not happening.

There was no fooling herself—of course it was happening. She was sweating. The wet was seeping under her arms. She could smell her own fear. She was in panic's grip and would remain there for the entire concert, more than an hour and a half. No, she'd never last that long. She was starting on the final movement now, which had a frisky opening: allegro grazioso, but grazioso felt quite beyond her. She'd make a bargain with her panic: If it would let her get through the Mozart, then the Bach Italian Concerto and a selection of Bartók bagatelles, up to the intermission, she'd say she was sick and couldn't do the second half. Panic would win this round. A pity, because she and Cynthia had chosen the program so carefully, for con-trast—the second half was the Chopin barcarole and Ravel's *Le Tombeau de Couperin*—as well as to show Suzanne's range, which was unusual for so young a pianist. All that would be lost now. No matter. Please, let me last just until the intermission.

She barely registered the polite but mild applause after the Mozart, and promptly launched into the Bach, an exuberant piece and, mercifully, fairly brief. She could hardly tell anymore how the music sounded—her ears felt stuffed and distant, like the onset of dizziness. The notes and dynamics were correct, but it might sound as if it were being played by an automaton.

She waited during the applause and tried, not too conspicuously, to take deep calming breaths. As before, the applause was not thundering but well meaning and courteous. Of course: She knew so many people in the audience. In the front rows, though she couldn't see them, were her family and friends. Probably some of her mother's friends, too, primed for her first big success. Could they tell how badly she was playing, or was it enough for them that she sat on the brilliantly lit stage and produced the notes? Richard must be out there somewhere. Cynthia. Maybe some of her teachers from Juilliard. Mme. Kabalevsky had said she'd try to come. They would know exactly what was happening. They would know her shame.

And the rest of the audience, the strangers? Who were they and why had they come? Music lovers? People excited by the debut of a new performer? Or subscribers, lonely people who filled their calendars with places to go of an evening, better than numbing television? Maybe tired husbands, fighting off drowsiness, dragged by wives who wanted to swallow "culture" in a few easy gulps, like some of the neighbors she remembered from childhood, who boasted at the canasta table of the wonderful concerts and plays they had attended, never describing them, only listing, as if adding them to a resumé.

Or students such as she had been not long ago, students with buoyant hopes, imagining themselves in her place a few years from now. But they would do better, they must be thinking. How had she managed to get here anyway, or was she just having a bad day?

After the Bartók, when she went backstage, she would say she felt faint. She was coming down with something. The concert would have to be stopped. With this idea to bolster her, she struggled through the bagatelles. The mood shifts and irregularities of the Bartók usually exhilarated her, but now she felt like she was picking her way through a field of nettles. She imagined herself attacking the music the way some of the male students in the master classes at school had done, and while that bellicose approach lacked delicacy, it did have a mesmerizing power. She was giving a shape to the music's contrariety, and it fortified her. A pulse of excitement kept her going. I'm doing it for him, she thought. He tries so hard, I can't let him down. Never mind me and my idiot fears. Do it for him.

But this worked for only a short time. The ice crept up her spine and her forehead grew damp. Her fingers, those dutiful slaves, trained robots, were the only part that kept their facility, and she let them go as they would. It was like setting free a cluster of clever gadgets, and while they did not betray her— they were obedient and mindless—they played with a mechanical neutrality.

When the intermission finally arrived, Suzanne managed to stand up and bow, then walk slowly offstage, careful not to slip on the gleaming floorboards.

Phil was waiting in the wings. "Great!" he cried. "You're

doing great!" There was a crowd of faces, stagehands, people darting about on errands. "Oh, please don't. It was a disaster. I'm not going back out there."

"What are you talking about? You can't stop in the middle." He took her arm and led her back to the dressing room, where she collapsed on the ancient divan. The springs moaned beneath her. On the walls were dusty photos of the famous pianists who'd played here early in their career. She knew her photograph would never be among them.

"Look, I'm feeling sick. Tell them I'm sick and can't continue."

"It's ordinary stage fright, Suzanne. I'll give you a Valium."

"No. No drugs. They could mess up my mind, and then I'd do even worse." She sat up and bent her head over her knees.

"Valium is nothing. But okay, here, take some aspirin, then." He held them out in his palm.

She swallowed them with a glass of water. "But you'll have to tell them something. I can't go through with it. I'll pass out."

"That could ruin your chances after all this work. It'll give you a bad name. It'll be harder to get the next gig. Dozens of people were dying for this opportunity, and you won it. I'm not going to help you throw it away. You can get this under control. You know the techniques they showed you at school. You didn't panic when you auditioned at the contest, did you?"

"That was different. It was only a few people judging and I was one of a long line. It wasn't so focused on me." I pretended it wasn't happening, she remembered. That wouldn't work in a hall with so many people. Too much reality pressing in on her.

"Have some more water. You're going to be fine. The worst is over, now that you know what it's like out there. Pretend you're in a small room with a few people you know. Richard and his friends—they always made you feel confident, you told me. Or pretend there's no one out there at all and you're playing for yourself. You'll see. This half will go much better."

"I need to lie down. Leave me alone for a while, Phil."

"No, that's not a good idea. Sit up. Or go in there"—he waved at the small bathroom—"and splash some water on your face. It's almost time."

He wouldn't let her stop. He was going to make her stumble out into the hot lights and feel it again, just when it had begun to ease: the ice in her spine, her fingers cold and rubbery, her whole body melting down. Her leg muscles felt like sand, but they would have to carry her out there. Philip said she must. This was what he had promised, and he wouldn't go back on it. Once, right after they were married, when Elena's name came up, he took her in his arms and whispered, "I'll never hurt or betray you again. I promise." This was why she'd married him, was it not? The thought was so troubling that she wished she could wipe it away. Had she married the way some people marry for money or connections or security? This was what she'd wanted, and he had convinced her that he was the one to get it for her.

She splashed her face and fixed her hair and came back out.

"In five minutes you'll be playing the barcarole—you know that suits you, and it'll sound fantastic. You look better now. Here, let me straighten your dress." He tugged at the fabric around her waist and hips. "Just keep yourself under control, and it'll sound as good as last night at home. I wish I'd recorded it. Then you could hear how good you are. Maybe one of these days we'll make some tapes."

She was his prisoner. She let him lead her back into the wings, where he gave a gentle shove at her back and she was onstage again, in the shattering light. She didn't look at the audience, simply began to play as if that were her prison sentence. And at first the music did go better. She managed to keep a grip on her panic. It was a small squirmy beast she held tight inside, restraining it with her stomach muscles.

The barcarole demanded a limpidity that she tried for but knew she didn't attain, although the fingers worked for her again. But will alone wasn't enough to keep the creature from wriggling out of her grasp and scuttling through the pathways of her body. Surely the audience could tell. Almost anyone could tell, as she began the Ravel, that the rhythms were getting shaky, the transitions hesitant. She had the notes all right but couldn't control the inner narrative of the elusive music; it sounded weighty and deliberate, not at all as Ravel should sound.

"Remember, you're not just a transmitter," Cynthia used to say when Suzanne first began studying with her. "You're so skilled that you tend to rely on that. But you're also an interpreter. You need an interpretation. Think of those language people at the UN. People are hearing sounds they can't understand, and the interpreter gives them a meaning, makes them intelligible. You need to do that." That was especially true of Ravel. But she wasn't making it intelligible at all. The music might as well have been a foreign language, or a familiar language poorly spoken. She played the slow passages too fast. She was restless, unable to linger in the moment or the sound—all she wanted was to cut and run. She played the fast parts so fast that the intricacies of the harmonies were smeared by speed. Even the page-turner seemed confused, as she leaned over to turn at shorter intervals than she had planned for.

She rallied her strength—it would all soon come to an end. Tolerable, Cynthia would say if she'd played this way at a lesson. Tolerable, Suzanne, but it needs to be more than that.

She didn't stand up the moment it was over. She would have liked to sink into the stool until they all stopped their clapping and went home, emptied out the hall. The page-turner gave her a slight nudge, and Suzanne rose and bowed to the darkness. She was politely called back for one curtain call, and then it was truly over. In the little room where she lay on the couch, Phil told her there were people outside asking to see her—her family, Richard, Elena—but she would see no one.

"You're behaving like a prima donna," he said. "You haven't earned that right yet. They care about you. And it's not the end of the world, you know."

"Leave me alone. You go out and entertain them. Tell them I'm too exhausted and I'll be in touch." She disliked being rude; she would have loved her mother's consoling arms around her, but she knew the moment she saw anyone she loved she'd burst into tears of shame. How fortunate her father was not alive to see this. Not that he would have known the difference between a good recital and a botched one.

Phil shook his head in exasperation, but he did as she asked. Later, in the taxi going home, she wept while he sat silently beside her. Even he could think of no more to say.

The next day the phone kept ringing—her mother, her brothers, Richard, Elena, Simon and Tanya from Juilliard. Everyone congratulated her, and Suzanne did her best to accept their words with grace. Only with Elena and Richard did she speak the truth.

"It was pretty bad, wasn't it?" she asked Elena. "I could hear it. I was frozen."

"No, no, I wouldn't say pretty bad. You could probably play those pieces in your sleep. You have that stunning technique that never lets you down. And that came through. Look, I've heard you sound better, but it wasn't as bad as you think. There were parts that were very impressive—the Mozart. And the Bartók especially."

That was Elena being diplomatic. Suzanne could take no comfort.

With Richard she was even more frank. "Tell me the truth. It was dreadful, wasn't it? I was out of my head with fear. Everything I've practiced all these years just washed away."

"I'm sorry you had such an awful time. I could tell what was happening. But it had its good points. You started each piece very well, and kept on, until the panic set in. Well, next time you'll do all the anti-panic routines and do better. But it wasn't a bad start. The technique was obvious."

The reviews—in the *Times* and *Newsday*, and later on in a couple of the music magazines—were not as damning as she expected. "In her first New York appearance Ms. Stellman displayed a keen sensitivity to the challenging rhythms and dissonances of the Bartók bagatelles" and, "She played the Bach Italian Concerto with admirable precision, if a bit apathetically as she proceeded." "Her interpretations of both the Mozart sonata and the Chopin barcarole began with promise, and though they remained technically accurate, they all but ignored the subtler textures and undertones." The worst, as well as the most just, in her view: "Ms. Stellman is obviously a pianist with extraordinary technical gifts, but she somehow made all the selections sound alike. The shimmering hues of Ravel have little in common with the more abrasive Bartók tonalities, and yet Ms. Stellman did not make much effort to distinguish them. In short, a proficient but mechanical, even somnambulistic, performance."

"Oh, blah, blah, blah," said Phil. They were sitting on the living-room couch with the papers spread around them. "A lot of pretentious words. Don't even read them. It's not worth it."

How could she not read them? She read them over and over, practically memorized them. She never said they were unfair. It was Philip who complained. "Okay, so you weren't in top form, but why dwell on the negative? They love to do that. Couldn't they hear the intelligence, the facility, the background you bring to the pieces? They should understand about stage fright in a newcomer. They could cut you a little more slack."

"Why? There are plenty of people just as good who don't go numb. Audiences pay money. They shouldn't have to listen to something mediocre, whatever the reason."

After all her years of work, to come to this. It was over, she said.

"That's nonsense. It's just beginning."

"Okay, whatever you say. You're the boss, right?"

He turned away. She showed him her bitterness, but not the

perverse pleasure she took in the reviews. Tepid as they were, they existed. They confirmed her existence. They put her name in print in what her father used to refer to as the newspaper of record: proof that she had been judged worthy to perform on that stage, however disappointingly. Years from now, someone going through old files might see her name. Long after she was dead, someone would know that she had existed. But this secret pleasure was too shameful to admit to anyone, even Philip.

He was patient while she brooded about the house, a week of watching television and reading mystery novels. Like a good nurse, he was all solicitude. Before he left in the morning he would bring her coffee and a fresh roll from the Italian bakery across the street, arranged neatly on a tray as if she were an invalid: coffee cup in the center, roll to the left, jam and butter just northeast of the coffee. Meanwhile, she canceled her students for the week and called in sick at the ballet classes she accompanied. In the evenings Phil brought home pizza or Chinese food, then insisted she get dressed and walk through the Village with him at sunset. It was early spring; the streets were crowded. He pointed out the first blossoms, the forsythia, flower of their home borough, he reminded her, embarking on its brief season. And they both laughed because they were alike in this: They had no use for nostalgia. They missed nothing of what they had left behind.

Philip was full of plans. His vigor drained what little energy she had. If only he would stop talking and simply walk beside her. They sat down at an outdoor table and ordered coffee, while they gazed at the sun sinking over the river, the endless traffic, the cyclists, and the handful of indefatigable runners in the midst of traffic. Suzanne marveled at their will. What made them feel that anything mattered so much? They walked and ran and drove so briskly, day after day. They were simply carrying on their lives, Phil said, as she'd done up till now and as she would do again. She was young, she'd have other chances. As soon as she was feeling better in a few days—he'd make sure of it. Already he was hatching plans, so she shouldn't let up on her practicing.

His words troubled her, his plans. He *would* make sure of it. With his contacts, his persuasiveness, his perpetual motion, he would find gigs for her, if not in New York then back in the smaller venues, where the audiences were not quite so demanding or couldn't afford New York prices. For all she knew he'd have her flying to obscure hamlets all over the country, sending her off into the chilly embrace of panic.

The following week she tried to get moving. She had to keep her job at the ballet studio and see her students. The trays of coffee and rolls stopped arriving every morning. Obviously Phil thought she had mourned enough. She practiced, but halfheartedly. The worst way to practice, as she well knew. If you can't put yourself into it, don't do it at all, Richard used to say. Wait for another day. Do something else, study scores, listen to recordings. Don't play using half of yourself. Cynthia, on the contrary, believed in putting in several hours no matter how you felt. Don't let your fingers start forgetting. They're your most loyal allies. The rest will come back when it's ready. As in school, there were too many opinions to choose from. She had to decide for herself, and while she leaned toward Cynthia's view, she couldn't always carry it out.

In the afternoons she lay on the couch, going through new

scores, looking over the piano works of John Field, the Irish composer famous in his time who created the nocturne form that influenced Chopin. But soon the pages would fall to her lap and she would question every decision she had ever made. Invariably, the interrogation arrived at the decision to marry Philip. It went back all the way to that first coffee with him after the Serkin concert at Carnegie Hall, and oh, the glamour of the place. Who could have imagined what that meeting on the stairs would lead to? Maybe the man she lived with, ate with, slept with, was all wrong for her. Had Elena been right, that day at the Juilliard auditions, when she said he was superficial? Was there really nothing more to him than the self-assurance, the glib words, the easy competence? If she hadn't been so hasty she might not be lying here on this couch, waiting for him to come home, dependent on his words, his plans. . . .

But who else would try to help her as he did? No one else could or would get her what she dreamed of, and that she seemed unable to get for herself. She didn't have the temperament, she'd once overheard her father saying to Gerda. "She looks fine and she can get by on charm for a while, but for the long run she's not tough enough." Maybe he had known her better than she imagined.

Philip had the temperament, she thought as they made love late at night. Here as in everything else he was energetic, managerial, effective, as if he were directing a performance and must make sure all went off splendidly. And Suzanne would think, Why complain of this? He does it so well. He makes me feel so good. He is my husband, after all. It's not hard to love him as I'm supposed to. Still, the voice she dreaded would intrude in a murmur, even during her pleasure. It spoke not in words at those moments, but in insinuations, images. Maybe she could be someone other than this cosseted creature, object of these lavish attentions. What else or how else she might be, she didn't know; she hadn't enough experience. She wondered about other possible lovers, no one she knew, imaginary men who might make bizarre demands, who could elicit something in her that she sensed obscurely but that had never had the chance to assert itself.

When it was over she retreated back into remoteness, even while folded in his arms or holding him as he lay with his head on her chest. She quickly felt separate. Philip remained present, connected, talking, wanting to maintain the intimacy. Maybe he had no private self to retreat to. The longer they were together, the better she understood that his staying connected was his mode of being in the world: Movement, intrusion, management were his way of affirming his reality, just as long ago, playing the piano and being recognized were hers, and showing her off had been her father's. She was the instrument of Phil's becoming real. Her success would make him super-real; then she would truly be his creature, at the piano no less than in bed.

⌒

Two weeks after the recital Suzanne privately labeled a nightmare, when her last student of the day had left, she lay on the couch watching a late-afternoon talk show, something she would have scorned before as wasting precious time. For years, she had regarded every moment as time to be consecrated to her work, her aspirations. There was no spare time to squander. Now, time was plentiful; it stretched out farther than she could see. She could barely manage to practice an hour or two at a stretch, and did so only out of habit and a sense of obligation.

On the TV screen, a fat, curly-haired, thirty-ish man—his size made him look older, but he had a baby face—with puffy cheeks and sloping shoulders was telling the unctuous host about the miracle of Overeaters Anonymous. It was those rounded chipmunk cheeks that first stirred a sense of familiarity, and then the voice, soft and husky for a man, as if pulverized by the rolls of flesh it had to pass through before emerging. She had heard that voice before. After a few moments, it hit her: Arnie Perchusky from her old block in Brooklyn, whom she had not seen or thought of for almost fifteen years.

An odd figure to serve as her personal madeleine. The images returned not in a rainbow of revivified sensation, but in waves of distaste and humiliation: Arnie Perchusky, the Cyclone, the sickening plunge, the sea below, the surf curling up like bits of abandoned confetti. The years she could not wait to be done with, years of waiting for her life to start. Waiting for now. And here it was, now, and what was she waiting for?

That summer evening she was sitting on the stoop of Eva's house with Alison and Alison's older brother. Before long, a group gathered. Eva was preening and tossing her head to show off her new feather cut with blond streaks. Her older sister, in an identical hairdo, had just gotten her driver's license, which she displayed proudly. Alison's current boyfriend turned up (they changed every few weeks, but there was always someone—it was those phenomenal breasts, the girls agreed), a freshman at Brooklyn College, along with two of his friends. Paula brought a cousin visiting from Philadelphia. The Schneider brothers from around the corner were there, the older one home from his first year at an upstate university, the younger a high school sophomore but reported by Paula to be a great kisser and to keep a stash of marijuana in his underwear drawer. And Arnie Perchusky, the enormously fat boy who lived down the block with his fat brother and sisters. Arnie wore a gray gabardine windbreaker over Bermuda shorts, despite the heavy, humid evening. To hide his fat, Suzanne thought.

Alison's boyfriend suggested they all pile into cars and drive to Coney Island to celebrate the end of the term. There were enough of them with driver's licenses, enough parents willing to hand over the keys. Suzanne drifted along in a mood of lassitude. She rarely joined in group sprees, but she loved the sea and couldn't pass up a chance to be there. The sea at night, the stars—yes. She could wander off from the others and dip her feet in the surf. In the car, driven shakily by Eva's sister, Elvis crooned "Love Me Tender" on the radio and they sang along. As always when she heard music, Suzanne couldn't help playing the notes silently with her fingers, against her palms. A hot breeze blew in the open windows, tinged by salt as they neared the ocean.

They walked on the boardwalk in twos and threes. Across the wide beach the surf was loud, the waves high and swift, roughing up the few twilight swimmers, who surfaced, shook themselves off, and dived into the next one. Suzanne was heading down the steps to the sand, when the boys insisted they must all go on the roller coaster. The Cyclone, guaranteed to make the girls scream, their stomachs flip. Suzanne refused. The Cyclone terrified her, but the girls urged her on. "You've got to try it. Just once in your life," Eva said. It was Eva's idea to pair her with Arnie. "He'll protect you," she whispered. "You'll be wedged in so tight, there won't be any room to fall out." That was loud enough to be heard, and Suzanne felt sorry for Arnie, who must have noticed the giggles and smirks.

To silence them, and because the hot night and salt air cast a spell of passivity, Suzanne agreed. It wouldn't last long. She'd hardly ever spoken to Arnie alone; he was simply a fixture of the street, occasionally latching on to their group. Now they were wedged tightly into the seat of the car, the metal bar as it clicked into place making a furrow in Arnie's soft, thick middle. He smiled wanly, no more eager than she, it appeared, to be on the Cyclone. The flesh of his hip and thigh pressed hotly against her. In the car ahead of them were Alison and her boyfriend, arms wrapped tightly around each other.

As the car began to move, Suzanne and Arnie exchanged a look of mortified resignation. Suzanne shrugged and tried to smile. At least she didn't care what he thought of her; had he been a boy she wanted to impress, she would have to pretend to be enjoying herself. With Arnie, nothing mattered. Ten minutes from now it would be over, she would have done it, no one could tease her for being scared.

The car ascended slowly at a forty-five-degree angle with deceptive calm, but she knew the descending angle would be sharper and rapid. As it paused, quivering at the crest of the highest curve, she looked down at the people strolling about far below, and at others on the Parachute, the Whip, the Ferris wheel. The carousel music was a mere tinkle in the distance, like wind chimes, and way out at the edge of the ocean, the surf was squiggly lines drawn in white chalk. When the inevitable plunge came, they were almost vertical, and her insides fell into her throat. She screamed louder than she thought she could, a monster-movie scream. From then on there was no relief: It was either the plunge or the anticipation. At each plunge, she screamed and thought she would die, yet knew she would not; the contradiction and the captivity enraged her and left her throat tight. In between the plunges she told herself it would not last forever, but the few minutes stretched out surrealistically.

Arnie did not scream, boys couldn't allow themselves to scream, although once or twice she heard something like a squeaking yelp. He held his breath and clutched the bar. They didn't exchange a word. She didn't even feel an impulse to grasp his hand. Despite his enormous presence, his soft sweating flesh against her, she felt utterly alone.

The ride didn't last forever, but the view from above and the sick dizziness did last, a sensation she could call up from memory at will—and often did. The ride came to evoke her entire childhood in Brooklyn: looking down, helpless, at the whirling, chaotic, beautiful world—crowds, motion, music, roiling sea, glimmering first stars in a royal-blue sky—but fearful she would never return to it, trapped by Arnie's mound of soft inert flesh and, at her middle, by the cold metal bar.

When they got off, shaking, they edged away from each other, embarrassed—strangers who'd shown each other their fear. All the rest of the evening she could call up the damp warmth of his flesh pressing against her. On the ride home she made sure they weren't in the same car.

At some point since that night some dozen years ago, Arnie had apparently discovered Overeaters Anonymous. On the TV show, he did look less fat than in adolescence, but clearly he was not yet finished with the twelve-step program, which he credited with changing his life. He spoke at length, more than Suzanne had ever heard him speak before. "I learned that if you persist, with trust in yourself and faith, you can accomplish anything you set out to do."

She switched off the set and sank lower into the pillows. It was more than the Cyclone that Arnie on the screen brought back: It was the entire block where she had grown up, embedded in her, an enclosing frame for everything that had happened since. She had left it as soon as she could, moving uptown to Mrs. Campbell's apartment near Juilliard. Her parents had fretted, but Richard helped convince them that the long subway ride twice a day sapped her energy. Since then she had returned only to visit, as seldom as she could, but the people in each of the small row houses remained as vivid as they had been back then, a tableau she could not expunge: the Schiffs, who owned the funeral parlor half a mile away and kept a somber black Cadillac in the driveway; the podiatrist and his placid wife, who sat on the porch all weekend and from that high perch smiled beatifically at everyone who passed; the girls she played with, whose idea of the exotic was Eva's father's dentist books with pictures of blighted mouths; the kindly Grubers next door to Richard, who in vain set an example of friendliness and said he was a good neighbor. And especially their daughter, Francine, who worked at a publishing company in the city and in the evenings sat on the porch chatting as she waited for her date to arrive: the law student. At some point, Francine had vanished for a year and returned polished and brightened, a blank gloss over her face and words. She had a breakdown, Gary told Suzanne, because her fiancé—remember that fellow who used to come round for her?—ditched her and she fell apart. That girl had no inner resources, Gerda murmured, standing at the sink. After her return, Francine vanished into her bedroom for a while. But soon she was up and working in the city again, not bothering with the suits or high heels any longer. She grew frumpy and sat on the porch in a cotton shift on the summer evenings, smoking cigarettes and staring into space.

It was the sight of fat Arnie and the memories he called up that roused Suzanne from her stupor. It wasn't over yet. She'd managed her escape from that cocoon, and she must not go back. She was not Francine; she had inner resources. She'd let Philip make plans and would do what he proposed. If that was why she'd married him, so be it. He promised, and he would keep his promise. It was his way of propitiating the gods who had ruined his childhood. If he did well enough, they would not ruin his adulthood as well. Or was it his way of ensuring his reality, just as her father had had to show her off? She would help him, as she had helped her parents when she was a child.

She told him she was ready to try again, and he hugged her. "That's my girl," and a shudder snaked through her.

ON THE STRENGTH of her winning the contest, and of that single New York appearance, disappointing but fortunately not lethal, Philip again began arranging appearances for her in small towns all over the East Coast, places Suzanne had never heard of. No matter that it felt like a step backward. She must keep going—that was the main thing. She traveled; she kept a bag packed with necessities; she got used to folding up her concert clothes (she exchanged the severe navy blue dress for a red one that showed more leg and less cleavage) at short notice and heading for the train station or the airport. She got used to nights alone in motels with plaid bedspreads and paintings of dogs and horses on the walls, to bad coffee, to playing on unfamiliar instruments, to meeting people and behaving like a professional—polite, cooperative, self-sufficient. She dreaded each new performance, each new trip. The bookings were in smaller and smaller places: a party for a volunteer ambulance squad; a benefit for a local Little League team held in a high school gymnasium for an audience of unwilling teenagers and their teachers; once, a ticket to her recital was the reward at a silent auction for a nursery school.

But the panic didn't change, and this she could not get used to. Every time she came onstage it was the same: the ice creeping up her legs, the sweating, the sense of distance and unreality, her fingers moving of their own volition. She did the exercises, the breathing, the mind games, and she managed to play adequately while battling the panic, but she could take no pleasure in it.

She no longer yearned for the panic to disappear; it was a part of her, something she carried with her like the nightgown and toothbrush permanently packed. Each time, she thought she couldn't go through it again, but she kept going because she could see no other path. She was hardly aware that over the years of practice she had developed a will of steel.

After a matinee performance with a string quartet in Silver Spring, Maryland, a benefit for a Catholic charity, she'd hardly been able to stand up and take her bows, her legs were so shaky. The charity's director, an elderly man whose finely tailored suit hung loosely on his bony frame, asked if she was all right, if he could get her anything. It was mortifying, he so old and frail, so courtly and concerned, and she so young and strong, barely able to move. She was fine, she said, trying to smile, and yes, maybe he could get her a glass of water. He was planning to take her out for an early dinner with the other performers, but she pleaded a family emergency. He was disappointed; she regretted offending him but couldn't explain. They barely spoke as he drove her to the station.

This must stop, she thought as she left the train at Penn Station. She'd tell Phil she needed a break. She wouldn't go home right away, not until she could summon her strength. She knew what his arguments would be, and his ceaseless encouragement, which had begun causing her mild nausea.

"Why don't you give it up?" she said to him once, nearly a

year ago. There was no need to explain what she meant. He looked at her with a stunned face. He was holding a container of milk, about to pour some, and he put it down because his hand shook. "Give it up? This is what we planned from the very beginning. Things are moving along. All you need is patience. Do you want to waste your God-given talent?"

God-given. She'd never expected to hear a word like that from him. If anything, the talent had begun to feel demonic. "Sometimes plans don't work out. If I can accept it, why can't you?"

"You don't have to accept it so fast." He came over and took her in his arms. "I know it's hard. But try just a little longer. One of these days the panic will simply go away, and then you can do what you were born to do."

He didn't understand. When she was in high school, then at Juilliard, she'd thought she would want to die if she couldn't play the piano onstage. Now she was ready to relinquish it. Not happily, but with resignation. What she had planned to do all her life was simply not within her powers. She wasn't one of the lucky ones, like Elena. She had the talent, but not the grit. Very well, she had no choice but to accept it. But there was no arguing with him.

When she got out of the subway, she decided to stop in a coffee shop in the Village on her way home. It was an early evening in June, close to the solstice, just the kind of weather she liked—mild, the sky pale, nightfall not yet near. She'd sit outside with a magazine and think of nothing, just delay the moment of going home and reporting on her day.

As she approached the Café Borgia she saw Richard sitting at a table outside. His back was to her but he was unmistakable.

His hair was graying and there was a slight droop to his shoulders, but his body kept its grace and ease. Success agreed with him. His music was played often, and the reviewers called him one of the most innovative new composers. His opera opening in the fall was based on Marguerite Yourcenar's *Memoirs of Hadrian*, he'd told her when they last spoke a few weeks ago. He was talking animatedly to someone across the table, but his body was blocking his companion. Suzanne quickened her step—surely he'd ask her to join them and she'd be distracted. She could forget the failed afternoon and relax. As a waiter came to his table, carrying a tray with two cups of coffee, Richard moved aside to give him room.

Now she could see. The person facing him was Elena. Suzanne retreated into the doorway of a shop that sold men's leather goods and paraphernalia: thick black belts, heavily studded black vests, pants festooned with sequins and chains. Two men came out, more boys than men, really, with spiky purple hair and bare tattooed arms, laughing, brushing against each other; one bumped into her and muttered a hasty apology. Elena tossed her hair off her face with a quick gesture. She was laughing at something Richard said, her mouth wide open, her lips red and glistening. She wore several ropes of heavy beads that glinted in the sun. She reached out her hand toward Richard's on the table, and he clasped it. Then they opened their hands and he played with her fingers. Lovers' gestures. Suzanne felt a wave of nausea and weakness. She turned onto a side street and hurried home. Philip was out. She flopped facedown on their bed, felt the whole front of her body sink into the mattress, sinking so deep that she felt part of the bed, merging with the coverlet.

She herself had introduced them at Cynthia's party—that was

the worst of it. Well, not exactly. Elena strode over and introduced herself. But it made no difference. They would have met that night sooner or later, and because of her. How could he? He knew she and Elena were good friends. And she thought he didn't . . . with women. But of course that was so naive, almost as naive as her not recognizing years ago, at seventeen, that Greg was his lover. Possibly the other men, too. And then there was Cynthia. How had she forgotten about that?

She was supposed to meet Richard for lunch in a few days. She'd invited him over for dinner several times, but he preferred to see her alone rather than with Phil, whom he seemed not to trust. But she couldn't live with this new knowledge until then. She called him the following morning.

"Suzanne, how are things going? You're running around a lot, aren't you?"

"I'm okay. I'm getting tired of it, though. I think I'm going to stop for a while."

"Do you still freeze up?" he said tenderly. But the tenderness was the kind he would use with a child.

"Cut it out. You don't have to keep being my protector. God knows I get enough of that."

"What's the trouble?"

"I saw you with her."

"With who?"

"You know. With *her*. At the Café Borgia yesterday. You're with her."

"Elena. You can say her name."

"How could you?"

"What do you mean, how could I? You sound like a child. We're all adults here."

"It was at my party that you met."

"Yes."

"I never imagined . . ."

"Do you realize how you sound? It's not as if you and I are married. You're married to someone else. This is absurd."

"I thought . . . I thought . . . you know."

"For chrissake, Suzanne. You're . . . what? Twenty-seven, twenty-eight? Do you know what you're saying? At seventeen, okay—"

"Please, don't remind me of that."

"But it's the same thing. How innocent can you be?"

"Too innocent, evidently."

"Let's get something clear. This is not a betrayal. I'm still your friend, the same to you as ever. I'm not taking anything away from you. This concerns my life, not yours."

But you chose her over me, she thought bitterly. "And what kind of life is it, anyway?"

At that, he hung up without a word.

$\curvearrowright$

As it turned out, there was no need to argue with Philip about future performances. A few days later she discovered an excellent reason not to continue traveling so often. She was pregnant. It was unplanned, but a relief, such a relief that she wondered why this escape route hadn't occurred to her before. It explained the tiredness, the nausea, the fretfulness. Even Philip couldn't expect her to go gallivanting about feeling this way.

He received the news happily. "But once you're over the first few months, we'll go at it again."

"I don't know. I'd rather wait."

"Okay, it's up to you. But let's not wait too long."

The pregnancy was like a gift: no more performances, no more fear or sickly dread, no more having to report to Philip when she came home.

Philip was excited, giddy, like an expectant father on a TV sitcom. She had to laugh when he whispered sweet nothings in the direction of her stomach—who knew he could be so silly? He anticipated changes they'd have to make in the apartment: no sharp edges, no open electrical sockets . . . But of course he'd had a younger brother, Suzanne remembered, a brother he'd doted on. Billy. He'd already said that if it was a boy he'd like to name him Billy.

Suzanne allowed herself to relax; it was as if her emotions were lying in a hammock whose slow, gentle swaying lulled her. She kept up her lessons, kept playing for the ballet classes, but there were no more hurried trips to Penn Station or to the airport with an overnight bag containing the required elegant but simple noncreasing dress, the shoes, the all-important music. That was over. Forever, if she had her way.

To go along with the baby, they needed a house, he decided. He was doing well enough to afford a house now, the kind of house he had dreamed of ever since he was so abruptly exiled from his suburban home. He suggested the idea to Suzanne and she nodded without much interest.

"Sure, if that's what you want."

She didn't care to go house hunting with him, so he went by himself and found a modest but attractive three-story remodeled Victorian with solid old mahogany wainscoting, high ceilings and fine woodwork, a small back porch, and space for a garden in front and back, a house far larger than they needed even with the baby—or two babies—but he planned to turn one room into a studio so he could work at home. It was in Nyack, right in town—he knew Suzanne hated new tract developments—only a half hour's drive from the city.

"You'll love it," he said.

She agreed almost too readily. She wasn't even eager to drive up and see it, but Philip insisted.

"You're right," she said. "It's a lovely house. Let's do it."

She knew very little about babies, had rarely been with one up close. Almost everyone could have one; in that she was hardly special. Several of the girls she'd grown up with had already accomplished that: Eva, Paula. (Suzanne had sent the requisite gifts, feeling sorry for Eva's baby—what a mother.) Suzanne could do it, too, even if she hadn't especially craved one. She couldn't yet picture the baby as a reality, just the way she hadn't been able to pay attention when Mrs. Gutterman in the fourth grade had explained what the prime meridian was, or when the science teacher in junior high had explained the whys and wherefores of precipitation. It was as if their voices faded into the walls and at the same time a dark curtain descended between her and the sound, and she withdrew into her own head until a bell rang to rouse her. There would be no bell this time, but a needy baby who must be attended to. She would love it once she had it, she was sure of that. But she would rather have had the other—she couldn't lie to herself.

When Richard called to wish her well, she was surprised.

"I heard your news," he said. "That's lovely. You'll make a wonderful mother. You're patient and gentle. I'm looking forward to seeing you with a baby."

How had he heard? From Elena? Were they still together?

She couldn't possibly ask, after their last conversation. And how would Elena have known? Well, one way or another, the rumor mill in the classical-music world was still functioning efficiently. "Thank you. But it's been weeks since we spoke. I thought you were still angry, or I would have called to tell you myself."

"We've been friends too long for me to stay angry when I hear something as nice as this. Let's just get past it."

"I'm so sorry. I can't tell you how sorry I am that I spoke that way. I didn't mean it."

"Sure you meant it. But that's okay. I remember how you were brought up."

"I've tried so hard to escape all that."

"Well, keep trying. Meanwhile, I want to take you out to lunch to celebrate. Before you get too big to sit at a table."

"That's a ways off," and she laughed. They made a date for the following week. Being in his presence, sitting opposite from him, brought out more truth than the telephone had.

"Richard, how will I ever do this? I don't know the slightest thing about babies. I never even wanted one."

"Well, is it too late to have an abortion?" he asked calmly.

How could he consider that, after his warm congratulations? "Oh, no, I don't want to do that either. There's no reason to. And Phil is so happy about it. No, I guess it's just nerves. I'll be fine." There was no one, it seemed, to whom she could talk about her bewilderment at the whole enterprise.

Two months passed, they prepared for the move, and then, abruptly, one rainy night, the need to talk about the baby collapsed. It began with waking in the night to a feeling of wetness, wallowing in a puddle, and when she nudged Phil awake and he turned on the lights, they saw that the wetness was blood. Then the rushing about, the towels, the taxi ride through the dark streets, and finally the blessed injection, the falling into darkness.

Better not to think of the baby anymore. Yet once they had put away the catalogs of nursery furniture and the books of advice on how to get a night's sleep, she found she couldn't stop thinking about it, imagining what and who it might have been, how it might have felt to hold it, watch it sleep, feed it, see it learn to walk, to talk . . . all the things that had never interested her before.

She mourned for the baby as if she had really wanted it, and Phil, who had really wanted it, mourned with her. Suzanne knew she was grieving over her life, the failure she had accepted with stiff resignation but never cried over. Phil's grieving was edged by memory, too: a reenactment of the long-ago grief he had dreamed would somehow be compensated by the child, his only close blood relative. Their griefs, different as they were, brought them together, especially when the doctor told them there would be no more children. There was damage to the fallopian tubes or the uterus—Suzanne never quite understood the technicalities; she only understood the result, irreversible.

And now what? they both thought as they came home the next day, pale and shaken. Now what? Phil didn't dare suggest more performances, certainly not until Suzanne was stronger. But he knew what was ahead for him: He would work harder than ever. He was gradually building up the recording business, with recommendations from satisfied clients like Cynthia, who'd recently signed on, and some young artists she'd introduced him to. Besides that, he would devote all his spare time to establishing an independent label and promoting his own recordings. CDs were taking over the market, and he would work on them until he became the best in the business. He could do it, he was sure. And of course he must take care of Suzanne.

They had to delay the move for several weeks. Suzanne was slow to recover from the miscarriage, even though the doctor pronounced her fine in every way. Only she must try not to get pregnant—it could be dangerous. She knew very well how not to get pregnant—she'd been doing it for years. What she didn't know was how to pull herself out of the pit of despair. Less the loss of the child—though that weighed heavily—than the loss of a future. The years ahead had always seemed too few and too short to accomplish all she had to do. Now they were too long, and too many. Time to be filled, no different from the ordinary people she had grown up with. No longer special.

She was tired yet suffered from sleeplessness, various aches and pains, sometimes spasms in her lower back. And she was barely thirty. If she felt this worn-out now, she wondered, how would it be at sixty? How would she pass all those years?

Gradually she resumed her teaching and returned to the ballet class for which she was the accompanist; the adolescent girls, it seemed, had not only grown taller but grown more proficient in the weeks she'd been away. They were aspiring to join the company, buoyed by the kinds of hopes she had once nurtured. She thought about them while she played bits from Bach and Mozart for their barres. Later in the class she gave them lively selections from Prokofiev and Milhaud as they whirled and leaped across the floor in their complex patterns; while she played, she wondered how many of them would be able to live their dream. It was an advanced class, and to her they all looked superb; she didn't know enough to distinguish between degrees of excellence. Had they been musicians, she could have spotted the chosen ones in an instant. Meanwhile, to them she barely existed, was simply the accompanist, providing the music they needed. She didn't need to be real.

When they finally moved to Nyack she spent time on furnishings, something she had never taken the slightest interest in. She learned to cook seriously and began preparing elaborate dishes, greeting Phil in the evening in an apron dotted with flour and spots of sauce. "It's great, of course," he said, "but when did you have time to do this? Aren't you practicing? You know, you've got to start again one of these days."

"Why?" she said flippantly. "Why can't I just cook? It's a very respectable life. My mother did it. Thousands of women did it and still do. We have a house now. Where is it written that I have to achieve something? Some people just aren't suited to that."

"What's this? Your evil twin talking? You're not the same girl I once knew."

"Sorry to have to spoil your dream, but it looks like that's who I am now. If you wanted to hook up with a sure thing, you should have stayed with Elena."

She was furiously pulling the dishes out of the new dishwasher. Phil was expecting that some would land on the floor. He had never heard her raise her voice this way, but from his experience in the studio with many frustrated artists, he knew enough not to answer, to let the fit play itself out. He couldn't believe she was serious about cooking; it was simply the most contrary image of herself she could conjure up.

To Philip's surprise, he began to see cookbooks of all nationalities appear on the kitchen shelf, formerly bare except for a *New York Times* cookbook. He discovered that Ralph Nader's mother had written a Lebanese cookbook with a charming essay at the end about bringing up her large family. Under Mrs. Nader's influence, Suzanne spent a great deal of time scouring the county for greenmarkets, and in the refrigerator Phil would find odd-looking raw vegetables whose names he didn't even know.

He didn't dare arrange any more concerts, but he did venture to ask, one evening after an excellent couscous dish at their new dining-room table, whether she was still practicing.

"Oh, of course," she said. "Hours and hours. I've always practiced. My mother never had to nag me, either."

"I hope you don't think of me as a mother."

"Sometimes I do. You'd make a good mother."

More and more she left him speechless. She grew quiet and withdrawn. Though she said she was practicing, sometimes the music spread out on the piano didn't change from one day to the next. He heard she had babysat a couple of times for the young couple next door. When she was sitting down, her restless fingers drummed musical phrases on the tabletop; he wanted to ask her what she was hearing in her head, but he hesitated. He knew she still went into town to accompany the dance classes. Then, one Sunday morning, as he was bringing in the newspaper from their front steps, she announced that Richard had asked her to help him rehearse the singers for his new opera, to open in the fall. This would be a lavish production based on the life and death of Roger Casement, the Irish patriot, something on a scale Richard had not yet attempted.

"Sounds great," said Phil. "So, you're going to do it?"

"Sure, why not? It should be fun. And I haven't worked much with singers before."

"I thought you and Richard had some kind of quarrel. You haven't mentioned him in ages."

She'd never told him about finding Richard with Elena at the café, and about the awful thing she had said to him on the phone. She was too ashamed. "I wouldn't call it a quarrel, exactly. Anyway, he called a while ago and we both apologized, and it's over now. We were too close to be on the outs for long."

"Well, that's good. By the way, in case you're interested, he and Elena are no longer an item," Phil said. He was getting out his tools, preparing to work on the back porch he was building. He wanted it to be ready for the summer.

"I didn't know you knew about that."

"I know everything. I have my sources. Anyhow, it wasn't a big secret. Why should it be? They're both free to do as they please. It didn't last long. He's back to men and she's got a new interest. Or so they say."

"What do you mean? Who?"

"Well, I'm not sure if there's any truth to it, but they say she's been going around with Paul Manning."

"Her stepfather? I can't believe it." She moved the heavy newspaper over and sat down next to him on the couch.

"Yup. The cellist. They go to concerts and parties together, and she hangs on his arm. They make a good-looking couple, too—she's still snazzy and has her hair either piled up like a tower or hanging down to her ass, and he's the distinguished, gray-haired older gentleman. You should come into town with me more often at night, you'd certainly run into them. You do know her mother died recently? I should have said that first. She had an aneurysm."

"I didn't know. When?"

"Close to a year ago, I guess. So this is not as outrageous as it sounds. Only a little bit outrageous."

"I wish you'd told me about her mother, Phil. I would have written a note or something."

"Well, it was during the time you weren't very communicative, and I just forgot. Anyway, what does it matter who she's going around with?"

It mattered, but she couldn't say quite why. Elena's sheer audacity had always troubled her, made her feel wanting. A sexual adventurer, too. Could this have begun while her mother was still alive? If it was true, that is. No, even Elena wouldn't do that. Elena was always up for adventure, even risk, but not for crass subterfuge. She'd told Suzanne when one of the professors at Juilliard had pursued her with extravagant promises, but she made it clear she wasn't interested. He was married, for one thing. And too short, for another, she said, giggling. Hairs in his ears. Suzanne had laughed along with her, recalling all the while that Elena didn't need to do anything for favors, not with Paul Manning for a stepfather. Now, with her busy concert schedule, when did she find the time? An affair probably took less time than a marriage, especially if Elena had remained in the apartment after her mother died. How convenient.

Phil had gone outside and was standing on the raw wood of the unfinished porch, cutting swaths of screening—a typical Sunday suburban homeowner, she thought impassively. Where had he learned to build a porch? Or to make the fireplace work, or refinish the basement, or install new storm windows and hook up the washer and dryer? He was really extraordinarily gifted. He could do anything with his hands. She ought to appreciate him more. When the porch was finished, he said, she could use it in the hot months, to read or study scores.

Or just lie on a chaise, if that was what she preferred.

⌒

For a while Suzanne was caught up in the excitement of the rehearsals: Richard's opera was panoramic, beginning with Casement's work investigating human rights abuses for the British government in the Congo Free State and in Peru, and including dramatic scenes of the Easter Rising in 1916. There were even appearances by Yeats, Synge, and Lady Gregory of the Abbey Theater. The opera's climax was the hanging of Casement as a spy: In the midst of World War I he tried to get the Germans to provide weapons and leadership for an Irish uprising, thus diverting troops from the war effort. But the British government's most incendiary evidence against Casement was a purported diary that revealed homosexual escapades. His many political supporters, along with Yeats, George Bernard Shaw, Sir Arthur Conan Doyle, believed the diary to be a forgery perpetrated by his enemies. A forgery that claimed a life.

It was clear why this material would appeal to Richard. Working with him was a pleasure: They understood each other so well, communicating with just a glance or a few words. The work made her feel useful again. Opening night was a huge success, with a party afterward for the cast and friends; Suzanne got tipsy on champagne and felt benevolent toward the world.

Quite late in the festivities, Elena sailed into the room on the arm of her stepfather. "Hey, it looks like you might be right," Suzanne murmured to Phil. It was only natural that an air of intimacy should surround them, but Suzanne couldn't be sure if it was familial or erotic. She'd met Paul a number of times during her first year at Juilliard, when she would occasionally stay over at Elena's Park Avenue apartment instead of taking the long subway ride home. Paul was tall, much taller than Elena, with fine features and an elegant bearing. He looked the way Suzanne imagined statesmen or diplomats had looked in an earlier, more formal era: suave, confident, successful. He certainly didn't look his age, which must have been around sixty. Not so old, really.

Suzanne left Philip examining the array of hors d'oeuvres— he often judged the status of party-givers by the quality, quantity, and decor of the food—and went over to greet them. Elena beamed and held out her arms for an embrace. Paul leaned down to kiss Suzanne's cheek and asked, in fatherly fashion, how she was doing.

"I'm fine. Quite fine." She wanted to say something about Elena's mother, but this surely was not the moment. "Wasn't the opera wonderful? You were there, weren't you?"

"Of course. I wouldn't miss anything Richard did," Elena said innocently. She had no idea, Suzanne saw, how much pain that affair had caused her. Elena, too, was innocent, in her way. She had no agenda except the scramble for professional success. She sashayed through her life as she had done through high school and college, making the most of every opportunity. The pain, Suzanne realized, had been self-inflicted.

They exchanged the requisite bits of news, though the party

was too noisy for Suzanne to catch all of Elena's and Paul's latest exploits. "It's a pity we never see each other anymore," Elena said. "How did that happen? Can we have lunch, or take a walk, or do something?"

"Sure," said Suzanne. "Give me a call."

She was making her way back to Phil, tottering in her high heels from the slight shock of seeing Elena, as well as from too much champagne. Someone caught her arm and she turned: Richard.

"I hope it's the music that's made you so dazed with emotion," he teased.

"It's everything," she said, smiling. He put his arm around her waist to support her, and she felt a quickening inside, the kind of feeling she imagined she would have known when the baby started to move, but it hadn't lived long enough for that. "I'm so happy for you," she said. "Everything went off perfectly."

"You were a great help."

"Oh, come on, anyone could have done what I did."

"But everyone isn't as lovely to work with," said Richard.

Was it possible he was flirting? No, she must be mistaken, or more drunk than she realized. She slipped out from under his arm and went to find Philip.

The morning after brought a headache and letdown: no more rehearsals. Back to the dailiness. Some days Philip would come home to find a student in the living room with Suzanne; she had quickly gained a reputation in their new surroundings. But more often he found her drifting about, looking half-asleep. If he asked what was wrong, she said she was tired. It was clear she didn't wish to speak of how she felt. He suggested she see a doctor and for weeks she resisted, then finally agreed to have

a series of tests. The results were inconclusive. Stress, the doctors invariably pronounced, though to him her life seemed too
easy. Depression, they suggested. Philip was slightly afraid of
her now. She seemed so remote, so cocooned. Only her fingers
were never still. When she sat in a chair staring into space or
watching television, they drummed absently on her knees.

He didn't dare bring up the question of more performances,
even though, with his business flourishing, he had many more
contacts. He could easily have arranged some gigs, even in
Manhattan. He hesitated to ask if she was practicing. Only
now and then did he hear her, on the weekends. She didn't
seem to have lost any of her technique or expressiveness. It
was amazing, he thought, how brilliantly she could play when
she was alone at home, and how the panic that overcame her in
public could destroy that virtuosity. If he had her talent, they
wouldn't be able to drag him offstage. He would play his heart
out in front of thousands, if he could.

He rarely touched the piano these days, and never when
Suzanne was home, a timidity alien to him. She certainly
wouldn't ever say anything critical; it wasn't an area where they
competed, but he felt the piano was no longer his. He loved
making music as much as he had as a boy, though, and so
he took up the recorder. He bought a beginners' book and
taught himself, and evenings after dinner, while Suzanne read
or watched TV, he went upstairs and played his recorder. He
even had fantasies of the two of them playing duets—just for
fun, of course—when he was more advanced. He had no idea
how much the thin, piping sound, with the occasional beginner's squawk, grated on her. If she was reading, she would put
her hands over her ears to shut him out.

Part 3

PHILIP NEVER DID go back to Elena's interview until six weeks after Suzanne's death; he dreaded reading the rest. Once again he fortified himself with bourbon, although it was only one o'clock on a Sunday afternoon, and scrolled down to the place where he had left off.

"What was your reaction to the recent article in the *New York Times* regarding certain sections of Ms. Stellman's CDs? I mean the one that named a number of the selections on those CDs that were allegedly taken from other pianists?"

"Well, I was surprised, naturally. And saddened."

Ah, yes, saddened. That was good. She was clever, always had been. A diplomat.

"You were one of the artists whose performances were used. One of her victims, as it were. Didn't that make you angry?"

"Well, no, I wouldn't say that. I felt bad for her, but not exactly angry. And I certainly wouldn't consider myself a victim—that's far too strong a word. I wasn't harmed in any tangible way, only startled. It didn't harm my reputation. Or that of any of the other pianists."

That's for sure, Phil thought. Some of them were very little known, at least outside their country. That *Times* article could only have helped their careers, revealing such high praise from reviewers. Incognito, that is. Naturally, the journalists wouldn't be pleased: It showed the vagaries of their critical judgments.

"Of course, it was very wrong," Elena went on. "I'm not saying I condone anything of the sort, or take it lightly. But I frankly don't think she was aware of . . . I don't think she knew there were passages from other pianists inserted, or sometimes entire movements used. And to tell the truth, I don't really know why they were used. She certainly could play well enough on her own."

The nerve, he thought. What could she possibly know about their life? The times when Suzanne's illness got the better of her, when she flagged and slumped over the piano, too worn out to continue. The numbers of repeats when she couldn't get a passage right and lost patience, wanted to give up the whole idea, and he had to persuade her to try again another day. For there were days, many days, when she played splendidly, as well as she used to as a girl. It was impossible to predict. Then, toward the end, her arms and hands grew weaker and occasionally trembled. But he couldn't give up his project in the middle, could he? Remembering, he noticed that his own hand trembled slightly as he lifted the glass.

He mustn't get rattled over this. He'd come so far; he'd keep his cool till it blew over. Why was everyone making such a fuss? It wasn't as if he'd stolen huge amounts of money from anyone—it was never for the money. If it had been, he would have gone about it differently, with advertising campaigns and publicity. The amount of money involved was relatively small, compared with the revenue from his other clients. Where was the great harm? It didn't hurt the music. They were fine recordings. They honored the composers. They made listeners happy. They made Suzanne happy. She deserved to be happy. She deserved better—such a promising career, so cruelly cut short.

"You knew her husband as well, didn't you? Philip Markon. He was her manager and also the recording engineer and owner of Tempo Recordings."

"Yes, I knew him. Or, I used to know him, would be more accurate. I haven't seen him in quite some time."

Now she wanted to disown him, he thought, just as he had thrown her over more than thirty years ago. *Used to!*

"He's recorded a number of prominent artists, hasn't he?"

"Oh, yes. Tempo does quite well. Or so I've heard."

Or so she'd heard? She knew very well that Tempo was thriving. Can't commit herself, the bitch?

"It's generally assumed that he must have doctored the recordings himself. Do you have an opinion about that?"

"No, I don't know very much about the technical side."

Well, that was certainly the truth. She knew nothing. None of them knew a thing. They assumed it was a routine matter of pressing buttons and adjusting knobs. None of them had any idea of the precision involved, the complications, the placement of the mics and keeping them balanced, correlating the scores, the sounds, and their musical representations on the computer screen, keeping track of the relations of bass and treble, unwanted accents, the dozens of details that made the performances sound as good as they did. They all wanted to sound perfect, and you couldn't really blame them. In live performances human error was tolerated, wrong notes no big deal. An occasional slip here and there was more than compensated for by the living, breathing artist right in front of you, the spontaneity of performance. But with CDs the public had become used to an aseptic perfection. The artists didn't like it and neither did the technicians, who had fostered it in the first place, imagining they were producing something for the ages. Now everyone had to submit to those rigid standards. None of Phil's clients were aware of the time and effort he put in, what blunders he had to smooth over in the master tapes, in order to achieve that perfection. They listened to the finished product and thought it was their own genius they were hearing.

"But it couldn't have been anyone else, could it?" the interviewer persisted. "He wouldn't have had an assistant handle his wife's recordings, would he?"

"I really can't say. I have no idea how it happened or how he runs his business. Producing a CD is a complicated procedure, and no one should jump to conclusions."

Well, at least she wasn't accusing him outright. She was answering like a politician, noncommittally. Probably she figured that was safest all around. She was adept at that.

"Do you think they worked on them together? What I mean is, don't you think Ms. Stellman must have been aware of those substitutions? Surely she listened to the masters and would have recognized segments that weren't her own playing?"

"Again, I really can't say. Things can be changed after the master tapes, and not all musicians listen to their CDs. It's hard enough making them, believe me."

"Did you ever discuss the recordings with her?"

"Only to congratulate her and say I was pleased for her. As I said, we'd been out of touch."

"So, you never noticed your own playing? You never confronted her about it?"

"No."

This, of course, was an outright lie. Good work, Elena. Excellent. He wouldn't have expected it of her.

⌒

Again he thought of the Polish pianist Kosinski, that first recording he'd altered ever so slightly. As he'd expected, no one ever noticed the substitution of a few bars in the first Chopin nocturne, not even Kosinski himself. It was just afterward, a dozen years ago, that he'd persuaded Suzanne to try recording in the studio.

Philip worked very hard on that first recording, and it took him longer than most to edit. Suzanne never asked about it, and when he finally had it done and asked if she wanted to hear it, she shrugged. She was sitting in the living room, reading Ned Rorem's journals, and didn't enjoy being interrupted.

"I'm sure you've done a good job. I know how I sound."

"Are you really sure? Don't you have any curiosity?" He held it out like a surprise package. "Look, there's a photo of you, and liner notes and everything."

She finally took it and perused it. "Okay, why don't you play me a bit? Not the whole thing, just enough so that I get an idea."

"Well, thanks," he said, with some slight sarcasm. "I did it for you, after all."

"I know. I'm sorry. The whole issue is just . . . you know . . ."

"It is now. But if this one does well, that'll change over-night."

She listened for about fifteen minutes; Phil selected the passages carefully. In fact, despite his disappointment at her lack of interest, he was also relieved. He'd made one or two tiny substitutions, as he'd done for Kosinski. (Alterations, he preferred to call them.) He was fairly sure she wouldn't detect them, but you never know. She had an amazingly keen ear.

That first Chopin CD did well. Although coming from a pianist who was little known and hadn't performed in public for years, it was fairly widely reviewed, both in print and online. It was the very oddness of Suzanne's obscurity, perhaps, that earned the attention, not to mention Phil's intense networking, calling in favors from what he termed the favor bank. There were deposits and withdrawals. Ever generous by nature, he had done a lot for his colleagues over the years, and now was the time to make his withdrawals.

The next time they went to the studio they did several Mozart sonatas, and the next time Beethoven, and then Suzanne said she'd like to try something different, so they did some Debussy and Ravel's *Le Tombeau de Couperin*, one of the pieces she'd struggled with at her New York debut years ago.

"You see?" he said. "You can do it. This one is a marvel."

After those first two or three, she never wanted to listen. "I trust you implicitly," she said gaily, throwing her arms around him. "You're a miracle worker." She'd just read the latest review in *Gramophone* of her Mozart recording: It used words like "pellucid," "luminescent," "poignant." She had the old intensity back; she was closer to the girl Philip had been so drawn to in their early years. He remembered that same transformation in high school, from the timid freshman to the talkative and sparkling girl he took under his protection. Now that it was happening again, he felt even more powerful. He didn't have to ask her anymore about practicing; she was so busy preparing for the recordings that she had to give up two students.

But there were spells when she was still plagued by the

mysterious symptoms no one could diagnose. Every couple of weeks she would spend a few days in bed, achy, weary, and when she came to the studio she could rarely play in top form for more than an hour and a half. She was willing to come back for more repeats, but most of the time Phil didn't push her. He didn't want to wear her out or discourage her.

"I don't know what's the matter with me," she said. "I have no energy anymore. I should be able to do this. At school I could play for hours at a stretch. Do you think I'm getting lazy?" She cocked her head and gave a wistful smile. "Or maybe just plain crazy."

"Of course not. Don't even think such things. You're a little down, that's all. Maybe it's the rainy weather." They had just finished a takeout pizza after a tiring session in the studio.

"Come on, weather never stopped me from doing a Schubert sonata. I was stumbling all over the place."

"That's okay. I can fix those parts."

"What do you mean, 'fix'?"

"Okay, yeah, we've got to do that one rough part over. But it's amazing how much I can accomplish with the technology."

"Really? But is it still me?" she asked querulously. "If it's all edited by machine? If it makes me sound better than I am, or even different? Then what are the reviewers reviewing? Me or the technology?"

"It's still you, don't worry. This is how all CDs are made."

"I wonder if listeners know that."

"They don't have to know. As long as they get the music sounding as it should . . ."

"Well, I guess if everybody does it . . ." But she looked dubious. She wasn't quite sure what he meant by "fix," but it was simpler to trust him—he was so competent at his work. If she pushed him further, there would be complicated technical explanations that would only baffle her.

He didn't say any more, just started cleaning up the crusts, then took his recorder and went upstairs to practice. Soon the reedy, piping noise she had gotten used to would begin again. Handel tonight. It never lasted for more than an hour or so, though.

It would be so ungrateful, she thought, to object to his methods, his "fixing." He had done everything he promised, as far as she would allow him. It wasn't his fault that she hadn't achieved a brilliant career as a performer—onstage, that is. She was entirely to blame for that failure and accepted the responsibility. If it were left to Phil, he would have kept arranging gigs for her, but she refused. True, the very thing she had longed for, she could not have. But this was the next-best thing and it made her happy, happier than she had been since her hopeful days at Juilliard. Her CDs were having an unexpected success, even selling well and bringing in money, which neither of them had counted on or even cared much about. If pride and ambition were her sins—their sins, for they were in this together—and perhaps a tinge of envy as well, she consoled herself by thinking that greed certainly was not.

At first she'd read the reviews in *Gramophone*, *Chanticleer*, and the other music magazines with astonishment. Was that really her they were talking about? "One of the most vigorous and lively performances of Beethoven's Opus 10 Piano Sonatas we've heard in a long while." "A masterful interpretation of Rachmaninoff, faithful without being slavish, played with keen understanding and consummate skill." "A pianist with an extraordinary range. It's amazing that we haven't heard of the reclusive Ms. Stellman before, but wherever she is, we hope for more of these profoundly sensitive recordings, and of course hope to hear her perform in public." They were the kind of reviews she used to make up in her head when she was still a teenager in high school. Or with her friends at Juilliard, before the pressures of the contests and the uncertain future sobered them. Her reviews nowadays reminded her of those absurdly overblown fragments they would compose, sitting over coffee after the day's classes.

None of it would have happened without Phil's urging, his efforts, his encouragement. Or what she occasionally called— in petulant moods—his badgering. "It's my badgering that'll get you what you want—don't forget that," he would say, undeterred.

Now he never needed to ask what she did all day, as he had done tentatively, those years in their Greenwich Village apartment and after they first moved to Nyack. Then he had dreaded asking, and she had dreaded hearing the questions and giving her vague replies: She took walks, she cooked, she read, gave her lessons, practiced. Now, besides the practicing, there were letters from fans, addressed to the studio and brought home by Philip. There were her polite responses to other recording companies making offers. She thanked them for their interest, but she worked exclusively with Tempo Recordings. She was sought out by more students than she could handle, and had to limit herself to only a few advanced ones, who came to the house.

And a year or so after the CDs started appearing, there were the interviews. At first Phil had thought it better if she handled them by phone, and she did two that way, for the online magazines. But when one website, called TheWholeNote.com, ran a feature headed "Does the pianist Suzanne Stellman really exist?" she insisted on allowing the reporters to come to the house, or even meeting them in midtown. She knew the headline was a joke, but when she remembered her childhood fears about not being real, it gave her chills. "Of course I exist. They can come and see for themselves."

"If you're sure you want to," Phil said.

"Why not? Are you afraid I'll say the wrong thing?"

"Not exactly. But we ought to go over what you'll say."

"You mean, to be sure it fits with what I said to the others? I can remember what I said."

"No, not necessarily. But journalists are very tricky, especially if you sit down and have a drink with them. You think they're being friendly, so you relax and forget it's an interview, and later you'll find every chance personal remark exaggerated. Did you tell the others you had studied abroad, as I said?"

"Yes. I was kind of vague about it, though."

"Vague is good. Though you might mention a few names this time. Paris, say. Nadia Boulanger. Milhaud. Emil Gilels. You might well have met them. Actually, Milhaud even lived here for a long time."

"You're kidding. It's one thing to say I studied in Paris—okay, I can live with that—but I can't say with a straight face that I knew those people."

"That's what I'm concerned about. If you can't say it with a straight face, then you should do it on the phone or in an email. And you don't have to tell them all the same thing. Tell one you were in Paris, and for the other, say . . . oh, Vienna."

"I don't get why we need all this lying."

"It's not exactly lying. It's just sort of stretching the truth. You did study at a major conservatory in a large city. It's good to have an aura of mystery. Then they'll talk about you—who is she and where did she come from? By the way, you can be vague about where you're from, too. Lots of artists say they moved around in their childhood. You have no idea of the fantasy lives they create for themselves. And by the way, don't forget to mention that you studied with Madame Kabalevsky. She's legendary now. You become attached to the legend."

She was reluctant, unaccustomed to stretching the truth, as he called it. But after all, it did no harm in the end. The facts of her life didn't matter; only the music mattered. She didn't lie in the music—there was no way you could lie in music.

After the interviews appeared and the CDs continued to sell well, she was invited to give a master class at the Manhattan School of Music, which occupied the old site in Morningside Heights where Juilliard used to be, while Juilliard itself was long since settled in its more lavish quarters at Lincoln Center. The streets and the old rooms were very familiar, even if the administration was a different one. The students seemed the same, too: eager, anxious, a curious blend of confidence, awareness of their own gifts, and fear. As for her, she felt no anxiety at the prospect of demonstrating a passage, or even a large part of a movement. Her panic always let her have a few moments of grace at the beginning, a short-lived generosity that made its succeeding cruelty worse. And it was the students being judged, not her. Remembering how she'd felt at the master classes at Juilliard long ago, she was kind. She didn't interrupt unless it was absolutely necessary, and she preceded her corrections with kind words—she could always come up with some merit in the student's playing. She played with virtuosity and grace; her visit was a success, and led to more.

"We were told you were very reclusive," one of her hosts remarked over coffee after the class. "But here you are, and you seemed quite willing to appear."

"Oh, yes," Suzanne said, laughing. "I heard there were rumors that I didn't exist, that the CDs were a kind of . . . I don't know, emanation. But I assure you, I'm quite real. And so is my music."

⌒

That summer she and Phil treated themselves to a trip abroad. Phil left the business in the hands of the assistant he'd hired two years ago, after the work became too much to handle on his own. Naturally, Phil had offered to arrange concerts for Suzanne—his contacts had now spread across the ocean: Kosinski, for one, would surely help him out, after Phil had gotten him off to such a good start in the United States with those recordings of the Chopin nocturnes years ago. And there were others like him, in Italy and Austria and Russia. But Suzanne said no, she wanted this to be a true vacation, though she would like to visit the conservatories she had heard so much about. This, too, was easily arranged. With the reputation she had earned from her recordings with Tempo, and from the online reviews and interviews, she was invited to conduct master classes at the Moscow Conservatory and the Vienna Conservatory. There were two students in Moscow who she told Philip were extraordinary; Philip asked them to stay in touch and consider visiting the States.

Soon after they returned home she met Richard for lunch

in an outdoor restaurant across from the park. Richard lived on Central Park West now, with his latest lover, a younger composer who taught at Hunter, just as he himself had once done. In love with himself, Suzanne thought, a younger incarnation.

"You're looking wonderful," he said. "Are things going well?"

She told him about their trip. "Imagine," she said, "the first time I've been to Europe. At my age! Except for those few contests, I mean, when I hardly saw a thing, I was in such a fog. We did all the touristy things, the Trevi fountain, Big Ben, the Louvre. It was glorious. And I met some wonderful musicians in Moscow. Of course, we needed a Russian translator." At that she immediately thought of Elena and regretted even this remote allusion. Fortunately, their salads were set in front of them and they were silent while the waiter fussed.

"Well, good," Richard said with a crooked smile. "Meanwhile, I've been reading a few interviews with you. I never knew you studied at the Paris Conservatory. Nadia Boulanger? How did you manage that while you were across the street from me the whole time?"

"Oh, come now. Are you scolding again? Like you used to? I didn't think it would do any harm to make myself sound slightly more interesting."

"And in another one you studied in Vienna. Don't you imagine some of the same people read both magazines?"

"So? They'll be slightly puzzled, is all. I'll be enigmatic."

"That doesn't sound like you at all. I hear the voice of Philip behind this."

"What's wrong with that? He always has good ideas about promotion, that kind of thing."

"Do you think lying is a good idea?"

"Do you know, you sound more like my mother now than you ever did twenty years ago?"

"And do you remember I told you your mother wasn't always wrong?"

She looked at him ironically from under lowered lids, like a chastised but still naughty schoolgirl.

"All right, I won't sound like a schoolmaster. Sorry. But seriously, Suzanne, it's not a good idea. Someone's sure to notice. They'll spread rumors—you know how fast they fly on the web—and soon they'll get suspicious."

"I have been to the Paris Conservatory, actually. Just last month. I visited them all. I think I phrased it in such a way that it might sound as though . . ."

"Oh, if you're into sophistry we'd better talk about something else. Your husband may go for that, but not me. So tell me what your plans are now. The Rachmaninoff CD was fantastic, by the way. You're sounding better all the time. How are you feeling?"

When she got home she reread the interviews in the online magazines and the two in print. She had only skimmed them before. What did it matter what they said about her life? What mattered was her playing. But when she'd read through them, it did seem as though she'd contradicted herself a good deal.

"Phil," she said, as she stirred spaghetti in a large pot. "Do you really think it was okay to tell all those stories in the interviews? Richard thinks maybe I shouldn't have done it."

"Oh, Richard thinks this and Richard thinks that." He rarely showed anger, and even now he didn't raise his voice, but it had a sharp edge of bitterness. "Where do you think you'd be if you'd listened to him all along?"

"I don't know where I'd be. I didn't see him for a long time after we married. He never gave me practical advice, I mean, not since I was a child."

"I didn't mean literally. Suzanne, you have to trust me in this. Have I ever steered you wrong?" He came over to her at the stove and put his arms around her waist from behind.

"I don't think so. But it's not over yet. Watch what you say— I'm standing in front of a pot of boiling water." She laughed and leaned her head back as he ran his hands over her breasts. "Please, I really need to drain this spaghetti."

"Later, then."

"Okay. Later."

"Not much later. Like, how about you finish the spaghetti and we take a glass of wine to bed and eat afterward?" He was still caressing her as he spoke, and he put her hand on the front of his pants. She didn't want to wait either.

"Okay, okay. Just let me finish this. You think you're changing the subject, but I won't forget."

"Oh, you will," he whispered in her ear, congratulating himself on the clever way he was handling it all.

He was pulling at her clothes as they went up the stairs, and they hardly made it to the bed. She was as aroused as she used to be years ago when they first married.

It was over quickly and they were hungry. They ate the spaghetti and finished the bottle of wine on the screened-in back porch Phil had built. They'd both changed into shorts and shirts, and sat with the plates on their laps and their bare feet up on the railing. High above them a gibbous moon shone, that odd shape, not quite a perfect circle yet, unsettling, unfulfilled.

"Oh, you know what I heard the other day from Alec?" Alec was his assistant. "About Elena. She's getting married."

"Married! Why didn't you tell me?"

"I'm telling you now."

"I mean before. So, who's she marrying? A musician? You're not going to tell me it's her stepfather?"

"No, no, they didn't need to get married. They were already family. She's marrying an investment banker. Works for Lehman Brothers, I think."

"I wonder how they met."

"I haven't heard that yet. But no fear, she'll probably invite you to the wedding and you can ask her."

"Me? If anything, she'll invite us. She wouldn't invite me separately."

"Maybe not. But I've always felt she's still pissed at me."

"What? You can't mean from high school?"

"Yes. Because I broke up with her."

Suzanne shook her head. Let him think that, she thought, if it makes him happy. On the rare occasions when his name came up in college, Elena had spoken of him dismissively—he was not even worth her contempt. Superficial, she called him. She'd sent him on his way. Suzanne would never forget those harsh judgments. Surely by now Elena had changed her mind: Phil had done so well, and all on his own. But if it placated his male ego to imagine he'd been the one to end it, let him.

"I'm sure she's gotten over it by now," Suzanne said, nudging his bare foot with her toe. "Especially as she's found an investment banker. She's certainly embraced the American dream, hasn't she?"

A s HE'D PLANNED, Philip had turned a spare room of the house into a soundproof studio where he could work at night, editing his recordings, a small room Suzanne rarely entered, crowded with a console and screens and tape machines and wires, all a mystery to her. It was too small for recording, and so Suzanne kept going to his studio in New York. Over the next few years her work there was often as dazzling as ever, Philip said; remarkable, the reviewers called it. Philip allowed a few journalists from small magazines to come to the house for interviews—to show she was real, Suzanne always said jokingly when they arrived. To them she spoke less about her background and more about the music, her interpretations.

But she grew tired and frustrated ever more quickly. Philip was required to do more and more alterations on her recordings; it was occasionally necessary to substitute an entire movement from his vast library of recordings by other pianists. What worked best were recordings made in his own studio, with the same room sound, so he found himself bringing out CDs nominally by Suzanne that competed with his earlier issues. Or he had to seek out older recordings made in similar studios. All this required a good deal of legwork, but it was worth it, he never doubted, for Suzanne. She was doing the best she could. It was not her fault that her powers were so uneven. If not for the bad luck of her illness, she could have been one of the great pianists of her generation.

For they had finally found a neurologist right in Nyack who had diagnosed Suzanne's mysterious on-and-off symptoms as a form of fibromyalgia. She was frightened when she first heard the words, then somewhat relieved when the doctor described the illness at length—elusive and difficult to diagnose—and said that hers was a relatively mild case. She was lucky that it hadn't progressed very far by this time—Suzanne was in her forties. If her luck held and she didn't succumb to depression again, it might not get much worse.

"We need to make clear," said Phil, who of course had accompanied her to the appointment, "that my wife is an important pianist. A major artist in the middle of a successful recording career." Suzanne shot him glances to make him stop, but to no avail. "She's been managing to play up to now, but we need to know the prospects for the future."

"It's hard to predict with fibromyalgia," the doctor said. A Chinese woman probably twenty years their senior, with a severe white coat and an array of diplomas on the wall, she seemed unfazed by Phil's boasting. "But I'd advise you, Mrs. Markon"—and here she turned back to Suzanne, who didn't interrupt to explain that she used her original name—"to go on as you've been doing, get exercise and plenty of rest, and, as I said, if you're lucky you'll be able to continue your work. I certainly hope so, and you should come in every couple of months so I can have a look."

The doctor wrote out several prescriptions and though both reached for them, she handed them to Suzanne. "You're fortunate that it hasn't affected your arms and hands any more than it has. I know it must sound odd to use that word, fortunate, in these circumstances, but you may come to see it that way once you get used to the idea."

"Frankly, I'm relieved, in a way," Suzanne said as they got into the car. "Not knowing is worse. At least I know it's real, it's not depression alone, or I'm not indulging myself. Did you think I was just, you know, avoiding . . ."

"Of course not," said Phil. Although he had at times thought precisely that. His sympathy and encouragement had grown slightly worn and thin, like an old coat its owner is thoroughly tired of but can't afford to replace. Now he could be freshly sympathetic and useful; it was bad luck, nothing psychologically torturous or self-destructive. He must see that she kept playing as long as possible. In any event, the recordings could continue; by now they had an independent existence.

⌒

Months passed and Suzanne was no worse. Indeed, she seemed better, more energetic and lighter in spirit, since the doctor had given her condition a label. She still enjoyed cooking. One winter evening she'd made an elaborate cassoulet, and as she was setting it on the table she said nonchalantly, "You'll never guess who came over today. Elena."

Philip put down his glass of wine and stared. "You mean turned up, just like that?"

"No, of course not. She called last week and said she wanted to see me. I wasn't eager, but she really pressed. So finally I said she could come today."

"You didn't tell me. Well, how does she look?"

"The same as on the posters. Even better. Still glamorous.

Very well cared for. The same faint remnant of an accent. I think she keeps it on purpose."

"What did she want? I assume she wanted something." Philip played with his fork, running his fingertips along the tines.

"She said . . . I hardly know how to tell you this. . . . She said a couple of passages in the Chopin ballades . . ." She had sliced the bread and brought the salad to the table; there was nothing more to delay her. Suzanne sat down, pushed her hair away from her face, and looked at him. "That very first recording we did, remember? She said passages were copied from hers. I'm sorry, I don't know how else to put it. You know, pasted in, or over, however it's done."

She watched him carefully, but he revealed nothing. He looked blandly at her, began eating the cassoulet, and made appreciative murmurs. When he looked up, Suzanne was still gazing steadily at him. He remembered how shy she was when they first met, or maybe it wasn't shy, maybe simply an innate reserve, an instinct of vulnerability that kept her from meeting people's eyes. He had taught her, when she first began to play in public, that she must look at people straight on, that otherwise they would distrust her. She had learned her lesson well. She stared straight at him; it was he who had to look away first.

"And did she say how she came up with something so preposterous?"

"Well, she heard something on it that rang a bell, and then she listened to my CD and hers, one after the other. Hers was a few years older, also done in a small studio, maybe that same place on West Twenty-fourth Street you used to rent. She sounded very specific about what she heard, but I didn't want to know the details. Still, I thought I'd better check with you. She didn't seem angry, only puzzled. Why did I do it? she wanted to know. Of course, I said I did nothing of the sort."

"Of course not," said Philip.

"I got flustered. I think I was kind of rude, at the end."

"That's understandable. Who wouldn't be? It's a serious accusation."

"It wasn't an accusation. I mean, she didn't threaten or anything like that. We're friends, she said. She just wanted to clear things up. But in the end I asked her to leave. I was in the midst of doing the cassoulet—that was the truth. It takes time."

He grunted and continued eating.

"Well, Phil?" That steady gaze from her large dark eyes was making him flustered as well, so rare a sensation that he hardly understood what it was.

"Well what?"

"Well, did you do that? It doesn't sound like something she'd invent."

"Okay, look," he said after a long pause. So long that there was nothing else to do but admit it. She'd get it out of him eventually—why let it drag them into an unpleasant scene? "It was only a few seconds, not even worth mentioning. When I did the editing I could hear that you were tired. I didn't want to make you go through it again. You'd already done several takes. It was our first time, remember?" He knew each CD, each date, each recording session with Suzanne in the studio; they required so much patience. "You weren't used to recording. You didn't have the . . . the confidence you have now. A couple of seconds—nothing really. It's a fluke that she caught it. I didn't want to bother you about it when you were off to

such a great start. Where's the harm? I mean, it's your performance, the whole thing. It's just a sort of . . . a Band-Aid."

"A Band-Aid?" She laughed, a harsh brittle laugh. "You're
calling part of a Chopin performance a Band-Aid?"

"Okay, I'm sorry. That was a stupid phrase. Just a little
adjustment."

"Did you do this 'little adjustment' in any of my other
recordings?"

"No! I certainly did not."

"Do you do it with any of your others?"

"No! Well, maybe once or twice. No one realizes how hard
it is to produce a perfect CD. It takes a hell of a lot of work.
Musicians are all the same, all of you. No one wants to keep
repeating a few bars that didn't come out quite right. Or they
want to play the whole piece straight through again. Sometimes you get five, six, ten takes and you've still got a couple of
doubtful patches. So . . . I'm not the only one, believe me."

"I'm not sure I do believe you. Did you do it with any others
of mine?"

"You just asked me that and I said no. Don't you trust me?"

She didn't answer that directly. "Don't do it again with my
work, Phil. I mean it. It's not right. You know it's not right."

"It's not any worse than plenty of other stuff that goes on."

"I don't care what else goes on. If it's not me playing, then
it's not me . . . it's not my . . . I mean, how can I feel any sense
of accomplishment? How can I read the reviews without feeling sick?" She remembered when she entertained her parents'
guests, the Woodsteins, with that section of the Rachmaninoff
prelude she passed off as her own composition. And her mother's stern disapproval, and Richard's. It must be tempting for

someone like Phil. It was easy to understand how, with so much technology and skill at his command, he might be tempted.

"Oh, I bet you can." He looked wily, and this time it was she who couldn't meet his glance. "I know what you want. I've always known what you want."

"I don't want it that way."

"And if that's the only way?"

"Just don't do it, okay? Besides the fact that it's wrong and it's . . . it offends me, it could get us into a lot of trouble."

He didn't reply, and she pressed him no further. The meal was over. They'd barely eaten, and they cleaned up in silence. Suzanne was about to throw out the rest of the cassoulet, but Philip put it carefully in a plastic container, a habit he had learned from his aunt Marsha. "It was very good. It'll be fine for another night," he said. "I've got some work to finish." He washed his hands at the sink, went into his studio, and shut the door.

Suzanne stretched out on the sofa in front of the TV. It was another of those crime shows. A suspect was being grilled in the small cell-like room by two detectives. It involved an international counterfeiting scheme—politics and terrorism were part of it—but as the scenes continued she couldn't follow the intricacies of the plot. The commercial was even more obtuse: A car slammed to a sudden stop, perched precariously on the edge of a cliff above a roiling sea. She should be working instead of sitting and staring at nothing. She was too tired to practice at this hour—nearly nine—but there were scores to go over. Phil wanted her to work on the Schubert Impromptus. She'd studied them in school, they were a staple of the repertoire, but that was a long time ago. Still she didn't move.

It felt good to hear voices in the house, even the harsh voices of the detectives and the district attorney. Voices that smothered the voices in her head, her own and Elena's.

She hadn't told Philip the whole truth about Elena's visit, only the bare minimum. Least of all how much it had shaken her. The phone rang when she was at the piano a week ago, practicing the Impromptus. The machine was turned down low so as not to disturb her, and she nearly forgot about the call. Later, when she saw the blinking light and heard Elena's unmistakable voice, she felt a shiver of apprehension. The voice conjured Elena's image. Suzanne hadn't seen her in ages. She and Phil had received an invitation to her wedding but they had invented an excuse. And Richard had mentioned something about a baby, but Suzanne never got around to calling.

She had followed Elena's musical endeavors more attentively than her domestic ones. Elena generally played in New York several times a year, with the Philharmonic just a month ago, then with a chamber group at the Ninety-second Street Y, and she toured and made recordings with one of the large corporate studios. She was leading the life Suzanne had expected for herself, and she couldn't help feeling Elena had stolen it from her. Just as she had stolen Richard and, years ago, Philip. She couldn't get over the notion that her own life would have been entirely different had Elena never come from Russia and turned up in high school. It was as if they were characters in a fairy tale and Elena was the fortunate sister who wins the prince and the kingdom, while the other sister, not as lucky, is hustled offstage to a hovel in the forest. Although Snow White and Rose Red, as Mme. Kabalevsky used to call them at school, had both wound up happy in the end. Snow White married the prince and Rose Red got his brother. Suzanne had actually looked up the Grimm story to remind herself.

"Suzanne?" The voice on the message was low, softened by trepidation, not at all like the usual Elena, bold and sure of herself. "I know it's been ages. I hope you're feeling better. The last time I ran into Phil he said you weren't feeling well. Listen, I'd really like to see you. There's something I need to talk to you about. Can you give me a call?" Aside from the faint accent, her English was perfect, colloquial, no more of those quaint textbook constructions. Those had disappeared long ago, by the time she got to Juilliard. She was nothing if not adaptable.

Suzanne didn't return the call. She had a good enough life now, thanks to Phil. But if she couldn't have Elena's world, she didn't want to be reminded of it. When the phone rang two days later, she picked up because Phil had said a reporter from a French magazine might be calling.

"Suzanne, I'm glad I got you. Maybe you didn't get my message. How are you?"

They exchanged banalities as if the gap in their friendship had been accidental, as if they'd simply lost touch and were cheerfully catching up.

"Look, I really need to see you. Can we arrange something? If you're in the city, maybe we could have—"

"I'm seldom in the city these days."

"Well, okay, then I'll drive up. Where is it, Westchester somewhere?"

"Nyack. It's in Rockland County."

"Nyack. Fine. I can get there."

"I'm not sure it's a good idea. I'm so busy right now, and you must be, too. . . ."

But Elena persisted, and Suzanne was no match for her determination. Elena always got what she wanted, she thought as she hung up. And now she wants me. For what, she could not imagine. She brooded about it for days.

The appointment was for late afternoon. Suzanne purposely occupied herself with the cassoulet, but nonetheless she was watching from the kitchen window as the car pulled up. A small black foreign car—she couldn't tell the make, but an expensive car. She would have expected something more gaudy. Nor, when she came in, was Elena gaudy. She was dressed soberly. She didn't need flashy clothes—success was a glow surrounding her. She was slim and her hair was slightly darker, with coppery tones in the blond, cropped short now and with that billowy, recently washed look usually seen only on TV commercials. She wore narrow black slacks and a gray silk blazer, and Suzanne immediately wished she had thought to dress for the occasion. She was wearing jeans and a black turtleneck, as she used to as a student. She felt older, dowdy, although Elena exclaimed about how wonderful she looked.

"You're as stunning as ever," Elena said.

"Me, stunning? I never was."

"Oh, come on, Suzanne. You know you always had that mysterious, secretive look, like, who knows what's going on behind that face? You still do. Anyway, so here I am. I never thought you'd move to the suburbs. You always used to say how you loathed visiting your brothers when they moved out of Brooklyn."

"That was Long Island, all that tract housing. This is different, it's a real town. We can walk to shopping, the bookstore, the cafés." Why was she accounting for her house, her town, her life? Already she was on the defensive.

"Well, it's a lovely house, and right on a corner, too. And that beautiful garden out front. Who takes care of that? Is Phil the gardener?"

"I am. I learned. I love it, and it's not hard, really."

"Aren't you afraid of hurting your hands?" Elena spread her own hands out on her lap, the thin fingers splayed. The hands were pale and perfect, articulated and alive even in their stillness.

"I wear gloves. I'm careful." Suzanne wanted to spread her hands out as well. They were every bit as good as Elena's, if not quite so white. But she restrained herself. Enough competition. "And you? You're still in the city, aren't you? And you have a baby?"

"Not such a baby anymore. Petey's almost three," and she smiled with the irrepressible joy parents always have when speaking of their young children. Suzanne had seen it on their other friends from school—Tanya, Rose Chen, even Simon Valenti—all of them now teaching and raising families. "We bought a town house in the East Seventies, room for the baby *and* the nanny. And not far from Paul. He's getting on, you know. I don't like to be too far away. Also because of Petey. Our boy."

"Your boy?" Suzanne repeated, puzzled.

"Yes, Petey is Paul's child. Oh, don't look so shocked. You must have known. We never tried to hide it."

"I . . . I suppose I did. I was never quite sure, though. And I certainly didn't know about the boy."

"Well, it's nothing we needed to advertise. And it's fine with

Oliver. My husband. He can live with it, and in fact soon we'll be having one of our own."

"That's great," Suzanne said. So, the rumors about Elena and Paul had been true. Of course they were true. Rumors about love affairs generally were. And now Elena had everything, plus a baby from each man. "You're not showing yet."

"No, it's early. I just found out a couple of weeks ago. Are you really shocked?" Elena followed Suzanne into the kitchen while she got the coffee ready.

"Not anymore. No. You always did things your own way." Suzanne grinned and Elena grinned back, and for a moment it was as if they were girls again, girls who understood each other well and wordlessly. As soon as she felt that kinship, she realized how much she missed it.

"Are you still in touch with Richard?" Suzanne asked. She poured carefully, no longer looking at Elena.

"Of course. He's got a new opera opening next season. This is some Chinese folktale theme, I forget what. Didn't he tell you?"

"No, I read about it in the papers. It's been a few months since I spoke to him. You know how New Yorkers never like to leave the city. I'm surprised you found your way up here." The moment of intimacy had passed. She hoped it wouldn't be long before Elena got to the point. Surely she'd come for a reason.

"But you and Richard were such close friends! Why are you burying yourself up here, Suzanne? Everyone you know is in the city. Even Phil's studio is there."

"I like it well enough. I don't feel buried."

Elena sat down on the couch and set her mug in front of her on the coffee table. "Well, I guess it's not my business. I'm sure

Richard'll send you tickets to the opening. Listen, I've heard some of your CDs. They're fantastic. And I saw some of the reviews in the music magazines. I'm glad for you."

"Yes, they're doing well. You know Phil, once he gets an idea in his head. He talked me into it."

"Really?" Elena turned to look at the piano. "I see it's the same Steinway. I remember it from your apartment in the Village."

"It's still in good shape. I practice on it, but for the recordings I go to the studio in town."

"I wanted to talk to you about the Chopin CD," Elena said. "The one with the ballades. It's a wonderful performance, of course. You were always fantastic."

Suzanne smiled. Maybe this was nothing but a friendly visit. Maybe now that she had established a reputation, Elena wanted her friendship again, or thought she or Phil could be of use, though she hardly seemed in need of anything.

"There was just something . . . something that bothered me."

"Don't tell me I made some awful gaffe. Philip would have caught it."

"No." Elena stayed silent, her mouth open, as if the words were stuck in her throat. "I don't know how to say this, but . . ."

"What?"

"I thought you would know. But maybe you don't. In the third ballade, the second and third movements actually . . ."

"Well, what?"

"Suzanne," she said. "Parts of them are mine. They're taken off my CD, the Chopin one I did way back when."

Suzanne set her cup down very slowly, as if it contained a

toxic substance, mercurial, that would spill at her peril. "What on earth are you talking about? I played them in the studio and Phil did the editing there, too."

"You know these things can be done, with all the fancy equipment they have now. I was shocked, but I know it's mine."

"This is madness. I don't even want to hear it."

"No, please. Please just listen a minute. Let me tell you what I heard. If you don't know, you need to know. I was listening to the second movement and something tugged in my ear, sort of like an itch deep in the ear. At first I let it go. But then a few minutes later, in that chromatic passage, you know, it happened again. Just like . . . I can't explain it, almost like a sense of déjà vu. So I listened all over again and it was that fermata, you know, after the runs . . . there's that fermata, and it was held just a little longer than it should be. I tried to remember where I'd heard that done before, and I realized it was me—I also did it the time I played it at Carnegie Hall. And the second time, a little later on, there was an ornament I added, a tiny trill—no big deal. But it's impossible that you'd do exactly the same thing. And if you did, it's odd that it got onto the CD. It probably shouldn't have gotten onto mine, either. What I couldn't figure out is why he'd copy a passage that had that. Maybe he just liked it."

Suzanne stood up. "I can't even keep track of what you're talking about. This is absurd. Stop it. Just stop it. You're saying he took your recording and put my name on it? That's crazy." Could he have done that? Even as she denied it she felt a shiver of dread. He was capable of it. Of course he was. There had been hints all along, but she hadn't allowed herself to pay attention to them. What had she been thinking? The fear shot through her and left her sick.

"No, no. Mostly it's you playing. He just inserted those Two-Parts. I'm not sure where it starts and ends, but I know there's a section of me in there. What I did was, I played my recording alongside yours. They weren't the same all the way through, not at all. Yours is even better in places, or at least different. Remember, we were always different? You were more restrained and I tended to go overboard. Not so much anymore, though. Anyway, it's just those two passages. I swear to you, Suzanne. Do you think I'd make this up? Listen for yourself. Here"—she rummaged in her big leather purse—"I brought my CD. Put it on and see."

Suzanne wouldn't look at the CD Elena held out. "Put that away. I don't want to listen. For all I know, you *could* make it up. You've always wanted to take everything away from me, from the very beginning." Suzanne stood up and turned her back to Elena. She didn't want to see or hear her. She wished she could make her disappear or pretend this was not happening. Out the window, three birds were pecking at the feeder; she felt as if they were pecking at her own skin. Elena was pecking, jabbing with her sharp beak. "First you took Phil. Then Richard. What is it now? Isn't your reputation enough for you? You can't stand that I'm having some success, too?"

"Suzanne! Phil was a silly high school romance, for God's sake. I thought we'd been through that over twenty years ago. You're married to him—what more could you want! I've hardly exchanged two words with him since. And Richard! I didn't 'take' him. He wasn't yours."

He *was* mine, Suzanne thought. Ever since I was a child. Mine.

"It was a brief fling, a few months, one of those things. It happens all the time. We became friends—it was you who wanted us to meet and be friends, remember? And then it just happened. It wasn't ever serious. Richard does that, you know, with men, with women. He's omni . . . omni something, or ambi . . . I don't know the word. Ever since that old boyfriend of his died—Greg, was it? And no, it wasn't AIDS, thank God, if that's what you're thinking. They were very careful. Anyhow, Richard flits around, I don't know, for distraction, maybe. It didn't mean he wasn't still your friend. I wasn't even very hurt when he ended it. I just . . . Look, I don't want anything that's yours. I never have. But you never trusted me. Just because I'm not the kind of person you grew up with. It's so provincial, my God. But look, Suzanne, what matters now is that if Philip is messing around this way, you've got to get him to stop. Someone's going to find out and there'll be trouble."

"I suppose you'll see to that."

"As it happens, I won't. I haven't said anything and I'm not going to. If that was what I had in mind, I would have let my agent handle it. You and I were friends. I came to ask you how it happened. You say you don't know, and okay, I trust you. But Phil is doing something and you can't let it go on."

Suzanne wheeled around to face her. "This is outrageous. *You* are outrageous. Why don't you just go?"

"Suzanne, I came here as a friend. You need to know about this."

"We have nothing more to talk about. It's a terrible accusation." It was, and more so because it might be true.

"I'm not accusing. But I did hear what I said I heard. I could let that go, I *will* let it go, but if there's more of the same, others are going to hear it, too, sooner or later. Maybe I should talk to Phil. Is he around?"

"No, and I'm sure he wouldn't have anything to say to you."

Elena gathered the jacket she'd thrown on a chair. "I'm sorry it turned out this way. Will you at least talk to him about it? For your own sake?"

"He wouldn't do anything to hurt me."

"He may think he's helping. Not that you need help—the playing is fine. That's why I don't see why—"

"I've asked you to go. Will you go now?"

Elena took a step forward as if to embrace her or simply take her hand, but Suzanne backed away. A moment later the door closed. The car started with a low rumble, and Elena was gone. For ten minutes Suzanne sat looking at the half-empty coffee cups, waiting for her heart to stop pounding. Elena's cup had a bright red lipstick smear on the rim; that tangible evidence of her presence was infuriating. Suzanne took it immediately to the sink and attacked the smear with a soapy sponge. She would have liked to pretend the visit had never happened. Could what Elena said be true? And if it was, could she live with that knowledge?

Back in the living room she noticed the CD Elena had left on the couch, her recording of the Chopin ballades. Suzanne didn't want to touch it. She picked it up with two fingers as if it were something filthy or sticky. She couldn't think what to do with it, and finally put it on the rack with the others; she would never listen to it. She returned to the kitchen, tied a dish towel around her waist, and resumed slicing the sausage.

That was hours ago. Now, she forced herself to look at the TV screen. The culprit, once again seated in the tiny room with the false windows, persisted in denying everything, but it was clear that this time he was defeated; the police were breaking him down. Philip must not do that ever again, she thought. But could she control what he did? Was there any way to control Philip, so good to her, always looking out for her welfare, so elusive, so insistent?

Over the voices on the screen—the cops exultant, the criminal deflated—came a whisper from the voice inside that she couldn't suppress: If he had to do it, then she was glad he'd used Elena. Elena, who had taken so much from her. It was only right that she, Suzanne, should take something back. Of course he must never do it again—she'd find a way to see to that. But meanwhile, she couldn't prevent a smile at the thought of this small but useful betrayal. Now the jury was giving its verdict, but she no longer cared whether the defendant was found guilty or not. She knew he was guilty, but it really wasn't such a terrible crime. He didn't deserve a lengthy sentence. She fell asleep on the couch.

It was close to midnight when Philip came out of the studio and sat down on the edge of the couch. "Come to bed. It's much more comfortable there."

"Oh. Did I sleep long?"

"I don't know. Did you?"

"I guess so. Have you been working all this time?"

"Yes. I'm not tired, though." He put his hand under her sweater and touched her breasts. "You're not too tired, are you?"

She smiled. "I was, but I'm persuadable. Persuade me."

He lay down next to her and began caressing her. In a moment he had his fingers inside her. "You're not still upset, are you?"

"No," she whispered. "But you will do what I asked, won't you? No more of that?"

"Shh, sweetheart, it's all a fuss over nothing. Think about this instead." She was already moaning. It took no time at all these days. He dug his fingers in harder, and she was gasping and clutching at him. He smiled. He loved to watch her come—he felt he was seeing the secret Suzanne, the one no one knew but him, the one behind the music.

Finally she stopped and sighed.

"That was just for openers. Now we'll go to the bedroom for the real thing," he said. He felt, as always, that he was directing a performance, produced, stage-managed, all conceived by him. She was his material, his setting, his cast. "My star," he said, and led her to bed. Chances were, she would never mention that other business again; she'd forget, or pretend to forget. He knew her better than she knew herself.

He was right. She didn't bring the subject up for a long time after that evening, simply played and left him to go about his business. That was the best he could hope for. It was no surprise to Phil that she was ignorant of how the real world operated. No one had ever explained to her that the goal was to get what you wanted, by whatever means. What he did was harming no one. And look at the benefits: It made Suzanne happy. He'd certainly rather see her happy than moping around the house, as she had for so long. If she thought it over carefully, she would feel the same, he was sure.

⌒

Richard's new apartment on Central Park West was larger and mellower in every way than the small house in Brooklyn where Suzanne had first met him, and it was more spacious than the place in the West Fifties where he'd lived until his operas became so successful. The Persian rugs resembled the ones from the

Brooklyn house but couldn't be the same. Instead of the paper Japanese lanterns there were fixtures in odd curved shapes that shed a soft amber light. The old couch was the same, though, and the piano. There were still piles of magazines and prints on the walls. The heavy yellow crockery in which she'd had so many cups of coffee was the same—even when she was a child Richard had indulged her fondness for coffee, which her parents would not.

"Are you back to living alone?" Suzanne asked as she looked around. No need for awkwardness on that subject any longer; the small window of time in which there might have been something between them had slammed shut for good long ago. Or maybe had never been open.

"Yes, for now," and he smiled, almost flirtatiously. Only lately she'd noticed that he was a flirt, provocative with all; she had to admire all the more his restraint when she was a teenager. The perfect gentleman, as her mother would say, for all those years. If only he hadn't been. "But I've been seeing someone from the opera we're working on for next fall. The Chinese folktale one?"

"Yes, I read about that. Who is it?"

"The tenor," he said, almost shyly. "He's a little young, but after all, I am the composer. That's an attraction."

"Oh, you have other charms, too. Now, what was so urgent that I had to run into town immediately?"

"It's nothing funny. Let me give you a glass of wine first. Sit down."

He sat down beside her. "Elena called me yesterday." He waited, but Suzanne did not help. "She said she'd been to see you. She told me what you talked about."

"She talked. I didn't say much. It's never necessary, with Elena. She can converse for two."

"I think you may not realize how serious this is. What she told you, I mean."

"I do realize it's serious." She emptied half her wineglass. "Why do I have a feeling we've had this conversation before?"

"I know. I haven't forgotten. Rachmaninoff, right? That was actually pretty clever, that you could pull that off. I couldn't praise you for it, though."

"No. Not even a smile. You made me see how serious fraud is. But I haven't done a thing wrong this time. I go to the studio and play as best I can, which isn't bad, frankly. I don't have anything to do with the technical part except to repeat what we decide needs repeating. The rest is Phil's affair. I don't even listen to the CDs. I just want to play music, I'm not an engineer or a businesswoman."

"Suzanne, you are being so disingenuous. And you know what that word means now."

"I certainly do. You explained it very well, what, thirty-five years ago?"

"They're your recordings. They have your name on them. Your husband is your manager and your collaborator in making them. If he is . . . stealing—I hate to use that word, but it's the only one that fits—other people's work, you're involved in it, too."

"After Elena came that day, I made him promise not to do it again." Even as she spoke, she remembered this was not the precise truth. She had implored him, but had not extracted any promise. How could she make Phil promise anything? He was so slippery, she would never know whether he'd keep a promise or not. Her marriage, she felt, was the opposite of most: The single aspect of their lives in which she could place complete trust was his love and sexual fidelity; in every other way she could never be quite sure of him.

"And you believe that'll do it?"

She couldn't keep it up any longer in front of Richard. He was right—it was disingenuous. Or worse. "I don't know. It was the best I could do. How can I force him to stop?" It sounded like a plea.

"You can't force him to stop. I'm not laying it all on you. You're not responsible for his behavior. But you're responsible for your own. You're the one who's got to stop."

"Stop making the recordings, you mean?"

"Yes. That's the only way to be sure this doesn't continue. Or else record with some other firm."

"You know I can't do that."

"Well, maybe not now. But sometime—"

"I can't stop," she broke in. "It's totally unfair to ask that of me. It's all I have. You know I can't go back onstage. . . . You know how much I wanted that. Oh, it's all right for you to talk—you've got what you want now. You worked hard, you did everything you were supposed to, and it happened for you. And I'm glad, really glad. But it doesn't give you the right to go around telling other people to give up all their hopes—"

"You say it's all you have. But you don't really have it, do you?"

"What do you mean?"

"If he's used Elena's recordings, he must've used others', too. You've told me yourself, you can't play for long. You have an illness that makes you tire easily. He doesn't push you—that's his form of kindness. Why don't you listen to the CDs? Study those recordings and see which parts of them are genuine and which . . . you know. How much satisfaction or fulfillment can you get if they're not really yours?"

"They were very satisfying. Fulfilling, yes. I was so happy with them, until you and Elena came up with these . . . these accusations."

"Come on, Suzanne, you know she was telling the truth. She couldn't make something like that up. Would it have been better if she hadn't told you? Then you'd be satisfied with an illusion."

"And so?"

"Is that what you want? It's not something real. Yours. Aside from being dishonest to others."

"They are mine. They have my name on them." She was trying to stay calm. He was opening a door on a cabinet of doubt she kept secret even from herself. She refilled her glass from the bottle on the table.

"What does that signify? It's only your name. It's your playing you want to be heard. At least I thought so. But you don't really know—"

"I don't want to know!" she cried. "I don't want to hear any more."

"All right, all right, I didn't mean to upset you. I only—"

"What did you mean, then? Did you think I'd just laugh it off? Or did you think I'd give up an entire career to satisfy your high moral standards? You're a prig, you know? You've always been a prig."

"Well that's a new one. I've been called a lot of things, but never that. And I thought you were the genuine article."

"I am! When I played for you long ago, you said so yourself. I can play as well as Elena and any of them onstage right now."

"I'm not disputing that. I mean genuine in another sense. That you wanted the music first, above anything else. But no, you want the reputation more than you want the music. Your name even without the music. A hollow shell."

"That's not true!" She was standing now, and almost shouting. "I want both. Why can't I have both?"

"But don't you see? You don't have either. It's a house of cards. As soon as someone who's not a friend of yours finds out—and they will, believe me—you'll have nothing. Less than nothing."

She tipped the wineglass up and drained it to the last drop, then started toward the door. "I'm going to trust Phil to do the right thing. I've made it very clear that's what I want, and I have to trust him. He's always kept his promises." He's done so much for me, she thought. He delivered what he promised, and I let him. Is that so wrong?

"Will you come to my opening if I send you tickets?" Richard asked.

"Sure. If you still think I'm worthy of listening to your work."

"Cut it out, Suz—"

But she was out the door.

Part 4

I T WAS A mere few weeks after Suzanne's funeral when the news really surfaced. "Barely cold in her grave" was the unwelcome cliché that leaped from Philip's brain, promptly suppressed as too coarse, for Suzanne if not for him. She wasn't in a grave, anyway. She'd told him long ago she wanted to be cremated, like her father, and he had always waved it off, saying it was too far away to think about. But when the time came, he complied.

He followed the music websites daily; they had been her staunchest fans, spreading the word of each new CD with adoring, overblown reviews. Now, beyond the hints and suspicions, they were posting comparisons of one or two of Suzanne's recordings with several others, some sent in by skeptical listeners, techie nerds. Philip resolved to ignore them. But the allegations persisted and multiplied, racing from one site to another in a furious prestissimo, then moved to the print magazines, which were always slightly behind. Still he didn't defend himself, and screened all calls carefully. If he had to speak, he would deny everything. They couldn't prove anything. Or maybe they could, but the proofs would be so technical that no one beyond the world of computer-savvy critics and Internet music junkies would pay any attention. His clients would be loyal; he had done well for them and they knew it.

It was harder to ignore Richard's phone call.

No preliminaries: "What the hell did you think you were doing?"

"Richard?"

"You know very well who it is. I just read about it in *Andante*. They don't print such things unless they've investigated."

"Don't you know how these music sites and magazines operate? One false note and they fly into a tizzy."

"Philip, you're not talking to Suzanne now. We all know how gullible she was."

She was not quite as naive as they all believed, he thought but of course did not say. He himself had never been quite sure how naive she was.

"What possessed you?" Richard went on. "You went too far this time. Chamber music? Orchestral works? Are there any limits to what you'd do?"

"It's all totally mistaken. I know how that equipment works better than you do. You can feed stuff in and get any results you like. They're just vultures picking at the remains. It's disgraceful."

"You're going to deny it? You mean she played with the Vienna Symphony? With the San Francisco Symphony? With the Tokyo String Quartet? What world are you living in? You won't be able to keep that up, you know. Aside from anything else—and there's a lot else—it's illegal. You're in deep shit. You won't be able to keep track of the lawsuits. But I don't care about that. I care . . . cared about her. You ruined her. Don't you realize?"

"Ruined her? Are you crazy? I made her." The ingratitude of the man was unbelievable. And he professed to care about her. "Do you know where she'd be without all those recordings? Lying on the couch watching soap operas." Or cooking shows, but out of respect for her memory, Philip didn't add that.

"You made her! You're nuts. My God, the colossal ego. I knew her years before you did. I helped her all along. She was a significant talent. It was only after she got together with you that things started to go wrong."

"You want to fight over her, Richard? I'm surprised at you. If anyone ruined her, it was you, nursing those great expectations. The pressure she put on herself. As if without the public recognition she was nothing."

There was a silence. Finally Richard said, "I didn't do that. I only encouraged her to do her best. The rest came from her. Or her parents. Or, who knows, the miserable culture. That's all beside the point now, where it came from. What you did is criminal. I'm glad she's not around to see those articles online."

"I can agree with you there."

"I bet you can, you bastard. You took someone I loved and made a sham of everything she did and valued. And for what? Not even money. For fame. But it was based on nothing. It wasn't even real."

"The fame was real," Philip said quietly. "Her satisfaction was real."

"You are a genuine sophist. Don't you see? That reputation, it's all going down the tubes. All anyone will remember is the phoniness. The true talent will be forgotten."

"Who can tell what's true?" Philip asked calmly.

"Oh, don't go all philosophical on me. You're not up to it. You're just a tinkerer. A technician. You didn't respect her, and you didn't respect music."

"I respected her enough to give her what she wanted. Which is more than what you did. She never got over your . . . that business with you and Elena. She felt so betrayed."

"That was absurd and childish of her, and you know it. My personal life has nothing to do with this. You ruined her good name. You ruined what she cared about."

"She's dead, Richard. She had her good name while she lived. She can't be harmed now by any of these lies."

"I won't waste my breath on you anymore. And don't expect me to defend you for her sake. I can't defend those CDs." And he hung up.

Philip sat by the phone in the empty living room. It was winter; the days were depressingly short, approaching the solstice. The light from the west window was fading. There was only a dim light over the piano, with sheets of music on the rack. He hadn't touched them since her death. He had never touched them anyway—that was her domain. He sat in Suzanne's chair, the old easy chair with the ottoman where she put her feet up. Or sometimes she curled up in it with a book late at night; the last few years she'd started wearing glasses, round wire-rimmed glasses. He remembered exactly how she looked sitting there, her dark hair tied back, the wine-colored velveteen robe. If he came out of the studio to get a drink or a cup of coffee, she would lift her head from the book and smile at him. She was happy, those last few years, and all because of him.

No one understood. He had taken no one into his confidence, and now there was no one to whom he could justify himself. Suzanne. She was the only one he would like to explain it to, but she was gone. Even she, the reason for all his efforts, the one who profited from those efforts, even she might not understand what a coup he had pulled off. If not for the single listener who bothered to look at the credits that appeared on the screen when he slid the CD into his computer, and bothered to write to *Gramophone* and *The Half Note* about the discrepancy, whose editors then bothered to fiddle with their state-of-the-art equipment to try to unravel all he had done, the whole thing might never have come to light and Suzanne would be remembered as the great talent she truly was.

If it hadn't been Suzanne's reputation at stake, he might have relished the notoriety, even if it did land him in deep shit, as Richard predicted. Who else could have engineered an entire career using old recordings and the newest computer programs? Not to mention that in the process he had acquired an encyclopedic knowledge of the entire recorded repertoire. But any pleasure he might have felt was stopped at its source by their last argument, just a week before her death.

He was getting ready for bed while she sat staring at the screen of the laptop she kept in the bedroom. "Aren't you coming?" he said.

"In a few minutes. I'm reading something."

"Don't take long, sweetie. I'm lonely. I want someone to put their arms around me. Do you know anyone who could do that?"

She wasn't appreciating his silly jokes tonight. "Let me finish, okay?"

He was almost asleep when he felt her weight sink down on the bed. She turned the bedside lamp on. "Phil? Are you up?"

He turned around. "I guess so."

"I can't believe what I just read in *Platinum*."

"What? Another good review? What's so hard to believe?"

"Phil. It was a review of me playing the *Emperor Concerto* with the Vienna Philharmonic. And in *Gramophone* there was one of me doing the *Trout* with that group from São Paulo. These are Tempo CDs. What's going on? They must be mislabeled."

He was already sitting up, his mind racing. Reviews, of course. How could he have made such a slip? He had sent out the usual review copies along with her latest solo CD, a selection of Brahms waltzes, and not given it a thought. Carelessness, pure and simple. Although she hardly read the reviews anymore, unless he sent her the links. What made her start surfing the sites tonight? Still, it was his fault. He hadn't thought about her coming upon possible reviews—he'd been so caught up in the latest adumbration to his scheme: Suzanne playing chamber music, Suzanne playing orchestral works, who knew what else might be in the offing? He'd found obscure pianists, excellent but barely known, whose style was not unlike her own. He'd been so pleased with himself. . . .

"Phil. It is a case of mislabeling, isn't it?" When he didn't answer, her voice became almost a wail. "Oh, please, Phil. Tell me it's a mistake." She looked at him, not even angry, merely wretched with suspicion. More than suspicion.

She'd never asked him outright before, or not since Elena's visit two years ago. Now he found he couldn't lie to her.

"Oh. So, it's not a mistake." Her voice hardened. "So it's a big lie. The whole thing is a big lie."

"No, no," he said hastily. "It's just this . . . these last few . . .

I thought it was a smart idea . . . you know, branch out, not just your solo work. Show what else you can do—"

"But I *can't* do it. I didn't do those, at any rate."

"But you could if you had the chance."

"Oh, so the truth is just a technicality?"

"Suzanne, it's late. I had a long day. Can't we talk about it tomorrow?"

"As far as I'm concerned, there's nothing more to say. I'm finished. Do you understand? I'm not doing it anymore. Elena was right. Richard was right. I can't keep participating in this . . . this . . . I'm finished. I'm never going to that studio again. Do you hear me?"

"It doesn't matter at this point whether you go or not. The CDs can continue without you. You're a brand now." He rolled over. Tomorrow would be dreadful, when he faced her in the light of day, but he might as well get some sleep. "Oh, by the way, how were the reviews?"

"The reviews? They were excellent. 'Masterful, plangent, powerfully articulated, controlled but touching emotional force.'"

He grinned into the soft darkness of the pillow. He'd done it again. He reached over and stroked her hip, but she pushed his hand away and turned her back.

Since that night she hadn't wanted him to touch her. She never brought the subject up again, and neither did he. The next few days were strained, with conversation at a minimum, but there gradually came a thaw. She wasn't one for the extended silent treatment. She had things to tell him: an invitation to do a master class at Oberlin in the spring, to attend a series of concerts by a former student who had won a major contest, a note from a childhood friend, Eva, congratulating her on her success. "She was a real bitch. I can't imagine why she got it into her head to write to me." And Phil, likewise, brought her news of the studio and his other recordings. Before long, she'd come around, he felt sure. A few weeks, and things would go back to what they were before. Their good years.

Instead he had found her lying on the kitchen floor while a teapot screeched. Calling her mother was an agony. Gerda had grown more sentimental in old age. "My little girl. So young," she wept. "Such a talented little girl. She had a real gift. Didn't she? And those wonderful recordings! It just isn't fair. It doesn't seem right."

"No," Phil agreed. "It's not right. She deserved better."

He was alone in the house that first night after he called the police and made all the arrangements, after the body was removed. Two young men in down jackets had lifted her off the floor and placed her on a stretcher, as if she were only sick. He closed the door after them; he didn't want to watch the next steps. He wasn't used to being alone. With all the people he knew, all the business contacts, the networking, there was no one to sit with him and keep him company. He felt the desolation he remembered from years ago, the first few nights in his aunt and uncle's apartment. At least this was his own home, with his own things.

The house was too quiet. Maybe he should have followed those two young men to wherever they were taking her. He should have kept her longer; he wasn't ready to let her go. He went over to the shelves that held hundreds of CDs; he could keep her by her music, anyway. Wasn't that the wonderful thing about art, that it outlasted its creators? Life is short, art is long—some ancient said that, he couldn't remember who. Suzanne would probably have known. She wasn't altogether gone. There was the music. He picked out one of the recordings he himself had made, Suzanne playing the Schubert Impromptus, and slipped it into the slot. The opening notes were full of brio, exhilaration. For a moment it was as if she were back in the room, alive and eager. He remembered her playing it in the studio, and he remembered editing it. Was this the one where . . . ? Yes, it might be the one where she faltered early on and he had had to make several alterations. The pianist was well into the piece now, and Philip had to acknowledge that it probably was no longer Suzanne playing. He had done his job so well, even he couldn't tell where the cut came. He couldn't be absolutely sure, but he didn't think it was Suzanne. There was a whole shelf of her recordings, recordings that bore her name, and he would play them all over the next few weeks, to try to keep her close. But he would never really know if he was hearing her or some stranger. It shouldn't have mattered. That was what he had told himself all along. It didn't matter. It was the music that was important, and no one could deny the excellence of his recordings. But now, when he needed her and her alone, it mattered.

Author's Note

THE IDEA FOR *Two-Part Inventions* came from the case of Joyce Hatto (1938–2006), a British pianist whose husband and recording engineer, William Barrington-Coupe, produced more than one hundred critically successful recordings allegedly by Hatto, who became known as "the greatest living pianist no one has heard of." After her death, the recordings, by means of sophisticated computer technology, were found to be by other pianists and released under her name.

Aside from this initial idea, the setting, time frame, characters, and all other events in the novel are fictitious and have nothing at all to do with the facts of Hatto's or Barrington-Coupe's life, of which I know very little.

I am indebted to Mark Singer's excellent *New Yorker* essay "Fantasia for Piano" (September 17, 2007), which investigates the technical and other aspects of the fraud executed by Barrington-Coupe; to what extent Hatto was aware of his exploits is uncertain. It was that latter aspect of the affair that intrigued me most and that I decided to explore through imagination.

I wish to offer warm thanks to Martin Canin, pianist and former professor at the Juilliard School of Music, who kindly and patiently supplied me with expert information about the classical-piano repertory and about the curriculum and students' lives at Juilliard during the 1970s and early 1980s, the period in which my fictional protagonist attended. Emily Leider, poet, biographer, and longtime friend, generously described to me her experience as a student at New York City's High School of Music and Art.

My friend and fellow writer Ellen Pall was, as always, generous, astute, and scrupulous in reading the manuscript and offering valuable suggestions. Many thanks as well to John Hill, musician and novelist, who helped me with the technical aspects of the recording process and corrected many errors in my early drafts. I am responsible for any errors that remain.